COUNTDOWN TO
RAGE

RICHARD LARSEN

COUNTDOWN TO RAGE

by Richard Larsen

For Dad. I love and miss you so much.

PROLOGUE

TWO YEARS BEFORE THE RAGE

A mouse slams against the glass of its cage. Cracks form at the point of impact. Red eyes bulging, it continues to ram, bent on escape. A scientist paces back and forth, occasionally peeking into the cage. He removes his fogged safety goggles and rubs his sweaty forehead. Suddenly, a door in the back of the lab slams open and a man in military attire stomps in.

"Henry, tell me this isn't happening!" the man screams, the lights of the lab reflecting off the numerous stars adorning his lapel.

"The experiment went horribly wrong, sir," Henry says, cowering.

"What do you mean horribly wrong? You were supposed to contain the virus."

"It must have gotten into our water—"

"Our water supply?" The general steps forward and hits his chest. "You mean this could affect us?"

Henry steps back and gulps. "If by us you mean the human race, well, then… yes."

"How could this happen? This was supposed to create super marines, not infect citizens. You better tell me something can be done." The general walks to the cage, inspects the rabid mouse, and points at it. "Are humans going to become this?"

"Well, the Mus Musculus was affected—"

"The what? What the hell are you talking about?"

"I'm sorry, sir, the mouse. The mouse was affected by the virus, and his testosterone increased rapidly. We thought we could control the levels, but we cannot. It took the mouse months to morph. I figure it may take humans years. It has to do with the animal's age. Once it reached maturity, it transformed."

The general runs his hand down his face. "Tell me there's an antidote, Henry."

"No, sir. We can't seem to decipher what is causing this. The water will evaporate, and the virus will become airborne. The ramifications are mind-boggling. This has the potential to infect the world. We have to alert the public, sir."

"This is top secret. You'll say nothing. Work on an antidote."

"But sir, we have to warn—"

The general snatches Henry by the neck and shoves his face against the glass of the cage. "You're going to tell the public that they turn into this? Not a word, Henry. Do you understand me? Find an antidote. This information does not leave this room. And if it does…" He points at Henry, punches his open hand, then grinds his knuckles into his palm. "Got that soldier?"

Henry salutes with a limp wrist, his legs shaking uncontrollably. "Yes, sir."

CHAPTER 1

PRESENT DAY
FOUR YEARS AFTER THE RAGE

Everyone I have ever loved is gone. This is the persistent thought
that runs through my muddled mind as I stagger through the forest.
Struggling to navigate the terrain, I collapse, buried in a pile of leaves.
The devastation of losing Summer is too much. My entire family, now
her. The brooding pines and oaks tower above me. Their branches
bend in the wind, pointing as if to say, 'Move on." I push up to my
knees, then to my feet, and warily continue.

I reach the top of a hill and a dark shadow, wider than the fattest
oak, takes form in the distance. I drag myself closer and a small run-
down cabin appears. Shelter. With my last bit of strength, I force
open the door and a musty smell overtakes my senses. My foot bursts
through moldy, rotten wood, and my face smacks into something soft
and dusty.

***

I sit up and dust flies from the deteriorated mattress. It dances through the light spilling from the numerous holes in the roof. The smell of mouse droppings gags me. I cough violently, trying to clear my lungs. With fingers digging into the small of my back and shoulders slouched forward, I survey my cabin. A sunken roof, bulged by water, looks ready to fall, and spider webs cover every corner. It's not much but it's been my home for months now.

My stomach growls, and my tongue swells from thirst. It's been about two days since I've eaten and I haven't had a drink since yesterday morning, or was it the afternoon? Regardless, I have to find some food and water. I pluck my bow from the dusty mattress and slither my way through an opening on the side of the cabin.

Entering the forest, I arm my bow and search for game. Whenever I use it, I'm instantly reminded of Dad and Craig. Dad bought the bow for me when I was young, preaching it would teach me patience. Craig, though, is the one who taught me the art of killing an animal. How to sneak through the trees, invisible to his prey. Always ready. Man, I miss them. Memories of family constantly sneak in. I hate the pain that comes with them. When will that get better? Probably never.

The woods are silent as I scan the landscape. There's not much as far as food out here. It's always scorching hot in the middle of July and that makes it even harder to hunt. I try to move silently, but the dry leaves crunch like potato chips under my feet. I can actually see the animals raise an ear, look over, and dart away. Two trees ahead, I spot a squirrel perched on a branch, gnawing at an acorn. Not much meat but better than nothing. Before all of this, I wouldn't have dreamed of killing anything. I'd cry when Craig would shoot an animal. Now, I know I must kill to survive. I fire, and the arrow pierces the squirrel's side. Famished, I rush over and skin it with my hunting knife.

I pull the hood of my cloak over my head as I eat it raw, hoping to shield myself from the world, to hide from my depression. I feel the weight lift off my shoulders as everything closes in. The cloak's one of my few possessions and, besides my bow, probably my most prized. Summer picked it out for me at an old hand-me-down store. She thought it made me look like an elf from her favorite movie. Can't remember the name.

The night I lost her plays over and over in my mind, constantly invading my dreams. The creatures surrounding her, ready to attack. The beast tackling me over the edge. Could I have saved her? Probably not. I'm happy I didn't see them rip her apart like the others. But the ache of losing her never leaves.

After eating I slump back towards the cabin. I've decided to abandon it, don't think it'll stand erect another day. Some days I get ambitious and want to leave; other days I would be happy with curling up in a ball, crying myself to sleep. But I know now that the time has come. I need to make my way towards the city. It's most likely crawling with the creatures, but I believe it's the only place where I can find some answers. Why teenagers change when they reach adulthood? Why Mom and Dad transformed from loving parents into those things? I must find the reason. I owe it to my family and Summer.

I gather my meager supplies and carefully swing open the crooked door. The cabin sways back and forth and then settles. I wouldn't doubt it collapses soon. Almost want to come back to see if it did. Some justification that I made the right decision. Funny, I never needed praise before, yet now I yearn for it.

After some time, I come upon a good spot to camp. It's right at the base of a hill and next to a lake. I try to stay near water because the beasts don't swim very well. They move so erratically and aggressively that they sink like stones. Swimming requires grace, which they have none of. Man, I think about them all the time. I guess if something's trying to kill and eat you, you think about it.

There's plenty of wood so I gather some for the fire. This is the only time I start one, to cook. I'm deep enough in the forest though that it won't attract them. I hope.

I search my bag and find my flint. It's the first thing I grabbed when I fled my house. My sister was yelling at Craig and me to just get out, but I knew we needed it to survive. I strike the flint, and the sparks ignite the kindling. Smoke fills the air around me; a swift breeze lifts it towards a darkening sky.

"Who's down there?" a booming voice echoes. I dive under some brush and twigs, not much of a hiding place. My heart races. It can't be one of *them*. They don't talk. I peek over the brush. Nothing. I muster the courage to call, "Hello!" No one answers.

I stand to scan the area when a tremendous mass stomps towards me. I grasp an arrow, but a paw of a hand engulfs my face and slams me against the bark of a huge oak.

"Who are you?" a giant man asks, his voice bellowing through the trees.

"You're… a… man," I stutter through his sausage-like fingers.

"I know what I am. Who are you?"

"Um.. Kyle."

"So, Kyle," he says through clenched teeth, "how old are you?"

"I just turned seventeen."

He gets down to one knee, spreads his fingers and stares deep into my eyes. "Someone told me they were seventeen once. Tried to eat me a week later."

He stands, grips my neck, and lifts me off the ground, my feet dangling beneath me. I'm now face to face with the giant. I gulp and pain shoots into my shoulder blades. "I haven't turned."

"How do I know you're safe?" He moves my face towards his. His breath smells, oddly enough, like honey. He looks at me funny, then smiles. "Alright, you seem safe, kid." He drops me and dusts off my shoulder. I stagger from the tree, rubbing my neck. No blood, that's good. As he gathers his supplies, I stare at him. I guess he's not a giant, just very big. And he's older, which makes no sense.

"I can't believe you're a man."

He hits his chest with a fist. "That I am." No doubt he's a real man. His beard's thick and scruffy. Calluses cover every inch of his palms. His shoulders are at least four feet wide, and his biceps are the size of watermelons. As I watch him, he notices my extreme curiosity.

"I know. You think I should be one of them. I just haven't turned. Don't know why. I'm not gonna complain, though. I don't wanna be one of those freaks."

I strain my neck to look up at his face and raise a brow. "So, you never changed?"

"Nope. And I've heard there are others who haven't. A few have been this way since the beginning. They're thinking it could be permanent."

"Who's thinking?"

"Scientists." He scratches the top of his head. "Well, educated people, professor types, I guess. We're not all dolts like me."

"What's your name?" I'm usually too shy to ask this many questions, but I'm too curious not to.

"My real name's Bruce, but my family called me Brute and it stuck. Kinda like it."

I like it, too, and it definitely fits him. "What happened to your family?"

"When I say family I mean my survival family." I know exactly what he means. "Two of them turned, both males. It's hard to pinpoint when anyone will change. Females seem to change later. I knew a woman who didn't change till twenty-one. Thought she was immune. Males, though, they change at a younger age, like eighteen. You're seventeen, right? Gettin' close." He stares into my eyes again. "Gotta be careful with you. My friends both turned and attacked me. I knew they were changing. It happens over a day, but when they go berserk that takes a matter of seconds. I killed one of them with this axe." He holds up the large weapon, which looks like it's from medieval times. Pretty impressive. He has a second one attached to his back by some type of belt that wraps around his chest. "I beheaded my friend.

Hardest thing I've ever done. The other jumped right on his carcass. I was able to escape as it tore apart the body. Met you soon after."

"So they can be killed without drowning them?" I ask.

He shrugs. "Yeah, guess so. Seems that you have to behead them, but I guess there could be other ways. I usually wound, then run."

I listen intently, astounded by the new information. I've only seen one adult since this began, and he died soon after. I assumed he'd have eventually turned. So you can get past a certain age without changing. Maybe you have an immunity to it and will never turn. And they can be killed with a weapon. What a relief. I'll learn to behead them. I'll save Summer in my dreams.

The sun's setting, so Brute sets his tent while I stoke the fire. I shoot some fish with my bow and we eat, but we don't talk much. I wonder if Brute's shy also. Still, I'm so happy that I have someone, anyone, around. The fire dies out, and Brute insists I take the tent. It's nice to finally sleep in something that, if it collapses, won't crush me.

Waking up to Brute's like listening to someone chopping down a tree. Regardless, I'm beginning to like him.

"Hey, Brute. Whattaya want for breakfast?"

He sits up and rubs his face. "A big bowl of sleep." Yeah, I like him.

He tears apart a fish with his bare hands before gobbling down the meat. After he's done devouring it, I tell him about my plan to travel to the city. He agrees immediately, and after packing our supplies, we begin our journey.

We make sure that we stay in the woods. Brute thinks it will be safer than the highway. Plus, everything seems peaceful in the forest. The sun peeks through the clouds and the birds sing. It's like this part of the world was never touched by the devastation. Every once in a while, though, I'll notice a clearing and see the battered branches and splintered wood. I've seen the beasts rip through trees before, knocking them over like bowling pins. But the worst is when we stumble upon the dried blood that's mixed with leaves and dirt where they caught their prey. There's never much left of the victim, just the occasional skull or bones. I pause at one of these sights and pray that they didn't suffer; hope it wasn't a child.

We walk a few miles then stop to rest and I show Brute some of my bow skills. One of my arrows goes straight into a skinny sapling and sticks. "Not bad," Brute says as he whirls around, and with a flick of his wrist his axe flies through the air and shoots right through my arrow. It splits the young tree, and the axe carries the wood and arrow straight into a large oak behind it. He struts over, and with a quick tug, pulls out his axe. A wry smile crosses his face. I smile back, trying not to show how impressed I am.

For the next few hours, Brute teaches me how to use the axe as a weapon. He swings it behind his back and grasps it with the other hand. He keeps the momentum going, and with a few rotations, throws it through a baby pine, which topples with a loud thud. It's all done with such ease and fluency. I know it'd take months, if not years, to get even close to as good as him, but by the end of the day, I feel I can handle the axe well enough to protect myself.

All the while, Brute and I talk. He tells me about his biological family and how he felt like he was the outcast. "My dad was an army sergeant so he would bark orders at me all day. I guess I kind of rebelled against him. My brother, Hank, and I got into drugs and he could never forgive us. You got any brothers, kid?"

I nod, but struggle to answer. It's still so hard to talk about him. "Yeah... a twin brother, Craig."

"Twin, ha. How'd you two get along?"

"Okay. He was kinda mean when we were young, but when everything went crazy, we bonded. I miss him so much."

Brute starts to speak, then stops. He gathers himself quickly. "I miss my brother, too. We went down the wrong path, I guess. My dad forced my mom to abandon us. I was so mad at him." He squeezes his fists and then slowly shakes his head. "But I knew it was my fault. I was really close to making up with him when all this happened."

"My sister, Lauren, had a falling out with my parents."

"You had a sister?" Brute says with a smile. "Never had the pleasure."

"Yep, two years older than me. She was the rock star of the family." I strum an air guitar. I guess I'm starting to feel comfortable around Brute. "She would sneak my brother and me into concerts. My parents caught her and kicked her out for a time. She moved back right before all this."

"That's terrible." Brute shakes his head then sighs. "The world's become hell, kid. I don't envy anyone your age. Knowing you're going to turn. No way to escape it."

I start walking a little faster. "That's why we've gotta find the answers." Brute laughs and, with two steps, passes me.

The sun beats down, making sweat bead on my brow. Brute's beard is soaked, so he peels off his dirty jacket and shirt. He smells like a man, too. To say Brute's big is an understatement. He must be every bit of 6'8" and his huge muscles flex with each movement. He's far from fat, but you can tell he likes food. His arms are covered in tattoos, mostly tribal. A long scar crosses from his forehead, through his eyebrow, to the middle of his cheek. I figure he's about 30 years old. I'll ask him when I feel more comfortable. He's rugged, but I guess good looking.

I've been told I'm good looking. I don't know. I've never been the type to stare at myself in the mirror like those vain kids from the locker room at school. As long as I could play sports, I didn't care what I looked like.

Over the next day, we trek towards the city. Brute thinks it's at least a week out. I must have traveled deep into the forest, out of fear of the creatures I suppose. Even though we're far from the city the houses become more condensed. We try to stick to the woods but eventually have to cross streets and sneak through backyards. There's no sign of life here. The houses seem empty and I haven't noticed any carcasses on the streets, although the road is stained with blood. We hop one fence and enter a backyard. Brute freezes then points. I turn expecting the worst but see a hammock gently rocking between two trees.

"Let's rest here kid," Brute says as he hops into it. The rope's strain but hold. I pull up a lawn chair next to him; don't think the hammock will hold the both of us. I throw Brute some meat and as we eat I ask him more about his brother, Hank, and he tells me that he noticed the change in him first. He was the adventurous type, owned a Harley that he and Brute would ride together, and loved any kind of adventure and any kind of woman. Brute says Hank was always very aggressive, so maybe it was a shorter change. One day he seemed more agitated and started to yell at everyone over anything. Then his eyes changed. They always do right before they turn. Once they turn, all hell breaks loose. They get the strength of many men, and their whole body pulses with rage.

Brute was able to escape with his mom and dad before his brother fully turned. His parents started to become aggressive, and he knew they were in trouble. It's now four years, though it seems like yesterday, since adults started turning into horrible beasts and attacking their loved ones. Not many survived that awful day. But the few that did simply call it The Rage.

CHAPTER 2

FOUR YEARS EARLIER
THE DAY OF THE RAGE

"Get up, loser."

"Let me sleep!" I yell as I bury my head into the pillow. Craig's so annoying. I love him, but sometimes I wonder if maybe he was adopted. I love sports. He loves mini bikes. I love movies. He loves BB guns. I have brown hair and brown eyes. He has blonde hair and blue eyes. I'm more like Dad, laid back. He's more like Mom, can't sit still.

"Come on. We're going to the beach after breakfast," he says as he rips my covers off me.

"All right. Just give me a second." I lift myself out of bed and throw on my favorite shirt. Craig will make fun of the fact that I wore it again, but I'm so used to it that it doesn't affect me anymore. I drag myself down the stairs, into the kitchen, and open the pantry. What cereal should I have today?

The back of the Lucky Charms box has the usual jokes and crossword puzzles. I even read the nutrition info. I love to read, always have a book in my hand. Just another thing my brother and sister pick on me about. I slurp the sugary milk on the bottom of the bowl and place it on the floor for Cosmo, our black Lab, to lap up the rest while I continue scanning the box.

"Good morning, nerd," Lauren says as she whacks me on the head. She's stronger than she thinks. "You'd read anything, huh?"

"You going to the beach with us?" I ask, knowing the answer.

She rolls her eyes. "Uh, no way. I'm like hanging with my girls." Lauren's fifteen and at that age where she thinks she's cooler than everyone. She rolls her eyes at everything. I hope I'm never that way. Craig and I had our thirteenth birthday last month and she didn't even come. I wonder if she realizes how much that hurt me. I'm happy my parents let her move back in after dragging Craig and I to that concert, though.

"Is Eric hanging out, too?" I wonder.

"Of course," Lauren says.

Oh, man. I hate Eric. He's Lauren's mean boyfriend. He's more annoying than Craig. He treats me like I'm the biggest loser that ever walked the earth. It's funny how real losers are the ones that call everybody else losers.

***

I hang out the side of our beat up Jeep My hair whips in the wind as we drive to the beach. We pull into the parking lot, and the seagulls scatter. I leap out and my feet hit the scalding pavement. Heat rises in waves off the blacktop, and I tiptoe, trying to avoid the burn. Why didn't I wear my flip-flops? My t-shirt immediately soaks through with sweat. I hate when it sticks to my skin. I feel like everyone can see the fat around my belly.

The beach is crowded like always, and the refreshing smell of the surf is immediately overtaken by a wall of Coppertone. The overly tan sunbathers lay on their towels in a perfect row. One man's so burnt to a crisp that I imagine him spinning on a spit, apple stuffed in his mouth. The thought makes me laugh out loud, and he peers at me, annoyed.

"Hey, Kyle!" Dad yells. "Help me with the cooler."

"Sure, Dad." I lift it up, but it's too heavy to put on my shoulder. I have yet to develop muscles like I see on the older guys at the beach. In fact, I picture them kicking sand in my face as I lie on my towel, calling me twerp. Instead I pull the cooler through the sand, but the wheels dig in, getting stuck. At this point, it's like I've been in the desert for a week without any water and the vultures are circling. "Craig, help me out, please," I beg.

"Do it yourself," he says with a wide grin. My blood boils even more, and I throw the handle down in disgust.

Dad places a hand on my shoulder. "Kyle, leave that for now. Let's go throw the football?"

"Sure." My heart stops racing, and I start to breathe normally. Dad always knows how to calm me down. I love it when he asks me to play a sport. He doesn't really like any. He couldn't tell you one player on the Yankees. I could name the bat boy and maybe even the trainer. He enjoys working. At the age of just sixteen he started a construction company with my uncle. They now own two bulldozers and a Mack truck.

He's always busy with his business so he never really plays any type of sport with me. I guess that's why I'm jealous of Craig. Dad took him under his wing and taught him the business. Craig learned to operate the bulldozer at a very young age and is just as good as Dad by now. One time, though, he flipped the machine on its side. I was so scared that he was hurt, and I cried until I knew he was fine. I guess I really do love him, even though he drives me crazy.

We play catch for a few minutes before Dad gets bored. He shuffles through the sand to lie down on the blanket and relax. He places his hands on his chest, and they rise with each deep breath. A few times he has lain down this way and then fallen asleep and woken up with white handprints on his chest. Oh, we rib him about that. He always takes it, though. He has a great sense of humor. Man, do I love him.

I sprint down to the water and when my feet touch the surf I tiptoe out from the chill. Wading back in past my knee, my body finally acclimates to the cold. Big waves roll towards the shore, and timing them perfectly, I catapult over the crest, crashing on the other side. A few really cute girls approach, so I pull in my stomach and stick out my chest. They stare at me, whispering and giggling. I pretend they're saying great things about me like, "Wow, look how cute he is", and I keep jumping the waves, even higher this time, as they pass.

I'm a little old for it, I guess, but I have a cool parachute man that I throw in the air and try to catch before it plummets into the waves. It's fun to see if I can save it before it drowns. To be the hero for once. Mom says I have an overactive imagination, like it's some kind of disease or something. The same girls pass as I play, and they snicker at how immature I look. Maybe this is why I don't have a girlfriend.

"Hey, you!" someone screams so loud I cover my ears. "What the hell are you doing with my son's toy?" I look side to side. Oh, crap. He's yelling at me.

"This is mine, sir," I say with a whimper.

He snatches my parachute man and shoves me to the ground. "That's bull! I saw my son with it two minutes ago!"

Dad rushes over and pushes the guy away from me. "What the hell do you think you're doing?" I start to cry but hold back because I already feel people staring. Embarrassment crawls over me, and I start to get queasy. "My son came with that toy. It belongs to him."

"Bullcrap! This is *my* son's. Don't make me fight you for it." Dad looks over at me with a 'do you want me to beat the hell out of him' look. I know Dad could probably crush him. He's 6'2" and muscular from all the hard work he's done. His hands are huge and covered in calluses from digging all day. I give a look like, 'don't worry about it'. My brother jumps up and down next to me hoping for a brawl but I don't want Dad to fight. I love him too much.

"I'm not gonna fight you over this, so just take it," Dad says, tossing the parachute man at him. "You're a real class act stealing other kid's toys."

"Screw off, pansy," the nutty dad says. "Here, son. Go play with your stupid toy!" Man, I kind of wish I gave my dad that 'yeah, beat the hell out of him' look.

"That was so bizarre," Mom says as we return to the blanket. "That's our pharmacist, Mr. Klein. He's usually the nicest, most gentle man. He must be going through some really tough times."

Except for the crazy dude, which rattles me for a while, we have a wonderful day at the beach. I'm packing the cooler when I hear two men screaming at each other. It sounds like one man was mad that the other bumped into his umbrella. The umbrella was still standing so I don't understand all the fuss. The argument starts getting so heated that Dad hurries us to the car. As we pull away, one of the men lands a really fierce blow to the other man's head. I expect the guy to drop like a ton of bricks but he comes back with a hard right of his own. As we round the corner, the punches are still flying.

"Dad, why's everyone so angry at each other?" I ask.

"Not sure, son. I've never seen anything like it. Let's get home." He steps on the gas, and my neck whips back. "I think we'll all feel safer there."

On the way home, there are a few more brawls in front of the King Kullen and one outside of the deli. When we get in, Dad turns on the news. I guess he wants to know what all the aggression is about because he sits up on the front of his recliner, instead of his usual melt-into-the-chair position. I briefly hear the news reporter state that numerous fights had started around the city. I'm not interested enough, as my Yankees started 15 minutes ago and I might be able to catch my favorite player, Derek Jeter, bat. It's his last year with the team so I try to see him every time he's up. I watch as the Yanks win and start to drift off.

"Kyle, wake up," Mom whispers. 'Craig, you, too. There's something wrong with your father."

"What's wrong?" I ask, rubbing my eyes.

"He's been breathing really funny, and he just woke up to do some work outside." Mom looks around the room then back at me with worried eyes. "Your dad always sleeps through the night."

I try to gather my thoughts and then stare into her eyes. When she's not doing well, they open wide and seem wild. Mom's bipolar. She has her good months, where she's the best mom on earth, and she has her bad months, where it seems she's a different woman all together. After a quick examination, her eyes are normal and she seems okay.

"Where's Dad now?" I ask.

"He's—"

"What are you saying to them now?" Dad screams through the door. "Don't you lie to them. Let me in this room!" Man, I've never heard him this mad.

"I'm not saying anything," Mom answers, cowering against my covers. "I'm just worried about you."

No reply. Craig and I both sit up and yawn when the door flies open. Dad's hand reaches in and clutches Mom's hair. He drags her out of the room into their bedroom across the hall. I'm frozen in fear and look over to see Craig's eyes wide and mouth dropped open. You can hear the yelling coming from my parent's room. First, Dad's screams are the only loud ones. Then I hear Mom's just as loudly.

I hide under my cover with my toes curled under. It's the only place I feel truly safe. After an hour or so, the arguing stops. Craig has already fallen fast asleep, but it takes me a long time to calm my nerves. As I lie awake, I imagine I'm a super scientist who finds a cure for Mom's illness and Dad's crazy behavior. My thoughts must morph into my dreams and I'm awakened by a loud thud.

"Guys, let me in quick!" Lauren sounds frantic. I hop up and open the door. I know what caused the thud. Eric's lying on the floor, not moving. Lauren slides into the room and locks the door.

"What are you doing back?" I wonder, forgetting about Eric.

"Don't worry about that. Something's really wrong here. Mom and Dad are not right, and I've seen a few people that are different."

"What do you mean differ—?"

"Just shut the hell up for a minute! You're a stupid little kid and I need to think," Lauren screams as she wrings her hands. I want to tell her that I'm thirteen, not a kid anymore, but I know this is serious.

Lauren looks around the room. "Craig, do you have any of your guns?"

Craig jumps from the bed. "Not really. Dad doesn't let me keep them in the room. I know where he stashes them, though. They're in his closet, behind his suits that he never wears."

Lauren smacks her forehead. "Crap. I don't know how we're going to get to them. Kyle, do you have your bow?"

"Yeah. It's under my bed." I slip under the bed and reach around. I must touch every stupid toy before I finally find it. Gripping the handle I hold it out in front of me and pull the string. It's still tight but there's only a few arrows left in the quiver.

"Well, it's better than nothing," Lauren says. "Just know that you might have to use this on Mom or Dad."

"What do you mean on Mom or Dad?" Craig and I ask in unison.

"I wish I could say more. There's something wrong with them. They were yelling at me as soon as I walked in, and Dad went after Eric. Did you see Eric out there?" I nod. "Mom and Dad were in the living room so we have to sneak into their room. I think the door's unlocked. As soon as I open your door, we'll run into their room and lock it. Do you guys understand? We can't stop. Don't look for Mom and Dad. Don't look for Cosmo. Just get into that room."

I have to admit I'm pretty focused considering the situation. I understand every word Lauren says but I'm also stunned by how weird this all seems. Mom and Dad, besides the arguing, seemed okay yesterday. What could have happened? I want to run out and hug Dad and ask him what's wrong. I want to tell Mom I love her, but I stay focused.

Lauren reaches for the door, unlocks it, and starts to turn the knob. Suddenly, she stops. There's a dragging sound, and Cosmo barks loudly. Her barks cease instantly, followed by a whimper. I feel like crying because I know she's hurt. "I have to help her," I half whisper.

"Don't move. Just wait and focus on getting to that room," Lauren says. "Craig, stay behind me and make sure you grab those weapons from Dad's closet. We need something to protect ourselves. Once we have them, we need to get out of this house."

"What about Mom and Dad?" Craig asks.

Lauren crouches and stares into our eyes. She knows how bad our hearts are hurting. "I know this is sudden guys. I don't think Mom and Dad will survive this. I don't know what happened, but I think they're gone already. We just have to get through this and figure it out. I love you both, and you need to listen to me now. Okay?" Craig and I nod, then start to cry. Lauren seems different now, so mature. She was always the family screw up, but now she makes me feel safe.

Lauren turns the knob and pushes our door open. The door to our parents' room is unlocked. A sense of relief hits me as I sneak behind my brother. I turn to glance down the hall and am frozen. Mom and Dad are hunched over Eric and Cosmo. They stare at us with blood dripping off their chins as they rip through flesh. The image I will never forget, though, is their eyes. Small, red veins snake through white into their black pupils. With every deep breath, the veins pulsate. "Dad!" I scream. His eyes follow me, and he lets out a hiss. Blood splatters from his mouth onto Eric's forehead.

"Let's go!" Craig yells. I try to run but my legs seem frozen to the ground. Lauren grasps my arm and yanks me into the room.

"Holy crap! Craig, find the weapons and let's get the hell out of here!" Lauren yells. Her body shakes and she suddenly seems flustered.

Craig shoves Dad's clothes aside, grabs his shotgun, and stuffs it into his hunting bag. It looks like he takes a few knives also and forces them in. As he rummages through the closet a survival kit falls onto the floor and spills its contents. I snatch a flint and shove it in my pocket. If there's anything I learned from Survivor, it's that you need fire to survive.

"All right," Lauren says, "no more time. Let's get out through the window."

Craig struggles at first but is able to force the window open. A big bush sits right in front of it, so he struggles to get himself and the hunting bag through. Just as I get my leg halfway out the window, a loud bang rocks the bedroom door. I know who it is, but I try to erase it from my mind.

Lauren shoves me out the window, and I'm tangled in leaves and branches. She jumps through, lands on top of me, and I get jammed into the bush. The branches tear my skin, and I cry out in pain. My back slams into the ground as Lauren rolls over me. The rocks of the driveway seem to embed themselves into my side, and blood trickles down my back. Lauren pushes herself up and bolts towards the woods. I tumble, the rocks slipping under my feet, as I try to follow. I'm finally able to stand but am facing the window as I do. The door slams open and Dad bursts in. He scans the room with those eyes. I duck down and can't help but stare. He's taller, more muscular and his whole body pulsates as he breathes. He looks out the window and let's out an ear piercing scream. Turning away from the sound I see Craig and Lauren enter the woods next to Mrs. York's house. I have to keep up with them, can't be alone. I sprint towards the woods. Every stride, my thoughts race. How could this happen? Is this a terrible nightmare? Are my parents gone forever?

CHAPTER 3

PRESENT DAY

Brute and I leave what we guess was a small, upstate town and enter the forest. After a while, we exit the woods and a huge, breathtaking lake spans the horizon. The water stretches as far as the eye can see as fog rolls through tremendous trees that seem to touch the blue sky. The smell of fresh water and the moss hugging the rocks that outline the lake adds to its beauty.

Brute stands tall and scans the landscape. "Now this is what I call a view, kid."

We decide to stay for a few days to take in the scenery. Upstate New York is gorgeous. There are farms with big red barns and fields of wildflowers. Huge mountains kiss the sky. It's so different from the flatness of Long Island where I lived as a kid.

I figure we're a few days from the George Washington Bridge, or is it the Throg's Neck Bridge? I can't remember which comes first. I always called the Throg's Neck Bridge the Frog's Neck Bridge when I was young. I would travel over it with my family on our way to Oneonta. We had about ten acres somewhere near there. Dad really loved that property. Craig learned how to hunt there and honed his rifle skills. Dad taught him how to skin an animal and remove its guts. He was very proud of Craig's hunting prowess. I was jealous of Dad's praise for him. I knew I shouldn't have been and I felt like a bad person for it, but I couldn't help it.

Dad got as far as building a small cabin on the property, only the walls and roof, no electricity or anything. Craig's plan, when we first escaped our parents, was to travel to Dad's cabin. We never made it that far.

We set up camp on a man-made beach right on the edge of the lake. We need firewood so Brute lets me use one of his axes to chop some fallen trees. After about five minutes, he joins in. It takes me about ten swings to chop through a log. For Brute it takes two, three at most.

"Did you like hard work when you were younger, kid?" Brute asks between chops.

"To be honest, not really. I was more into sports."

"Oh yeah? What'd you like to play?"

I swing the axe like a bat. "Baseball."

Brute hacks at a log and splinters shoot above him. The smell of pine fills the air. "I was into wrestling and anything with a motor."

"You would have loved Craig."

"You would have liked Hank, too. Oh, I got some stories about him, kid." A smile crosses his face. "We would drive my dad crazy. Favorite story of all time is when he and I both got drunk on whiskey and decided it would be fun to jump Devil's Creek."

I raise a brow. "Devil's Creek?"

"Weird name, I know. Got it from two trees that stuck out from the bank. Looked just like devil's horns. The dirt around the trees made a perfect berm for jumping. My dopey friends," he points to himself, "and yours truly of course, would try to jump the creek on our motorcycles. No one ever made it." He lifts his pant leg to reveal a nasty scar on his knee. "Have the battle scars to prove it. Well, one day, Hank and I decided we would jump it with our dad's truck."

"Did you make it?"

"Slow down, kid. I'm gettin' there. I nailed the gas from about a quarter mile away. Must have been doin' 80 when we hit the berm. Truck went flying, but the bumper went soaring ahead of us. We landed and heard a loud crunching sound."

"The bumper."

"Right, kid. Of course we didn't know this, so we got out, high-fived, and jumped for joy. Heck, we had just jumped Devil's Creek. Hank noticed the mangled bumper first. 'Oh crap,' he yelled. 'We're dead meat.' We panicked, tied the bumper to the truck, and dragged it all the way home. Didn't know what to do. I think we duct taped it to the truck, hoping my dad wouldn't notice. To be honest, I don't remember much. I was pretty drunk. My dad woke up in the morning screaming to all high hell. He chucked his army boots at us. They hit Hank right in the noggin." He slaps his knee and leans against a tree. "Oh, kid, those were some good times."

We continue to chop wood and share more stories. I tell him about the time my brother shot me with a BB gun and the pellet got stuck in my leg for two months. Brute laughs so loudly that birds scatter from the trees. I find myself joining in. I haven't laughed in so long. Could my depression be lifting? Maybe. I show him the scar on my knee where the pellet entered. It's not as nasty as his, but he seems impressed nonetheless.

Brute also shares with me that he spent over a year in rehab, struggling to get over a heroin addiction. He had started experimenting with Hank, gateway type drugs, but they went too far. He met his only love there, June, and you can tell by the way he talks about her, that he adored her. He doesn't tell me what happened to her. Maybe he's not comfortable enough or it's just too painful.

I think Brute wants to change the subject because he says, "Hey, Kyle, we need some food. The meat's getting low. See if you can hunt something with your bow." I hate going into the woods because of the creatures, but we haven't seen any of them in a long time. Anyway, we need food, so I agree to go.

The forest is thick surrounding the lake. Tiny thorns poke my skin, stinging like bees, as I push through the dense bushes. Fortunately, it begins to thin out as I move deeper. There's not much as far as game in these woods, or at least I haven't noticed any. A few chipmunks pop their heads out of holes in the ground but I don't bother because their tough to hit with my bow.

The wet leaves are so slippery that I struggle to get up each hill. It poured last night, and it's difficult to keep my footing with any type of speed. I grab tree after tree, pulling my way up. When I feel stable, my feet slide from under me. It's very frustrating. I finally make it to the top of the hill and freeze. There, at the bottom of the adjacent hill, is a deer. How awesome would it be to get a deer? We'd have meat for a month.

I pull out an arrow and carefully place it on the rest of my bow. My heart races, but I creep along the forest floor, knowing that any slight noise will startle the deer. I place the nock of the arrow on the string and pull back. My arm shakes from the tension. Once I pull it all the way back though, I'm very still. I stare down the shaft, right through the arrowhead, to the rib cage of the deer. Its chest is rising with each breath, oblivious that its life will soon be over.

Out of the corner of my eye, I notice something ripping through the trees. It dives through the air and snatches the deer by the neck. It's one of *them*. I accidentally let my arrow go and it sticks into the ground next to the creature. The beast turns and stares at me with those eyes. I take a few steps back and slip in the wet leaves. My head smacks a rock and my eyebrow splits open. I cover the wound and blood oozes between my fingers. The smell of it makes me dizzy, but I know I have to bolt. The blood's scent will quickly attract it.

I get up and sprint as fast as I can. I want to yell for Brute but know I'm too deep in the woods for him to hear. I slip down hills and then half crawl, pulling as I try to climb up. I seem to be running forever when I turn and spot it. The monster's struggling with the leaves also, but it's so quick that it's gaining ground. There's no way I can outrun it. I fumble with an arrow and am able to fire right as it lunges for me. The arrow pierces the side of its leg and alters its flight. It slices its razor sharp claws, but I twist to avoid the blow. This sends me flying down the hill but actually helps my momentum.

The thick brush is straight ahead. If I can get there, I have a chance. "Brute!" I yell. "One of them's right behind me!" I dive through and land on my side, flipping wildly as pain shoots into my neck. Brute must have heard me because I see him chop down with his axe, slicing the beast's hand clean off. The creature falls to the ground thrashing about, writhing in pain. It rises and licks the wound.

"Into the water," Brute yells without hesitation. I get up and begin half-crawling, half-running into the lake, Brute dragging me most of the way. The creature pursues, but stops. It looks at us and slowly twists its head, which lets out a loud crack. I wonder if it knows it can drown. It again licks its wound at the wrist, but doesn't show any more signs of pain. The arrow still sticks out of its leg, and blood spurts with each breath it takes. The creature's breathing is as I remember it, fast and forceful. And those eyes, veins pulsating. The beast moves deeper in the water, up to its knees, and hisses at us. Brute and I start to swim into the lake when a loud scream, definitely not human, comes from the woods. The beast turns, screams, then bounds onto the beach and leaps through the brush of the forest.

Brute grabs my arm and pulls me towards the shore. "That was a close call, kid. Are you all right?"

"I'm okay," I lie, feeling like my heart will explode from excessive beating. "Just a little shaken."

Brute gets out of the water and collapses onto the sand. I follow, legs feeling like Jell-O. I rub my neck, and pain zings down my back at the slightest touch. We sit wet all night, miserable, not starting a fire for fear of the beast returning. We now know we are getting closer to the city and will probably see more of them. I have a hard time falling asleep, but when I do, I again dream of my family and Summer, and me falling out of sight as they kill her.

CHAPTER 4

FOUR YEARS EARLIER

As I flee, I sob uncontrollably. I never realized how hard it is to run and cry at the same time. Branches whip my face as I follow Craig and Lauren. There's not much distance between each house, so the woods are relatively thin. Porch lights make it bright enough to see, but I still occasionally fall and struggle to keep up.

When we come to a street we race across to get to the protection of the trees. As we travel, screams echo and I wonder if our horror is playing out everywhere. I want to yell and tell Craig and Lauren to stop. I need to talk with someone, anyone, about what's happening.

The route Lauren is taking is familiar, and I realize where we're headed. It's where all the teens go when they meet at night, Split Rock. Split rock is a huge rock that was split in two. The crack between the two pieces is big enough to walk from one side to the other, though it eventually narrows, forcing you to squeeze through. I've been there at night a few times. It's mostly a hangout for the older kids, though. My friends and I would go during the day and have seen the half-smoked cigarettes and empty beer cans.

It's a long way, and I wonder how we'll ever get there without stopping. Lauren's a smoker, and her coughs get nastier after each stride. We run for a few more minutes when finally she stops. "What…" she pauses, gasping for air, "the hell is going on?"

"We have to keep moving," Craig whispers as he pulls in short breaths. "I saw one of them coming out of Mrs. Blake's house. We're not safe here."

"You're right. Let's keep going," Lauren says softly through loud wheezing. "I can't run anymore, so we'll walk the rest of the way."

I feel much safer walking. We hide behind the bigger trees as we move and make much less noise. I'm also more aware of my surroundings. My breathing slows and that's when the horror becomes even more noticeable. Blood curdling screams come from every direction. The sound makes my skin crawl, and I try to drown it out by humming the theme to Star Wars. It doesn't work.

We finally make it through the houses and cross the last street to the outer edge of the forest. We still have a ways to go to get to Split Rock. The moon and stars shine brightly, so I can see relatively well. We walk less than a hundred feet into the woods when I hear a familiar voice. "Hey, who's there?" the voice whispers. It's my best friend Mark. Hearing him makes me smile for just a moment.

"Mark, it's Kyle," I say. "Thank God you're okay." I grab his arm and pull him in for a hug. It feels a little weird, but he's my best friend and I love him. I'd never tell him that, of course. One time, I invited him to my birthday party and he couldn't come. I cried for two hours straight. He ended up being able to make it, and I was ecstatic. Craig ruined it all though by telling everyone I cried. I'll never forgive him for that one.

Lauren and Craig pat Mark on the back when his brother, Doug, runs in right behind him. "Did your parents go nuts, too? My mom ate my freakin' cat." I don't know why I find that funny, but Doug always makes me laugh. He's the town stoner and class clown. I also hate cats, which adds to my awkward chuckle.

"Yeah, our parents killed my boyfriend," Lauren says, choking back tears.

"Everything's going to hell. It's like we're all instant orphans," Doug says. "We're headed to Split Rock to hide. Have you seen any others change besides your parents? I noticed a few more. It seems like all the adults are going nuts."

"I noticed a few as I was running," Craig says. "I think Mr. Lenahan got Steve. When I passed his house it looked that way." Steve Lenahan was good friends with Mark and me, and I suddenly feel sick to my stomach. Craig points towards a path in the woods. "Let's keep moving and be quiet. We'll talk when we get to the rock. I don't feel safe here."

We march in silence the rest of the way. It reminds me of some of the war films I used to watch with Dad. The soldiers would march silently into battle, knowing that most of them wouldn't survive. Memories of my parents pop into my head as I walk behind Lauren. They start with good thoughts, and then the image of them as monsters interrupts.

We're getting closer to Split Rock, and I look forward to talking to Mark, really just anyone. There's a small building with graffiti sprayed across it up ahead. Mark and I used to climb on its roof and jump off. Split Rock was on the property of an old nuclear power plant that was never in operation. Dad said the protesters stopped it from ever running and he was pissed because it caused his taxes to go up. I think the small building was an old security guard outpost, but I knew the rocks were just over the next hill. My legs start to burn, and I labor to climb when I notice lights flickering ahead. The tops of the boulders peek over the hill as flames reflect off them.

About 20 to 30 figures surround a fire. By their heights, I figure they're mostly teenagers. We approach with caution, but my sister recognizes most of them as kids from her high school.

"Thank God you're all safe. Did your parents go crazy, too?" she asks.

A tall teen steps forward to speak. The hair on my arms stands straight up. It's Ryan Murphy. Most people think he's cool, but I hate him. He picks on Mark and me relentlessly. He's one of my friend's older brothers and he's the bully of all bullies. One time, he got Mark and me to kneel in mud and kiss his feet in front of the school. That was humiliating. Mark actually cowers slightly when he steps forward.

"A few of us were here already," Ryan starts explaining, "so we haven't seen any of the crap going on. At first, I thought it was a prank, but I can see the fear and seriousness from whoever arrives. Everyone's said it's been the adults, but Nick said his brother went crazy, too. Right, Nick?"

Nick is Ryan's best friend and slightly nicer. I think he knows Ryan's a jerk but wants to remain in the cool group so he tolerates him. "Yeah, he came back from college last week. He started acting weird a few days ago. My parents changed much quicker. They were screaming earlier today and then just went nuts. They got Megan, man. My mom would never hurt Megan; she was her little princess. This is all too crazy."

The older kids are the ones dominating the conversation. I sit next to the fire, afraid to speak up. Ryan would probably push my face in the dirt if I did. Man, I hate him. "Hey, Kyle," Mark says as he sits next to me. "How you holding up?"

"Not so good." I cover my face and fight the tears. "I can't stop thinking about my parents."

"Yeah, first my dad, now my mom," Mark says. Mark's dad passed away two years ago. He had some form of cancer. He was a really nice man. Mark was devastated by it, and it took a long time for him to act like himself again. "I know it's really hard for us right now. But the saying 'time heals all wounds' is true. I never forgot about my dad and it still hurts, but it gets easier to think about him as time goes on."

Mark and I talk for a while. The older kids are still surrounding the fire. Everyone's telling the story of how their parents changed, and even the tougher kids start to choke up and have to stop. After a while,

I'm so tired that I scoot over and lean against Lauren, my head falling into her lap as I try to stay awake. I hear more kids arrive and more stories of horror being told. Lauren pats my head to soothe me, and the touch of her fingers and the warmth of the fire ease my shaken self to sleep.

CHAPTER 5

PRESENT DAY

Brute slaps my head to wake me, and I sit up rubbing the pain. Man, he's strong. After breakfast we decide to break camp and move on after last night's experience. The creature never returned, but we don't want to take the chance that it might. I push branches aside as we travel, and everything seems to startle me. A bird chirping in the distance, or the wind rustling some leaves causes me to arm my bow. It may take a little while for my nervousness to subside.

We trek through the forest over the next few days making sure to stay off any roads. Brute's ahead of me when he says, "Hey, kid, this way." He points to a small path. We follow it down a steep hill and out through an opening in the woods. Straight ahead there's a tremendous bridge. It's a mass of metal that juts over a huge river. The tall piers that hold it erect glisten in the sun. The bridge is so long that I can't see it touch down on the other side.

To the right of the bridge is the skyline of Manhattan. I've only seen it from a car, and from this angle, the buildings look humongous. Some of them push into the clouds and seem to rise up forever. The setting sun reflects off the building and shoots into the small waves of the river. I stand and stare with my mouth wide open. With the bridge and buildings together, it's the most majestic thing I've ever seen.

Brute begins to unpack. "That's the George Washington Bridge, and this is the Hudson River. We'll set camp right on the edge for protection. I know it's cold but no fire tonight."

Dusk settles in and there are still some lights on in the city, but it's not nearly as bright as usual. I sit at the edge of the river, Brute lounging in the grass next to me, and the stars twinkle overhead.

"This reminds me of my mom." I sigh, remembering the nights Mom and I would lay on the hood of her car and search for shooting stars.

"I used to live near here years ago. When the lights lit Manhattan, you couldn't see these stars. Hey, kid, you haven't said much about your mom. What was she like?"

I usually don't talk about Mom's illness, but after first telling Brute a lovely story about her, I open up.

"She had a serious mental illness," I say as the weight of never telling anyone lifts off my shoulders. "She was such a wonderful, loving mom and then, without notice, would turn manic pretty quickly."

"How so?" Brute asked, seeming extremely curious, as if he had someone in his family with a similar affliction.

"She had manic depression. Lithium levels in her brain would fluctuate." I sound so smart, but it was hours spent studying online, trying to figure out why Mom's mental state would change so rapidly. "If she didn't take her medicine, she'd start screaming at my dad and spending money wildly. She was also very sexual and would embarrass me in front of my friends."

"I know what you mean, kid. Months before he died, my brother was diagnosed with schizophrenia. It was so difficult because he wouldn't take his pills. It's almost like he enjoyed the high."

"My mom, too," I say, remembering the time I found a pile of pills hidden in the cookie jar, wondering why she wouldn't want to be better. Not knowing that she couldn't help herself, couldn't control it. I'd sit up night's crying, wondering why God would do this to me. Not realizing that it affects so many families. Thinking I was the only one. I instantly feel closer to Brute, knowing he has felt the same pain. I fall asleep peacefully, no nightmares, no feelings of despair. I know I have a friend, a really big one, and I'm not alone anymore.

Brute shakes me awake. He's probably trying to do it lightly, but with his big paws it's like a bear shaking a salmon. "Kid, get up. We have to cross the bridge." I sit up and rub the sleep from my eyes. It's dark. The sun has yet to rise. I want to ask Brute why the heck he'd wake me so early during my first good night's sleep in years, but I figure he wants to cross the bridge in the dark. When I first saw the bridge, I thought how beautiful it was, but now it dawns on me how dangerous it could be to cross. There's no escape route if we see one of the creatures. Yeah, it's surrounded by water, but the people that jump off bridges don't want to survive.

"Is there any other way into the city?"

"I don't see any boats, so a bridge is the only way. We could take the Verrazano, but the traffic's terrible on the Belt." Brute laughs so loudly I imagine it's how a giant would sound. I laugh more because of the way he reacts, but instantly cover my mouth looking around for them. We're closer to the city now, so we have to be careful. He's still smiling as we gather our stuff and head towards the bridge.

Brute explains that last night we actually traveled adjacent to the Palisades Parkway in order to move through woods to the bridge. He also felt it safer to follow along the water in case we encountered one of them. I agree with him and tell him how smart he is.

We pass through a park and a stench overwhelms me. There are carcasses of all different types of animal, mostly human, spread through the square. I pray I didn't know any of them and painfully move on. There's a highway sign that says, "Henry Hudson Dr. George Washington Bridge 1/4 mile."

"Hey, Brute, should we take the highway?"

He shakes his head. "We'll follow it, but stay in the woods as far as possible. Keep a keen eye. Once we get on the bridge, the water will be to our disadvantage. And stay close. I don't want to lose you." It feels great hearing him say that.

The woods thin out as we follow the road. Eventually, there are only a few trees and it seems silly trying to hide. Brute points to a service ladder that bypasses the tollbooth. We scurry up the rungs to the lower level of the bridge. No cars are traveling through, and the tollbooths are abandoned. I had half-hoped that the city would be bustling with everyday life, but I can see that hope is gone.

We climb up a skinny service walk, and we're able to stay off the road of the bridge. Cars litter the road, most overturned. Whoever was inside did not survive, judging by the blood soaking the pavement. There aren't any bodies in the cars or around them. Maybe the creatures dragged the carcasses to the park we had seen before.

I look over the edge of the bridge, and water glistens below as I follow behind Brute. From the back, his massive shoulders seem almost unreal. Can someone be that big? I have never noticed this before, but as he walks he squeezes his fists and his forearms bulge with every stride. He looks like he's entering a fight with each step he takes. I wonder if he realizes how intimidating he is.

On his back are two axes that cross each other. Every once in a while he reaches back and makes sure he can grab the handles of both of the axes. During one practice, he wields both and swings them with such power and grace that I clap at the feat. Brute bends down to take his bow when one of the creatures just misses him midair, its leg slightly brushing Brute's face. Oh, crap! Where did it come from? I fire my bow and shoot it in the thigh. It winces and yanks out the arrow. The creature charges, and I whip its face with the lower limb of my bow. This blinds it for a second. I snatch an arrow and stab it in the neck, hitting its jugular. The creature rears back, eyes blazing. Gobs of blood spew from the wound. It pushes towards me with its back legs pumping but slows quickly. A gurgled hiss foams from its mouth. It reaches for me, claws swiping the air, and collapses on the pavement.

The jugular, of course! I've found another way to kill it, and outside of drowning them, this was my first kill. I'm so proud of myself. During my elation, another creature leaps from behind a car. It spots me and advances, intent on ripping my head off. I arm my bow and aim for its jugular but before I can shoot Brute reaches behind his back and grabs both axes. He soars through the air, weapons converging as one. His muscles bulge as he lands and whips the two axes together. One axe collides with the other in the middle of the beast's neck. Its head pops up in the air as its body falls lifeless to the ground. I half expect him to say something cool, like those action heroes would say in the movies, maybe "I guess he won't be getting ahead in life" but I snap out of it. I realize this is no movie and these things want to kill us. Brute points to keep moving and as he glances over, I slice a finger through my jugular and he nods.

We duck behind each car as we gradually cross the bridge. I didn't notice the two that just attacked, so every hidden spot on the bridge is a potential ambush. I keep my bow armed and never lower it. Brute's muscles tighten when we pass each car and I know he's ready for anything.

We finally cross what seems like the middle. The other side looks clear of movement. The sun begins to peek through the tall skyscrapers. It's such a calming sight amidst all the chaos. I even notice Brute pause for a brief moment to gaze at the beauty. The sun keeps rising and I'm temporarily blinded, but the warmth feels wonderful. I take a deep breath and fill my lungs with the warm air.

It takes about two hours to cross the bridge. Brute spots another service ladder, and we climb down the side. There's a sign that says "Fort Washington Park" and we enter the woods there. I'm relieved to be off the bridge, knowing we're much safer in the forest and near water. I expected to see more of them and hope that maybe there aren't that many left. We set up camp next to the river and can see across to the other side. I vaguely spot where we stayed last night, scan the bridge, and realize how far we traveled. Brute's paw grasps my head and turns it back to the middle of the bridge. The hope I just had disappears.

A man's fleeing and about five creatures are in pursuit. They trap him up against the side of the bridge. He climbs over the edge. What's he doing? He looks down at the water and back at the beasts. He twists and leaps. One of the creatures follows, clawing at the man as they plummet. I can't watch, but a loud splash tells me his fate. He must've been so scared of them if he thought his best option was to jump. I feel real sorrow for him, even though we've never met.

I also realize that he was a man and that means that he was one of the immune. There aren't many of them. Brute's the first I've met, and now this bridge jumper. I'm guessing way less than one percent don't turn when they reach adult age.

Brute seems shaken. "Let's stay close to the river," he says. We travel about a half-mile and set up camp early. There will be no fire tonight, and I doubt I'll get much sleep.

CHAPTER 6

FOUR YEARS EARLIER

The smell of fire wakes me, and my eyes water as smoke wafts over my head. I'm lying next to Craig. Lauren must have moved me last night. My muscles ache, and the ground is so hard that my neck cramps as I turn to look around the base of Split Rock. Bodies surround the two boulders, only a few covered with blankets. One or two tents are set up and they are bulging with kids. I guess no one had time to think of what supplies to bring. They just wanted to get away from their parents. I don't blame them. I wipe the sleep from my eyes and notice Lauren sitting at the trunk of a tree, smoking a cigarette.

"How did you sleep, little buddy?" she asks.

"Not bad, I guess. How bout you?"

"Not much. I keep thinking of what happened last night and how screwed we…" She pauses and glances at me. I can tell she doesn't want to upset me. "Just had a hard time, that's all."

Craig opens his eyes for a moment, then rubs them with his fists and falls back to sleep. I lie next to him, needing more rest. I must have dozed off for a while and am wakened by yelling.

"Listen, we can't stay here forever," Ryan yells. He points his finger in Max's face. Max Keller is the toughest kid in Lauren's school. I almost expect him to snatch Ryan's finger and rip it right off his hand.

"I'm staying till we figure out what the hell is going on here!" Max screams back.

"And how we gonna figure it out genius?" Ryan yells. "Do you see any TV's here? No one's phone has reception this deep in the woods. We have no idea what's happened. We have to see if anyone's still alive." I'm starting to agree with Ryan, but I hate him so much that I don't want to.

Max turns and waves his hand as if to say 'screw you' and walks away. Ryan's friends surround him and pat him on the back. You can tell they're discussing what to do next.

My stomach growls, and I feel lightheaded. I hope that someone's brought food, although I'm sure they'd be resistant to share. Luckily, Mark walks over and hands me half a banana. "I stole this from some guy over there. That's all I could find. My brother thinks we should move on, try to find some food. Where's Lauren?"

I glance around and shrug. My mouth's full of banana as I mumble, "I don't know." Mark laughs at how stupid I look. He sits down, and we talk for a while about what's happened. We both start to choke up, so I suggest that we climb the rocks to distract ourselves.

Long Island was created by a glacier basically dumping its contents as it slowly floated south. At least that's what my teacher, Mrs. Lawson, told us. I can imagine this big boulder being dropped here millions of years ago. What I can't imagine is what force split this boulder in two. An earthquake, lightning, a huge Godzilla-like monster? Before yesterday I'd have thought the last one crazy.

We jump onto the base of the larger rock and slowly start to climb. I've scaled these rocks so many times that I know every nook and the best footholds, but because of some moss, I still slip on the way up.

The view's stunning as we stand at the top. To the right's a long stretch of marshland with tall grasses at the edge of the forest. Along the edge there are fallen trees that Mark and I would climb, and then jump into the pools of water below. Straight ahead is more marshland and a river that our town's named after, Wading River. Mark and I'd wade through that river all the way to the Long Island Sound almost every summer day. On clear days, you can see all the way across to Connecticut.

I turn left and immediately see the ugliest, sore thumb possible, the Shoreham Nuclear Power Plant. A lime-green monstrosity. It's a tremendous building with a round, cylindrical generator jutting out of the middle. It totally ruins the beautiful nature surrounding it. I look away and wish it wasn't there.

"Hey, Kyle," Mark says and points to a large maple. "Right next to that tree's the muck mud." The muck mud, as we call it, is right at the beginning of the river. It's a pool of the nastiest muck. It stinks like a baby's two-day old diaper. Mark and I used to go there, jump in the mud, and try to escape. If you struggled, you'd sink farther. I once dove in head first, my legs pointing straight in the air. After he finished laughing, Mark had to pull me out. I almost died, but I laughed along with him anyway. After that day, we scattered pieces of wood over the most treacherous spots.

Mark and I stand and stare for a few more seconds, then leap across the split of the rocks to the other side. The smaller rock's flat so it's easier to sit on and relax. I look over the edge and pockets of kids talk below. There must be about fifty now.

"Hey, pin heads." Ugh, I know that voice anywhere; it's Ryan. "Get off, you twerps. This isn't for the little kids." Mark and I obey and scurry down the side. We stuck up to Ryan once, and we both had black eyes for weeks; it wasn't worth it. I jump off the rock, and Craig and Lauren approach.

"We have to figure out what to do next. We can stay here or go," Lauren says. "The only problem with staying here is food."

"I can hunt," Craig says.

"I know but we can't just eat meat. We need variety. We also need fresh water."

"What about the river?" Mark asks. "There's plenty of water there."

"That water's brackish," Lauren explains. "It mixes with the ocean, so it's mostly salt."

"I know where there's fresh spring water," I say. About a week ago I came to the marsh on my own, and as I was exploring along the edge of the forest, I noticed two bricks sticking out of the bottom of the hill. When I inspected closer, there was clear water flowing out. The earth acts as a natural filter and it had a crisp taste to it. We're all thirsty and decide to head down to the spring.

It's right where I remember. Water pools in my hand and I slurp it up. The coldness slides down my throat, and it's as fresh as ever. We each take a few handfuls, and Lauren talks about how this might be a good place to stay after all. I'm happy. I don't want to leave.

The huge rocks peek over the trees as we make our way back. A few kids are sitting on the flat side, talking. The sun begins to set, and its rays scatter throughout the leaves. We reach the bottom of the boulder when suddenly one of the kids on the top stands and points off in the distance. "Look!" he yells. I can't see anything, but his screams cause everyone to stand and point.

"Over there!" someone shouts. Craig jumps up on the rock and covers his mouth in shock. I follow and finally see what's causing all the commotion. Running over the hill are two boys who must be younger than me. Not far behind are four or five of the creatures, ripping through the trees, converging on them. A beast slashes one of them from behind and drags him to the ground. It rips open the boy's neck then stares right at me with those eyes. It throws its prey to the side and tears straight for me. I'm stiffened by fear, unable to budge.

"Let's get outta here!" Craig yells.

Everyone in the camp scatters. A body plummets from the rock above, smashing into the ground next to me. Craig and I jump on the rock, but Lauren grabs us from behind, dragging us to the ground. My ears ring from the piercing screams, and my head starts to swim. I can tell Lauren doesn't know which way to run because I'm spun in a circle and this adds to my confusion. Everything seems to be moving in slow motion as I see a beast slam into a girl.

"In here." Lauren throws us into the split in the rock. She shoves us farther into the crack, and my ears stop ringing. Things seem to quicken. I can still hear screams, but they're deadened somewhat. The inside of the rock is ice cold as I hug against it. Craig pushes me and I slide along the wall, stopping in the middle. "Are you hurt?" Lauren asks.

"No," we both answer.

The screams seem farther away now. I peek out of the narrow opening about ten feet away, and there's no movement. I turn my head in the other direction. Craig's flattened against the wall, shaking. I can't see Lauren. I feel trapped. I'm gonna faint. My knees wobble, and I slump against the wall. I'm stood up straight by Lauren's screams and a sudden push. My face scrapes against the side of the rock. Wincing, I shuffle my feet towards the opening.

"Move," Lauren yells. A strong shove throws me out of the crack, and Craig lands on top of me, elbowing me in the nose. Pain zings into my jaw as I brace for Lauren's weight, but I don't feel anything. I look back and she's wedged in the crack, pulling her stomach in, trying to squeeze through. She reaches her hand out and stretches her fingers as if to say 'pull.' "Help me, please."

Craig and I jump up, grab her arm, and yank as hard as we can. All three of us slam into the ground with a loud thud. I sit up dazed. I turn to the rock and the creature's jammed in the crack. It reaches for us, flailing its arms wildly. Lauren plucks us off the ground. "Run!" The creature breaks loose and heads back through the crack, determined to eat.

The tall grass that outlines most of the marsh is straight ahead. Maybe it's a good hiding place. I trip over bodies as I run and hope the monster will stop to eat. I enter the grass, and my face is whipped by tall reeds. They move easily as I push them aside, not once turning to see what's following us.

"It's right behind us!" Lauren yells. We finally break through the grass, and the stench of the marsh hits me. My feet sink into the soggy ground, and I instantly know what to do.

"Follow me."

It's tough running through the marsh, and the creature must be laboring too, because it hasn't caught us yet. Even though I can barely see, I feel my feet cross over wood. Craig and Lauren follow, and as we navigate a few more pieces, we hear a loud splash. I look back and right away the creature's stuck. It tries to force its way out, pushing its claws into the muck. It jerks wildly, not able to calm itself, then slowly sinks out of sight.

We hug, and Craig and I high five. I'm so amazed that the plan worked and proud of myself that I thought of it. We start heading back towards the grass when the tall reeds rustle violently. "Who's that?" Lauren calls. No answer.

We freeze, glancing over at each other and Craig mouths "run". We turn and sprint into the marsh as two beasts follow.

CHAPTER 7

PRESENT DAY

The thought of the beasts chasing that man keep me up most of the night. I dream of him falling, and then hitting the water, which jolts me awake.

Brute sits up with dew on his beard and wipes it off with his big paw. It looks like he slept very well. He's like Dad was; as soon as his head hit the pillow, he'd fall asleep and stay that way until he woke. I'm jealous because I've never been that way. I'm a very light, restless sleeper.

We eat breakfast without making a fire. I'm hungry for some hot food, but I bite into my granola bar and rub my head awake. Brute picks up his axe and runs his finger along the blade. "We're going to head into the city today, so be ready for anything."

"What exactly are we looking for?" I ask. "Do you think there's a place where someone's trying to find a cure?"

"I don't know, kid. But we'll never find out wasting away here. Let's go."

I like how matter of fact Brute is so I gather my things and follow. We walk through another quarter-mile of woods, and there's a long stretch of highway. We cross over the wide road and enter the city. The street sign says 161st Street. I've visited Manhattan with my family a few times, and the buildings don't seem as big as I remember. I think the street numbers were much lower; 42nd street keeps popping into my head. I also remember visiting Times Square.

As we walk, Brute points to his eyes, then points towards areas that appear dangerous. I wonder if Brute was once in the military, although he never mentioned it.

We proceed with caution as we make our way to lower Manhattan. We pass a playground that looks like it hasn't been played on for a long time. I imagine the kids that used to have fun here, sliding down the slides and swinging on the swings. I'm enjoying that moment when Brute pushes me up against a car and holds a finger to his lips. "Shh."

He points to a street corner about a block down where a beast is feeding on a corpse. It hunches over the body, ripping flesh from bone with its sharp teeth. It's the only time they calm down slightly, when they're filling their bellies. It's the first time I've really seen one without fleeing in the other direction.

The beast's body is hairless. Its pale skin tight, veins strewn throughout. Its ripped chest and huge shoulder muscles rise and lower with every breath, blood pumping through its veins. A scream bellows from deep in the city. The creature cranes its head towards the sound. It snatches what's left of the lifeless body and bounds away.

My stomach begins to growl. "Hey, Brute, I'm starving."

"After that?" He raises an eyebrow. "Are you sure?" I nod, and he shrugs. "Alright, look for a store."

The city has a grocery on almost every corner, and we enter the first one we see. The shop's small and has one of those counters that's surrounded by plexi-glass for protection. I wonder if maybe this wasn't a safe area—I mean before the change; now no place is safe.

"Grab what you can, kid. This store's small, and I feel trapped. There's only going to be canned and boxed foods. Most of the boxed will be stale so let's stick to the cans. See if you can find a can opener. Only take what you need."

"Okay."

I didn't notice when I first walked in, but the store's a mess. What looks like cereal, and maybe crackers, are strewn all over. Someone must have been looking for food and found it stale. There's movement on the floor and I raise my bow, but it's only a rat, scrounging. I walk down an aisle and see Brute's enormous head extending over the shelves next to me.

I pick up a cereal box and start reading the back. I just can't help myself. I dump a few flakes into my hand and force myself to taste it. I close my eyes and bite what amounts to cardboard. I'm wishing I were the rat, willing to eat anything, when I hear what sounds like metal tap together. I peek over the shelves and Brute's arms are extended, clutching two cans of Chef Boyardee, a funny grin on his face. I giggle as I take out my hunting knife and stab at the top of the can. It just dents the lid. I stab harder, and the smell of sugary tomato sauce fills the store.

We can't start a fire for fear of attracting them so we eat it cold. I used to love Chef Boyardee as a kid, but have always eaten it hot. It's incredibly good cold. Brute grasps his can, dumps the contents into his mouth, and gobbles it down, unaware that a few of the little meat balls stick to his beard. I point to a mirror next to him, and when he glances at himself, he looks at me and starts bellowing so loudly that I spit a meatball on the floor and join in. We stay in the store for a while, covering our mouths to stay quiet, trying desperately not to attract them.

We eat our fill, gather ourselves, and walk towards the center of the city. The buildings begin getting much taller, which makes me feel much smaller. The streets are silent, and although littered with cars and garbage, there are always a few corpses in sight.

Brute doesn't talk as we walk, and I find my mind wandering. I expected to be attacked by the beasts every few feet, but we haven't seen any for some time. A few of the building's windows are reflective, and I pose in different menacing ways, my imagination running wild. I pretend to shoot my bow, saving Summer from her demise.

"Kid, pay attention," Brute scolds.

"Sorry. I'll stay alert." Brute nods and turns. I raise my bow, making sure he doesn't see, and continue my rescue.

When my daydreaming ends, I notice that we're crossing over 57th Street. Brute motions to follow him a block over to 7th Avenue, and when we turn left, there's a huge void. A tremendous black screen hangs on a building, and I can tell this is Times Square. "It looks so different without the lights," Brute says. He's right. I remember the lights and neon signs. The screen would flash with different advertisements. But now it's dark, and just doesn't have the same luster.

As we approach the square, it feels wide open. We pass a ticket booth, and I remember waiting on that line for cheap tickets. As we get closer, there's a terrible sight. About twenty of the creatures are feeding on human carcasses, tearing flesh from the bodies. The rotting smell is so awful that when Brute drops to the concrete for cover, the contents of my stomach go with him. I feel like I'm going to vomit again when Brute pulls me down into my puke. I throw up in my mouth and swallow, throat burning as the acid retreats.

"Stop it." Brute whispers through clenched teeth. "Don't make a sound." I want to stop, but I just puked in my mouth. It's almost impossible not to hurl again.

Brute grabs the hood of my cloak and begins to pull, then freezes. One of the beasts looks up, sniffing the air. I freeze too, body cemented to the ground. It twists its head and looks around, then continues feeding. I'm too afraid to move, and Brute seems the same. We're not really hiding, but we're far enough away to not be noticed. Yet. Do we run? Do we stay here?

I feel my heart beat as we lay sprawled on the pavement. I find it weird that it's a slow, rhythmic beat, then realize I haven't taken a breath and feel lightheaded. Suddenly, my throat begins to tickle. Crap, I have to cough. Come on, Kyle, not now. I squeeze my abdomen, trying to hold it in. Brute notices and reaches for my mouth to stop me, but he's too late and I cough into his hand instead. He grabs my shoulder and, although he probably wants to throw me against a wall after the cough, throws me into a dash. We take off down the street, the creatures screaming behind us. I sprint as fast as I can, slapping my head, thinking how careless I am. How Brute's life and mine will be shortened by a stupid cough.

CHAPTER 8

FOUR YEARS EARLIER

As we're running I can't help but think of Dad. It strikes me as weird that at the most stressful times I think of my family. I wonder if he's still out there, if he's the one who drowned in the muck mud, or if he's one of these two creatures about to devour us.

I peek over and see Lauren stumbling next to me, pulling in deep breathes as she wheezes. Stupid cigarettes! I'll never smoke. Craig's far ahead now, but his leg gets stuck in the mud and we catch up to him as he yanks it out. Even in the dark, I can run pretty well in the marsh. I know the little islands of land that are surrounded by pockets of water. I jump from one island to the next with each stride. I figure the creatures must be getting stuck, and hopefully they are falling behind. Up ahead, the moonlight reflects off the marsh. It must be the first part of the creek we have to cross.

The creek that makes up Wading River snakes through the marshland all the way to the Long Island Sound. At times it's really deep and Mark and I'd have to swim across; other times we could walk. If the tides were low, most of the creek was pretty shallow; at high tides most was deep. We approach the edge, and water's spilling over the bank. It's high tide. I turn to see the creatures' eyes and fangs glowing in the moonlight. Without hesitating, I jump. It feels like slow motion. Craig decides to dive head first into the water, looking like superman. Lauren's arms flail as she flies, not quite the superhero. I can only imagine what I look like.

Some of the channels of the creek are small enough to jump over, but in the dark I can't tell if I'll hit water or the mud of the bank. My legs hit first, smashing into water. My head enters next, feeling like its hit a brick wall. I'm flipped over and spun around. Already gasping for air, I push my legs to stand, but they sink into the muddy bottom. I emerge to gulp air and see Craig pulling himself up the other side. Reaching for the edge, I claw at the mud, but it's like grasping butter. I strain to pull myself up slightly, but slip back down the bank, submerged in the water again. I hear the splash of two more enter the creek. It's them. I look over and see the creatures struggling. They can't swim. Arms flailing wildly, a claw slashes Lauren's side. She screams and reaches for me. I clamp onto the grass and turn to help Lauren but don't spot her. Where did she go? Did they grab her? Did she go under or get swept down river?

The creatures' bodies flail, water flying everywhere. Lauren finally pops up, gasping. If I don't get to her, they'll tear her to shreds. I stomp one leg into the mud and it sinks deep. The mud adheres like cement, holding me secure. I extend my arm towards her. "Lauren!" She reaches and grabs my hand. The weight of her slaps my face into the mud, and I strain to hold on. I pull as hard as I can, but I can't lift her. Lauren slips from my grip, but she drifts to the side and is able to grab the edge. She slowly lifts herself over the bank and collapses. Heart beating out of my chest, Lauren sprawled on the ground in front of me, I see the creatures' claws clutch the grass and begin to pull themselves out. "Lauren, get up! Now! We need deeper water!"

"I'm hurt," she says, grabbing her side in pain, barely able to speak. "Just keep running." There's no way I'm leaving Lauren to be killed by these beasts, so I grab her arm and throw it over my shoulder. My legs immediately sink, and I can't lift them. I turn to see the beasts still stuck. Craig, muscles straining, yanks my shoulder, and my legs pop out. We grab Lauren and run.

There's a wide creek just ahead. If we can just make it to the water, the creatures will surely drown. Lauren's weight slows us considerably, and it feels like we'll never get there. I sense them about to seize us when I drop, dragging Craig and Lauren to the ground with me. The creatures soar over us, clawing as they crash into the water. They pop up and thrash their arms uncontrollably, then go under. Their heads emerge again, searching for air. Finally, they sink for good.

My face falls into the mud, the stink making it scrunch. I roll over and peek at the water once again just to make sure. Sitting in the marsh, every muscle beyond exhaustion, I wipe the mud from my face. "Are you okay, Lauren?

"I'll be fine," she says, "but I think we need to get out of the open."

"We should head to the Sound if they can't swim," Craig says. "We can stay in the water, so they can't get out to us." I agree with them both. And at least we now know a way to kill them.

We carefully walk across the marsh and follow the winding of the river. We want to stay as close as we can to the water, but because it's not a straight line, our progress is incredibly slow. I hear something in the distance and squint for focus. A figure is running across the marsh. We all dive for cover. It's not close to the size of the creatures, must be a kid. "Over here," Lauren calls out in a hushed voice. The figure turns and sprints towards us. As he gets closer, I can see it's Mark. He drops to his knees and pulls in a deep breath.

"Are you okay?" I ask, grabbing his shoulder to hold him up.

He grabs my arm and pulls me in close. "They're everywhere," he takes a deep breath, "and they're coming." He loses consciousness, and as his head hits the ground, three of the beasts emerge from the woods.

"Get up, Mark! Let's go!" I pull at his arms, but he doesn't budge. "Help me, guys, please."

Lauren and Craig rush over and we lift Mark up, but he's dead weight. We drag him while I slap his face, trying to wake him. "Just get into the water!" We get Mark to the edge and roll him into the creek.

I jump in and turn to look for them. My body's submerged, and my eyes float just above the surface like an alligator. Mark begins to drift away, and I grab his arm to stop him, pulling him next to me. Suddenly, his eyes shoot open and he shakes his head, a confused look on his face. I raise my finger to his lips. We float downstream and the sound of the beast's legs entering the mud gets louder. They stop at the creek's edge and peer around, noses sniffing the air. I look at Mark, Lauren, and Craig and can see the hopelessness in their eyes. A loud scream echoes from the forest, and almost as quickly as they appeared, they take off, bounding wildly back to the woods. I finally exhale, and Lauren pulls me to the edge of the bank. We lay in the mud, trying to catch our breath. I can't help but wish I were in bed curling my toes into my covers.

Mark thanks us and starts to weep. "I couldn't find Doug. I think he's dead."

"Have faith and pray he's alive," I tell him. Lauren consoles Mark with a hug, but he pushes her away

"I know he's dead. Everyone around me was getting torn to pieces. Nobody could escape that."

"How'd you escape?" Craig asks.

"I saw you guys run into the rock, but I couldn't get there. They came from all sides; it wasn't just the few we saw. There were dozens. I jumped under the side of one of the rocks, but a beast must have spotted me and grabbed my legs." He lifts his pants and his legs are scratched to his knees. "He was just about to eat me when Ryan cracked him on the head with a log."

"Ryan Murphy?"

"Yeah, Kyle. He yelled at me to run, and I fled into the woods. I only heard his screams."

"Why would he save you?" I say. "I don't get it."

"I don't get it either," Mark says. "Maybe he wasn't such a bad kid."

"Yeah, well, anyway, I'm happy he saved you," I say. It would be tough to lose my best friend.

As we start moving towards the Sound again, screams pinball through the trees in the distance. I try to drown them out by thinking of a special time with Dad. My favorite memory of him is when we visited my grandfather's island in Maine. Dad, Craig, and I would take a boat out there, and it would be just the boys for a day or two. Craig and Dad would fish and hunt and I'd search for wildlife, not to hunt but just watch. I'd see beavers, foxes, and the occasional black bear. At night we would build a fire and roast marshmallows while Dad told scary stories. If only he knew how scary reality is right now.

On the second day at the island, we started to run low on food, and a severe thunderstorm rattled the lake. The waves were so high we couldn't head back to the mainland. By the next day, all three of us were starving. We had a small canoe on the island and decided to paddle back along the shore. We laughed when we'd occasionally tip over. It was so much fun. When we reached the mainland, Mom and Lauren treated us like heroes because we were able to defeat the storm and get home to safety. I felt very proud, and Dad knew it. He made sure to tell me how proud he was of me, and that I was becoming a man. I will never forget that day, and it makes me cry that I will never see Dad again. He meant everything to me; he was my soul. And for this to happen to him, it saddens me beyond repair. *I'll miss you, Dad, and I'll love you forever.*

Emotionally and physically, I'm exhausted. Everyone else must feel the same as we all collapse to the grass. We haven't seen any monsters enter the marshland, and we're happy with staying here for now. "What should we do about eating?" I ask, "Do you think we should start a fire?"

"I don't know if a fire's a good idea. It might attract them," Lauren says. "But then again, my clothes are soaked and I'm incredibly cold." We decide on a small fire, just enough to warm us and to cook.

"I'll go look for something to eat," Craig says. I'm nervous for him to leave, but I can feel my stomach growling. Mark goes with him. They soon come back, and Craig holds up what looks like a freshly killed duck. "We found it just inside the grass reeds. I don't know how long it's been dead, but I think if we cook it well enough, it should be okay." We all agree to try it, and Craig starts to gut the duck.

He first cuts the legs and pulls them off. He then spreads the ducks wings. They are so wide that they must span six feet. He cuts them at the joint and throws them aside. "You might not want to watch this part," Craig advises, but I can't look away. He uses the hunting knife and carefully cuts into the duck right below its neck. He then slides the blade down the duck's stomach to its rear. Blood spurts as he cuts. He reaches his hand into the duck and, in one pull, tugs out its organs. Its innards plop onto the ground. Craig was right, I shouldn't have watched. "The organs are still warm. This duck will be good to eat."

Craig cooks the meat over the small fire, and it seems to take forever. Once it's done, he tosses me a piece. "Be careful," he says, "it's hot." The meat burns my hand, so I juggle it before tossing it into my mouth. As soon as I taste that delicious, juicy meat, I could care less how many ducks I had to watch Craig gut. We keep thanking him for the meal and eat until everything's gone. The fire crackles, and with my stuffed belly, I feel content for the first time in days.

"How screwed up is all this?" Mark asks. "A few hours ago I was watching the Yankees, and now..."

"I know," I say. "What do we do now?"

Craig leans in. "We live. We survive. That's what our families would want us to do. We don't give up… ever."

Survive. I don't even know what that means anymore. Does it mean to live, to breathe? Does it mean to find food and water to quench our thirst? Does it mean to stick with our family till the end? Or to just exist? My mind's still racing as I fall asleep.

I wake to Lauren lightly shaking me and holding me up to her face. She whispers very softly with fear in her eyes. "Quiet, they're here." We must have dozed off. Why didn't we have someone keep guard? It was still dark, so we couldn't have slept for long. Smoke rises from the fire. Its smell must have drawn them. The beasts walk into the moonlight, saliva dripping from their fangs as they sniff the air. We are all sprawled on the grass, hidden in shadows. I peek over the grass and see the creature's slash at pockets of tall reeds, searching. They're close. They'll notice us any second. I have to distract them. I turn and roll over the bones of the duck. I squeeze what I think is the spine and heave it as far as I can. The beasts turn and bound after it like a dog. I stand, look towards everyone and mouth, "Run".

There must be water nearby? The power plant's close to the left. I know the mouth of the river sits right in front of it. It's not too wide, and on the other side is a jetty of rocks. We just have to get there.

I leap over the bank of the river expecting water but hit hard sand. Crap, it's low tide. Everyone lands next to me and we start scurrying over the opposite bank and onto the rocks of the jetty. I twist back, and the monsters have stopped at the edge. My foot gets jammed in a rock as I climb. I tug, but it won't budge. Mark grabs my leg, pulls, and my foot pops out of my shoe. My sock's now hanging half off while I slip on the moss of what seems like every rock. I hear the beasts splash into the creek and their claws scrape against the rocks as they climb.

We reach a fence that surrounds the plant and my fingers jam into the chain link as I start to pull myself up. Craig has always been able to scale anything like a monkey, and he scoots to the top. He grabs Lauren, pulling her over. My sock keeps getting stuck, making it next to impossible to climb. If I can just make it over, I'm sure the creatures will struggle, too. I slip again and begin to fall when Mark's hand pushes my back, shooting me to the top. I wrap around the fence, grasp Mark's arm, and pull, but he won't budge. Mark looks at me, eyes widened with pain. I pull again, but he won't come loose. "Come on, Mark! Climb!" There's no response, just a dampened scream. His hand slips from mine and he falls. The beasts tear at Mark as I collapse to the ground. "Get off of him!" I reach through the fence but know there's nothing I can do. I cover my face and sob when I'm grabbed from behind. Lauren shakes me and yanks my arm.

"Move it, Kyle! Craig found a ladder!"

My legs feel weak and I stumble, but Lauren holds me up. My best friend's dead. He saved me and I couldn't help him. I look to see if maybe he escaped, but it's obvious he hasn't. Blood's splattered all over the fence, and the beasts are ripping apart what's left of his body. I turn back and see Craig already halfway up a ladder leading to the roof of the round building of the power plant. Rust flakes off as I grab the rungs and start to ascend. It's well lit here. Even though the plant has never been in operation, the lights are always on for some reason, so I'm able to look down and see that one of the beasts has already scaled the fence and is on the ladder. I'm almost to the top when Craig's face peeks over the edge.

"Move, Kyle! They're right behind you." My legs pump as he keeps calling. I feel the heat of their breath on my ankles so I kick with all the strength I have. My foot connects with one of the creature's jaws, and although unable to see, I don't feel them anymore. Craig reaches for me. "They're still coming!" He grabs my arm and throws me into darkness. The roof's edge shields me from the lights. I stand and am temporarily blinded. Stumbling and unable to see, I move towards Craig's screams.

Craig stabs his knife into the old screws on the top of the ladder. "Help me push!" Lauren and I run over and grab the top, straining with every muscle. The first few screws pop out with a ping, but the ladder only lurches forward an inch or two. "Keep trying. They're almost here!" We push, but it doesn't seem to budge. I expect them to jump over any second and start tearing us apart. I let go and step back a few feet. Lowering my shoulder, I smash into the top. The remaining screws snap and the ladder starts to tip. My shirt gets caught in the metal, the weight of the ladder pulling me over the side. Lauren grabs my arm and stops me from falling. I look down, and the beasts are still clinging to the ladder as they smash into the ground. They spring up, searching for their meal, peering up at us with those eyes. They let out a loud hiss, then leap over the fence, breaking trees as if they're popsicle sticks as they tear through the forest.

Craig and I collapse next to Lauren, and we lean against the edge of the roof. Exhausted, I try to catch my breath when I hear a faint whimper hidden somewhere in the shadows. "Who's there?" I ask. Whoever it is shuffles against the side, hiding in the darkness.

"Please, don't hurt me," a young girl answers. I crawl towards her, and her face emerges from the shadow. She's beautiful.

"What's your name?" I ask.

"Summer."

CHAPTER 9

PRESENT DAY

Brute, throwing me into a run, has propelled me forward and I feel terrible that he's now way behind. I hope the creatures don't catch him because of me. My arms and legs are pumping. I don't think I've ever run this fast, but Brute barrels by. "Move it, kid." He looks like a locomotive chugging down the street. I sprint even faster now. Sweat pours from my forehead down to my lips. I spit out the salty taste in between quick breaths. Glancing at the reflection from a skyscraper's windows, I catch a glimpse of the creatures, eyes bulging, bearing down on us.

We turn the corner, and Brute hustles down the stairs of a subway entrance. I follow and immediately lose my footing. I tumble down and crash into Brute. His huge chest is like smacking into a concrete wall. He lifts me up and ushers me around the stairs to hide underneath. We catch our breath, and Brute points to a subway ticket booth. The beasts stomp down the stairwell as we enter it. Brute locks the door, and we huddle under the desk, silent. Sweat beads down Brute's brow into his beard. How are we gonna get out of this one?

I don't know if they can smell us or saw us enter the booth, but the creatures start to bang loudly on the glass. The noise echoes inside the booth when Brute taps my shoulder. "Hey, Kyle, did I ever tell you about June?"

"No," I answer, wondering why he'd bring it up now, then thinking maybe he wants to tell someone about her before we die. Regardless, I'm all ears.

"She was the most beautiful girl I've ever seen." Brute beams as the bangs get even louder. "I'm not too good with the ladies. I've had my share of girls, but I'm far from smooth. June and I, for some reason, had a connection right away."

The walls are shaking as the monsters keep banging on the glass. It must be bulletproof because it doesn't shatter, holding strong against their powerful blows. The walls begin to buckle, though; they'll collapse at any moment.

"I met her on my first night in rehab. She was also struggling with a heroin addiction. She helped me get through those first few nights of withdrawal, shaking under my covers, wanting to end it all. I didn't feel much love from my family. We never really showed emotion, but I loved her with all my heart. Without her, I truly believe I wouldn't be here. Wouldn't have ever met you, kid." His eyes start to well with tears.

"Whatever happened to her?" I ask, gripping my bow as the door begins to collapse.

"She got sick a month after we met." His eyes close as a creature's claws slash at us through the door. "She died in my arms, Kyle. Me holding her, wishing I had met her sooner."

I close my eyes, and Mom appears in front of me. She's tucking the covers under my feet, telling me I'll be okay. Dad kisses her cheek. "Hang in there, buddy." Lauren and Craig walk in and pat my head. They all smile, such beautiful smiles. I sit up to hug them, but they're gone. I lower my head. Tears fall between my legs. A hand lifts my chin and delicate fingers remove the hair from my forehead. "Don't cry," Summer whispers and wipes my tears. Her beautiful hazel eyes stare into mine. She kisses me, so slowly, then backs away. "I love you, Kyle," she says, backing away farther, her face seeming to glow. Her beauty is suddenly replaced by a beast's horror. The door has succumbed and they're in. I turn my head, ready to die, when a loud noise echoes from the subway tunnel. The monsters turn and tear towards the sound. Brute looks at me and shrugs. We both wipe away tears and slowly peek over the counter to see… nothing. I reach for the door handle, forgetting it's not there, and a hand grabs mine. Someone drags us out of the ticket booth just before it collapses in a heap.

The air has a smoky smell to it, like a firecracker. I figure that's what the stranger used to divert their attention. We leap onto the subway tracks, and the sunlight that was shining down through the stairs dissipates. Slightly disoriented from lack of vision, I trip but manage to right myself.

There's a cracking sound ahead, and I see a faint green glow. The stranger shakes it, and the glow brightens. A glow stick. I can now see about fifteen feet on all sides. Brute's running next to me, and the mysterious stranger's ahead of us. He's wearing black jeans and a black hoodie. He has the glow stick in his left hand and what looks like a dagger in his right. Whoever this is has a cat-like quickness, and we struggle to keep up.

I feel like we're putting some distance between ourselves and the beasts when one of them pounces on Brute. Brute grasps the monster by the neck and hurls it against the wall. The stranger sprints ahead with the light, and we're surrounded by black again. The sound of Brute's axe slicing through air passes my ear. I hold up my knife and slash into the darkness when a glow stick lands beneath us. One of the beasts enters the glow and Brute hacks its neck half off, blood splattering my face. I wipe my eyes, unable to see. I don't know how many there are. For a second, I get the urge to flee, but I'm not leaving Brute behind. I'll die right here, right now to help him.

I stab with my hunting knife, and the blade enters flesh. The beast screams and grabs my neck. My eyes focus. Now able to see, I slice at its neck. I miss my intended target but hit its shoulder. It stumbles back, and then lunges at me. A hand pushes my head aside, and the monster's jaw slams into the wall. A blade flashes through the darkness, slicing its jugular.

Two burning fuses roll a few feet away, and a loud bang follows, making my ears ring. The air fills with firecracker smell. At this point, I don't know which ways up and start to stagger away from the light. A small hand takes mine and drags me into something cold and damp.

Brute pushes me from behind. I try to stand and run, but my head hits the ceiling so I crawl as fast as I can. The walls are circular and feel like cement. It must be some kind of drainage pipe. I can just imagine how Brute's fitting through and actually hear his shoulders rubbing against the wall. "They're right behind me," Brute threatens. Brute pushes even harder, and I struggle to crawl fast enough to stay ahead of him.

I can barely see past the stranger but notice an opening up ahead in the pipe. There's a waterfall on the other side, about ten feet across. A rope dangles in the middle, and the stranger swings across and hits a lever on the other side. A piece of wood pops up, diverting the water to the sides to reveal a large sewer pipe. He swings the rope back and points into the pipe. Without hesitation, I swing. My legs enter the opening, and I let go of the rope. My elbows smash the sides and pain shoots up into my neck, the coarse concrete tearing into my skin. I turn to see Brute lunging out of the opposite pipe, not waiting for the rope. One of the beasts follow, biting at his feet as he flies. Brute's arms, head, and shoulders enter the pipe, but his lower half slams into the wall. The beast grabs his legs and Brute begins to slip. I grasp his shoulders and pull as hard as I can, but he won't budge. The stranger swings down and kicks the creature's face, sending it smashing into the wall and then plummeting into the pit below.

The stranger pushes off the wall with his legs, swings back, and kicks Brute's lower body. He and I go flying and crash in a heap on the floor of a small room. I stand to see the stranger hit another lever. The small door of the pipe falls and water rushes over it. He slides into the room.

He takes off his hoodie and blonde hair flows as she shakes her head. "They won't try to get through the water," she says. "We're safe now." I almost fall over.

He's... a *she*!

CHAPTER 10

FOUR YEARS EARLIER

Summer's shaking as I crawl up to her and take her hand. I pull her in close and she whimpers. Lauren and Craig slide over, and we embrace for what feels like an eternity. Normally I'd feel awkward holding someone I don't know, especially a girl, but that feeling never surfaces as we breathe slowly, trying to calm our nerves.

After some time, Summer pulls away and stands in the light. She has long, brown wavy hair that reaches her hips. Her skin's tan, like it was just kissed by the sun, and she has these stunning hazel eyes.

She sobs and drops to the ground, her hands in her face. "I've lost everyone." My awkwardness settles in, and I can't find the right words to say. Lauren kneels next to her in the darkness and whispers something while patting her back. Summer continues to cry when Craig grasps my shoulder and pulls me to the roof's edge.

We sit in complete darkness. "Let's try to get some sleep. In the morning, we'll hunt for food."

"Craig," I reach to grab where I think his shoulder is but miss, "thanks for saving me again."

"No problem, bro." Craig never uses my name. "I know you'd do it for me. Now get some rest."

Summer eventually stops crying, and it's quiet, so I assume everyone has fallen asleep. I put my head down, hoping to feel a pillow but hit the rubbery material that makes up the roof. It's actually kind of comfortable but smells like those pink school erasers, and anything that reminds me of school puts a bad taste in my mouth. I toss and turn and can't sleep. Visions of Mark keep popping into my head. All the fun we had together. The pranks we'd pull. Memories swim for most of the night, and right before I fall asleep I say, hoping Mark will hear, "Thanks for being such a good friend."

My eyes open to the sun beating down, heat rising in waves off the rubbery roof. The eraser smell's so strong now that the inside of my nose burns. I sit up and rub my head, knowing last night wasn't a dream. Summer's talking to Lauren, and I scan the roof but don't see Craig. I jump up, alarmed. "Where's Craig?"

"Relax, little buddy." Lauren points to the other side of the roof. I hurry to the edge and look over. There's another ladder that reaches to the ground. I can see most of the forest from here. The hills stretch all the way to the winding road that leads to our middle school. On one of the hills, Craig's hunting.

"Hey, Craig," I yell and wave. Without looking up at me, he raises his hand as if to say "quiet". His calculated movements suggest he has his sights set on something. The sound of his twelve-gauge echoes through the forest, and a few birds scatter from the trees. Craig runs over and holds up his kill, a fat groundhog. He throws it over his shoulder and begins to walk back to the ladder when something huge moves a few hills away. Right away I can tell it's one of the beasts!

"Craig, run!"

He looks up at me and waves his hand like "I'll be there in a minute."

"No, it's one of creatures!" I point frantically, and this time he understands. He grabs the groundhog like a football and sprints towards the fence. Lauren and Summer hurry over to the edge.

"What's the matter?" Lauren asks. She looks at the beast charging over the hill. "Oh, crap. Craig, move it!" From this view I can tell how enormous and quick it is. The beast tears through the woods with such strength that he obliterates small trees, smashing them to splinters. Craig reaches the fence and heaves the groundhog over. He scales it and leaps to the ground. The beast slams into the fence with what looks like frustration. It slashes the metal and then bounds off into the woods. Craig's safe, and my heart slows its beat. I'm so relieved when he climbs the ladder and hops onto the roof.

"Man, I have to be more careful," he says between heavy breaths. "It's almost as if I forgot they were out there. From now on, if anyone goes down, we have to have a lookout."

Craig takes out his hunting knife and plunges it into the groundhog's fat belly. Guts spill onto the roof, and I decide not to watch this time.

I'm able to break some wood off the edge of the roof and use my flint to start a fire. As I'm making the fire, I stare at Summer. I can't help it. In the daylight, she's even more beautiful. She has this really cool heart-shaped birthmark on her neck, and her hazel eyes mesmerize me. She looks up, and I turn away. I hope she didn't notice. I want to gather the courage to go talk to her, to walk up and say hello, but I just can't get over my shyness. She turns away and stares at the ground, twirling her hair. I wonder if she's shy, too. She's only talked to Lauren since we found her.

The fire's hard to start with all the wind, so I try to block it with my body.

"Need help?" Summer asks.

"Uh… sure." The words get caught in my throat. Smooth, real smooth. Summer kneels next to me and touches my shoulder. I feel like I'm going to die. She reaches down, her hand brushing mine, and throws in more wood. My head spins. She flips her hair back. I can't take it anymore. I stand up and escape to the other side.

"Is something wrong?"

It must take me a minute to answer. "No, I'm... sorry. I'm... just trying to block the wind."

"Oh, okay." She raises an eyebrow and walks back towards Lauren, shrugging her shoulders. Ugh. Why couldn't I talk to her? It was my chance to get to know her. I suck. My shoulders droop, and I stare at the fire, hoping it'll start itself. I pull in a deep breath and strike my flint again. The sparks turn to flames, and Craig tosses the groundhog onto the fire.

Summer asks Craig how he was able to catch the groundhog, and he's so smooth explaining how he did it. Craig was always good at talking to girls. He's already had like two girlfriends, and I've had zilch. Now I'm depressed and jealous.

Craig tells Summer what we've been through the last two days, and she finally opens up to us when he's done. "I was at the beach visiting my family. I had never been to Wading River before. My uncle rented a beach house for a week." She stops talking and lowers her head. She lifts up and tears race down her cheeks. She tries to start again, but can't.

Lauren pats her shoulder. "You don't have to tell us till you're ready."

Summer takes a deep breath. "I'm sorry. My uncle was so precious to me. He was always so nice and gentle. I was on the beach sunbathing, enjoying what I thought was a beautiful day, when he ran out of the house chasing my cousin. I just figured they were playing a game. He tackled Anna, and they rolled in the sand. But when they stopped, she was covered in blood. My uncle had his jaws clamped on her neck and was ripping it apart. I screamed but couldn't help her. I was so scared. I ran into the water and swam across to the jetty. I watched my uncle and aunt tear apart their family." She stares towards the beach and shakes her head. "Others ran out of their houses. It was a slaughter. I climbed the fence and found the ladder. I feel so guilty for leaving them."

"If you didn't, you'd be dead, too," Craig says.

"I know. I hid here and don't remember much. When you showed up I was terrified, but thank God you came. I wouldn't be able to survive on my own."

"What happened to your parents?" I finally work up the nerve to talk to her.

"I'm not sure what happened to my mom or dad. They live in Portugal. That's where I'm from. I wonder if the same thing's happening there. I actually live with my grandmother. She's been watching me since I was five."

"I'm really happy you're with our family now," Lauren says, "but we have a decision to make. Although it's safe, we can't stay on this roof forever. The rubber smell is nauseating and it's too difficult to get food. Plus, we need vegetables, fresh water, and to find some answers. I can only see the top of Split Rock, and it'd be nice to know if there are any survivors." She points towards the beach. "A few of the houses seem to still have power, and I haven't seen any of the monsters near them. Maybe there's food and water."

"I agree. We have to leave," Craig says, "but while we have protection, let's allow our injuries to heal."

We spend the next few days going up and down the ladder. We feel safe staying within the perimeter of the fence. It's much nicer on the ground, and I can't stand the smell anymore. A few of the beasts have been moving through the woods, but if there's any trouble, we can just climb up the ladder to the safety of the rooftop.

I explore the power plant and find that it's huge. The circular roof we've been staying on is one of three similar structures. Each has a large building underneath, and I search them for any supplies I can find. One building has an old cafeteria. I push its door open but don't see any food. In the corner is an old sink, and the faucet turns with a squeak. Brown, rusty water spits out. I let it run for an hour, and we now have an endless supply of fresh water.

Craig and I venture outside the fence and hunt for game, but also search for edible fruit. I show him some red berries from a bush near the fence. "Hey, Craig, is this good?"

"No, bro. Those are poisonous. You want to look for the ones that aren't so bright red." He picks some that aren't as colorful. "Try them. They're very juicy." It tastes good to eat something besides meat, and the sweetness and tartness together make my lips pucker. I pick a handful more and stuff it in my pocket for the girls.

"Hey, look over there." Craig points to a tree in the woods. "Notice anything?" I look then shake my head. "Behind the tree." I step to the side and standing there is a large deer. "It's a buck," Craig whispers.

"Well, duh," I say, feeling stupid for not knowing.

"Quiet, you'll scare him. Take your bow and aim carefully. You want to hit him right here." He points to his rib cage, right below his armpit. I pull back my bow and set aim. I'm so nervous I start to shake and let go. The arrow sticks into the tree right in front of it. The deer jerks and looks towards us. Craig grabs my bow and fires. The deer drops, then stands up for a slight moment, before falling and becoming still.

"You got him," I congratulate Craig. "Sorry I missed."

Craig pats me on the back. "You tried. That's what matters. We'll practice, and you'll get the next kill." We approach the buck, and its chest is barely rising and falling. "We have to put it out of its misery," Craig says. He takes his knife and plunges it into the deer's chest. The smell of blood fills the air. The buck's head shoots up, mouth wide open, and then drops to the ground, black tongue lying in the leaves. "It's way too heavy to carry over the fence," Craig says. "We'll have to cut off a hind leg."

Craig pulls out his knife and hands it to me. "Here, you try it." I shake my head so vigorously that I'm dizzy, but I have to start learning how to survive, although I'm content with Craig doing most of it.

Craig notices my apprehension. "You have to do this. You've seen all the death. Who's to say that I'm not going to be gone soon? You need to be able to protect and provide for the girls." He pauses, and I can tell he feels weird saying this to me, like a father-son talk. "Just promise me you'll try."

I nod and grab the knife. Craig points to where I should begin. I close my eyes and push into the skin next to the deer's groin. "You have to stab for the first cut," Craig says. Oh, great. I take the knife back and, closing my eyes even tighter, stab as hard as I can. The knife breaks the skin, and blood gushes from the cut. I feel woozy but right myself, hoping Craig didn't notice. "You know," he says, "usually you should drink the blood the first time." Craig laughs and elbows me. He knows that's not happening unless he wants the berries staining his shoes.

Craig's finger follows the deer's groin up to the back of his leg, and I follow the route with the knife. I pull and saw and can feel the muscles and ligaments being severed. Blood and fur mix, and the smell's awful. I'm able to saw up around the leg and Craig helps with the last cut to remove it.

"Bro, I'm proud of you." I'm proud of myself, too, but my knees feel weak and I fall to the ground. Craig laughs and helps me up. We bring the leg back to the power plant and have a nice meal. Craig tells the girls I killed the buck, and they're impressed. It's an experience I'll never forget. I'm happy I shared it with Craig, and for the first time, I feel like I can survive.

Over the next few days, Craig teaches us how to better defend ourselves, and we spend a good amount of our day inside the fence practicing. I'm becoming accurate with the bow and can hit any tree, even on the run. I'm running low on arrows, so I try to make some out of wood and feathers I collect. They fly about as straight as a drunken snake.

"You hold the butt of the gun here," Craig says as he points to his shoulder. Lauren and Summer copy him and aim the shotgun, although they don't fire in fear of attracting the creatures. He also shows the girls how to use the hunting knives—block with the arm and quickly jab with the knife. After practice, Lauren walks over to the fence and leans against it.

I sneak up behind and elbow her in the arm. "You two are getting good with the knives."

She turns and her eyes are red from sobbing. I pull her in close and hug her.

"What's the matter?" I ask.

"I'm sorry. I don't want to upset you guys. I just can't stop thinking of Mom and Dad. I was only home for a few days before this crap started. I never really talked to them about how mad they were."

I lift her head and stare into her eyes. "They loved you with all their heart, Lauren."

"I know. But even you have to admit how tough I was to deal with." I don't say a word, just stare. "See. I know I was mean to you and Craig. I just wanted to hang out with Eric. I wish I had spent more time with you guys, and Mom and Dad. I really regret it now."

Craig must have overheard us because he steps in and hugs Lauren. "Mom and Dad were mad at you, but I heard them talking a few times. They missed you so much. They wanted you to come home so badly. You were their little girl, and you meant the world to them."

Lauren cries into her hands and pulls us both in. "Thank you so much. You have no idea what it means to me to hear that. I love you, guys."

Lauren's in a much better mood over the next week, and she and Summer are becoming good friends. The power plant begins to feel like home, but we know we'll have to leave soon.

One morning, we decide as a group that it's time to go. We need to find the answers to why this has happened. We collect our supplies and stuff them into some bags I found in the buildings. Craig checks all the weapons and makes sure they're filled with ammunition. He then plans how we'll get to the vacant houses to search for supplies. "Above all," he says, "stay next to the water." We start to climb the fence, and I turn back towards the power plant and realize that even though I hated how it looked and how it destroyed nature, it saved our lives, and I know we won't have its protection anymore.

I reach the top of the fence, and a light breeze carries the smell of salt water. It calms me as I pull in a long sniff. We descend into the water, and although it feels ice cold, I quickly adjust. It's not high tide, but its depth forces me to tiptoe across. At one point, Summer is lifted by the current, and I instinctively grab her so she isn't swept away. She looks at me and smiles. My cheeks feel warm, and I turn away. We get across the mouth of the river and ascend onto the soft sand of the beach.

The houses look abandoned, but we still approach them with extreme caution. The first house has three stories, and a deck wraps around the second. It's owned by a wealthy lawyer who had an older son, Mitch, and two twin daughters, Megan and Katie. He'd always yell at Mark and me if we crossed into his yard. I half expect to hear his intimidating voice as we approach the house. I hear nothing.

"Don't make a sound," Craig whispers. We tiptoe into the house through large sliding glass doors and arrive in the kitchen. Craig points to the cabinets. Summer and I open the squeaky doors and search for food. They're stuffed with all sorts of canned and boxed goods. What should I take? There are too many choices. As I consider what's good, Summer pulls out a box of vanilla wafers, shakes them, and smiles. I guess she really likes those. I'm not a big fan. Still struggling with my decision, I collect some cans and place them into my bag. I open the refrigerator door and find it filled with food. Man, I wish I had a cooler. I take water, apples, and some veggies, even though I know they'll spoil quickly.

Craig and Lauren go upstairs to search for weapons or ammunition, and I hope a few blankets. I miss the comforts of home and feel like sinking into the couch when I notice it in the living room. "Hey," Summer whispers, "do you hear that?" I listen, but hear nothing and shake my head. She motions me over and points to the pantry. I tiptoe towards it and hear the sound. It's a faint humming, and it's definitely coming from inside. She nudges me to open the door. Is she crazy? I don't know what's in there. What if it's one of the beasts? Not wanting to look scared in front of her, I reach for the door and gently pull it open. Huddled up in a corner is a little girl, weeping.

"Megan?" I ask.

"No." She whimpers.

"Katie?" She nods and begins to cry. Summer pushes past me and falls to her knees to hug the little girl.

"Craig, we found some—" I cover my mouth. What the hell's wrong with me? Lauren and Craig hurry down the stairs and shove me into the pantry. Craig turns and carefully pulls the door closed. They both place their fingers forcefully to their lips and switch off the light. I can barely see through the slats of the pantry when two beasts tear through the screen door, ripping it to shreds. They plow through the kitchen, searching.

Katie starts to whimper, and Summer covers her mouth. The beasts turn towards the sound, staring straight at the pantry. Their shadows cast through the slats as they lurch forward. Lauren and Craig raise their guns, and I steady my bow. Ready. Waiting. Suddenly, a clock alarm beeps upstairs. The beasts freeze, twist around, and bolt away. Their loud footsteps stomp up the stairs. We exhale for a moment.

Lauren picks up Katie, as Craig opens the door with a creak. With our weapons drawn, we sneak towards the sliding doors. The waves crash against the shore, and we break into a sprint, hoping to reach the water before the beasts notice us. Lauren labors as she carries Katie and falls into the sand.

Katie screams, and I turn to see the monsters through a large window on the second floor. The creatures smash through the window, shards flying everywhere. They crash onto the ground and continue the hunt.

Get to the water, I tell myself and dart towards the waves. "Run, Lauren, fast!" I scream. Lauren turns and grasps Summer by the arm as one of them lunges. Craig hits its jaws with the butt of his gun and stabs it with his knife. The knife enters the beast's chest and it falls, tumbling in the sand. It leaps up and charges again. I fire an arrow into the second monster's head. It backs slightly but still jumps and we enter the water with a splash. The monsters immediately struggle. Lauren and Summer are able to swim away, but Craig's taken under.

"Stop!" I scream. Like they'll listen. I dive where I think Craig went down. Blood fills the water around me, and the metallic taste mixed with salt gags me as I come up for air. I gotta find Craig. The beast's arms flail in front of me, and I stab with my knife but hit nothing. The creature lunges, and I spin, sinking below the water again. At this point, I can't tell which way's up and crack my head on the rocky bottom. Dazed, I'm grabbed by the beast. Its claws pierce my skin, and my blood stains the water. I reach for the surface, but only my hands break through. I need air. Water enters my lungs. Suddenly, the beast's grip loosens, and its lifeless body sinks to the sandy bottom.

Struggling for air, I fight to the surface, pull in a deep breath and cough up water. Craig's covered in blood as he continues to fight the last creature. Katie swims by me, kicking her stubby legs, trying to get to Lauren in the deeper water. I reach for her but have no strength and collapse. I float to shallow water and push my hands into the sand. They dig in deep, but I'm too exhausted to lift myself. The surf crashes over my side and rolls me towards the shore.

I come to and see Katie screaming, but I can't hear her. Water stings my eyes as I try to focus. I must have lost consciousness for a moment. I sit up turning quickly to look for any beasts, but the waves slam into me, knocking me down. I'm able to lift my head and see most of them on shore screaming towards Craig. One of the beast's charges at Katie and snatches her legs. Craig dives into the water and latches around her waist. She slips from his arms and is quickly dragged down. He dives under but comes up alone. Craig swims in to stand and screams as he swings his knife. Lauren and Summer hurry towards him to help. I try to stand but can only lift myself a foot or two when my arms fail and my face hits the sand. Everything turns black.

CHAPTER 11

PRESENT DAY

I still can't believe the person who saved us, who perfectly slit that monster's throat, is a girl. "How'd you do that?" I ask.

"Oh, that's nothing. I've been fighting my whole life. You guys are lucky I noticed you enter the subway. The Ragers are tough when they trap you."

"The Ragers?" I knew what they were, but found the name weird.

"That's what I like to call them. What do you call them? By the way, where you from?"

"I'm from Long Island," I say. "We've been hiding upstate for a few years now. I don't like to think about the creatures, let alone name them."

"Well, it's kind of my daily life, so I have to think about them. You can use the name if you like. Who's the big guy?" Brute sits up with a thud, wincing from his injuries.

"Name's Brute. What's yours?"

"Nightstar."

"It's catchy. I like it. What's your birth name?"

"I'm pretty sure it's Mary, but not positive. My parents died when I was young, around five I suppose. I remember them calling me Nightstar because I loved the stars at Central Park."

"I'm sorry about your parents," I say, feeling her pain. "So, where were you when this began?"

"I've been homeless since my parents died. I moved into this place before the Ragers. I just stayed here when everything went crazy."

I look around the room. Natural light spills in from a grate above, so it's easy to see. The space is small but cozy. I'm not really sure what it once was, maybe a utility room or something. I don't notice any doors or windows. Brute's sprawled across a bed that seems about half his size. A table sits in the corner of the room with an old laptop. There's a dresser and what looks like a small, but comfortable recliner. The walls are lined with rugs, but the floor is bare cement. I find that odd. A drain's right in the middle of the floor, and I can hear drops of water falling through. In a corner, shelves are stacked with boxed and canned goods, and there's a small nightstand with a lamp. The only way in or out of the room is the pipe

"This place is awesome!"

"I'm glad you like it. Let me show you around. It'll be a short trip."

She shows me the laptop and turns on the lamp. "Solar power. I snaked a wire to the road and hooked it up to one of the solar street lights. Gotta be careful, power doesn't last very long." She flips it off, then plops down into the recliner and pats the arms as if to say, "See? Comfy".

She rubs one of the rugs that hangs on the wall. "Used to have these on the floor, but they got so damp that I hung them up." I casually steer her towards the lever, and she nods and gives me a "pretty cool, huh?" look.

"How did you make it?" I ask.

"I actually made that before the Ragers. I found this place just exploring one day, and I crawled through the pipe. I knew I didn't want to get wet every time I got home. It just so happens that they don't like water. I got lucky, I guess. It's a simple lever, just used wood and rope. Might eventually change it to cable when I can. Rope's getting old and worn." As she's speaking, my eyes run over the lever. The rope's attached to a pulley that winds to the wooden door. I pull the door up slightly, and it's hinged to the pipe at the top. This looks anything but simple.

"Hey, you guys hungry?" Nightstar asks. Brute and I nod. She opens a can of soup and pours it into a pot. She lights a match and ignites a small Sterno can. Bending over, she opens a cooler and a mist pours out of it, covering the floor. A bottle of water lands in my lap, and it's ice cold. Dry ice? The water's great, and the soup's even better. I haven't had hot food in so long.

We eat and talk. I yawn so Nightstar offers me her recliner. It feels just like Dad's and I'm so comfortable that as soon as I put my head down I fall asleep.

It's dark when I wake. A very dim light seeps in through the grate, and my eyes begin to adjust. Brute's snoring, just as loudly as ever. I get up, and although inching forward, immediately knock into everything. The lamp falls with a crash, and Brute sits up, his hulking body turning then falling down, the springs of the bed straining to hold his weight.

"Nightstar?" I call quietly. No answer. I feel for the small door to the pipe and it's up. She must have gone out. I crawl to find the lamp, and my hands are quickly soaked by the dampness of the floor. The lamp lies on its side. I hope it's not broken; that would be embarrassing. I slide my hand up the lamp and flick the switch. It still works.

The light blinds me for a second, and I rub my eyes. It must be the middle of the night. I wonder where Nightstar went? I open the cooler—it *was* dry ice—and grab a water bottle. The laptop sits on the desk in the corner of the room. I sneak over, my curiosity consuming me, and look around. I turn on the power button, and the screen lights with a glow. It takes forever to load when I hear the outer door to the pipe. I grab the laptop and push it closed, sliding it behind me, hoping Nightstar doesn't see. She climbs through the pipe and hops into the room.

"What's up nosy?"

I look down, shaking my head as I step away from the laptop. "I'm sorry. I'm the curious type."

"There's really nothing on there. I don't have the Internet, and it doesn't power long enough to really do anything." I totally believe her and don't want her to think I was looking for anything. It feels weird talking for the next few minutes, but luckily Brute sits up and rubs his eyes, breaking the awkwardness.

"Water." I throw him the rest of my bottle, and he chugs it in about a second.

Nightstar laughs then sits next to Brute. "Guys, I was just wondering. Why'd you come to the city? You know this place is crawling with them."

"We're trying to get answers," I reply.

"Yeah, I know what you mean. You're seventeen, right? I just turned seventeen last month. You probably have two more years. Being a girl I might have a few more, but I'm still getting close. I can see your big friend there didn't turn. Lucky him. There are a few that haven't, but I'd say it's one in a million. It's like hittin the lottery."

"Is there anyone here that's trying to figure this out?" I ask.

"There might be. Or there used to be." She looks under her table and takes out a radio. She turns it on, and static emits from the speaker. "For years, someone would transmit a signal. It stopped about six months ago. They were asking people to go to a certain building to try to work on a solution. I never went. I've just always been on my own."

Brute sits up. "Where's the building?"

"It's near One World Trade Center."

One World Trade Center. That's the memorial that was constructed on the site where the Twin Towers collapsed. Craig and I were just babies when that terrible event happened. Dad said the world has never been the same. He knew a firefighter who died in the building. So many lives lost. I've visited a few times, and Dad showed me his friend's name etched in brass that overlooks waterfalls to a pool of water below. He thought the waterfalls meant God was crying for the fallen. "Such a beautiful, touching memorial," Dad would say, "but such a terrible day."

"We should go there and check it out," I say. "See if they're still trying to find the cause. Maybe the radio signal just stopped working. We have to do something."

Nightstar turns off the radio and slides it back under the table. "I've just been waiting for the inevitable. But if you think something can be done, a way to stop us from turning into those beasts, I'm all for it."

"We'll go tomorrow," Brute announces, "but first, let's eat!" Nightstar chuckles and pats him on the belly. He grabs his stomach and laughs, his belly moving up and down. We all laugh together, and for the first time in a long time, I don't cover my mouth. I feel safe, and I have Nightstar to thank for that.

CHAPTER 12

FOUR YEARS EARLIER

The water smacks my face as Craig drags me away from the beasts. I immediately spit, trying to rid my mouth of the strong salty taste. Craig turns and looks past me. "Stay on the edge of the deep water; if they come closer, we'll swim farther out." I try to stand, but Craig yanks my arm and my head goes under again. He doesn't realize I've come to. Between waves I see what must be more than ten monsters on the beach, following us as we move with the current.

Lauren pulls Summer through the water. "Stay close together!" I'm finally able to stand when a monster charges towards me, claws raised. It gets so close I can see the veins in its eyes; then it stops. They know they can't swim.

"Just stay deep enough," Craig says "They won't come any farther."

We make it to the mouth of the river, and although the current's strong, we swim to the opposite beach. The other side of the river's empty, so we step onto the shore, collapsing in the sand. The beasts' screams echo off the high dunes surrounding us, but I'm sure they won't cross to our side. We're safe for now.

"Is everyone okay?" I ask. "Where's Katie?" My mind flashes back to her drowning and Craig trying to save her. Lauren shakes her head, and Summer starts to cry. I slap my forehead. Man, do I have to learn to shut up.

"We have to stay close to the water," Craig says. "Make our way up the island. There are a few houses a couple miles down that are right on the beach and might be safe. We'll enter one of them and look for food. The cliffs are too high here to try." We all glance up. Craig's not kidding. The cliffs are enormous. Trees lean over the top edge, looking ready to tumble, their roots twisting out from a wall of darkened dirt. Islands of bushes and grass dot the mass of white sand, which eventually spills onto the beach. It would be impossible to climb.

"Were we able to save anything from Katie's house?" There I go saying that name again. Stupid.

Lauren and Craig check themselves over and shake their heads. Summer just stares at her feet as her tears fall to the sand. I search myself and still have my bow and knife but must have left the food in the house.

"Let's get going," Lauren suggests. "We have to find food and water." Lauren hugs Summer and whispers to her as Craig and I follow behind.

"How ya doing, Craig?" I ask.

"All right, bro. It's just so crazy what's happened."

I kick a pile of sand. "I know. I miss Mom and Dad so much and seeing Mark killed…"

"I can't stop thinking about Mom and Dad, either. I feel terrible about Mark, too. He was a great guy. I wonder what happened to all my buddies? I hope they're okay."

I hadn't put much thought into what happened to Craig's friends or any of my other friends, besides Mark. Craig and I didn't hang out with the same people. He played with kids that liked dirt bikes. My friends and I played sports. Once in a while though, we'd all get together. We'd play capture the flag (his team always seemed to win) or we'd swim at someone's pool.

"You know," Craig says, "if we didn't lose everyone, this would be kind of cool, like two heroes fighting evil monsters." He cocks his rifle and does an action pose. I arm my bow and pose. Craig laughs and slaps my back. I join in, throwing my arm over his shoulder.

As we walk down the beach, we pass an area that Craig and I know very well. "Hey, Craig, look. The cliffs."

He winks at me. "We had so much fun there."

Craig, me, and all our friends would walk to the cliff and hang out, staring at the water below. It wasn't very often, we didn't like each other very much, but if we got especially bored we'd go. One day, being stupid kids I guess, we decided to jump the edge and run down the cliff. After many bumps and bruises, we actually got very good at it. The cliff was mostly soft sand. If we picked the right route we wouldn't hit the thorny bushes or islands of grass. We'd start running down and lose our balance going forward, but then flip straight over and continue. Sometimes we'd tumble over and over, but if we maintained our balance, it wouldn't hurt and we'd eventually start running again.

I'm staring up at the cliffs reminiscing, when a loud crash echoes down. Lauren turns. "What was that?" The sound seems to have come from high up the cliffs. We look and two monsters crash through the trees, falling onto the cliffs below them. What are they chasing? I look a little lower where a figure is leaping down the cliffs, flipping over with perfect precision. It must be someone we know. The monsters aren't so lucky and lose control right away. They look like pinballs, bouncing off of every bush and tree.

"I know that form anywhere," Craig says. "It's Donny." Donny's one of Craig's friends and is probably the best cliff runner there is. He used to come on his own to practice. At this point, he's way ahead of them and almost to the bottom. He does one last flip and is on the beach.

"Hey, Donny, over here!" Craig yells. Donny looks over and smiles. He enters the water, and they hug. "Dude, thank God you're okay!"

"You to, bro," Donny says. He points towards the creatures. "Those things are coming. We have to get out of here!"

Craig pulls Donny back, deeper into the water. "Don't worry, man. We found one of their weaknesses. The suckers can't swim."

The creatures flip the last few feet and smash into the bottom of the cliff, beaten and bruised. They immediately rise and charge towards the shore entering with a loud splash, water flying everywhere. We back up in the water, deep enough for them to drown, but they continue their pursuit. Crap, they're not stopping. I start to turn and swim, when they go under. They emerge again, eyes wild, but quickly go back down. Finally, silence. We look at each other, and Donny smirks.

"Dude, that's sick. How'd you figure it out? Let's get a boat and just live on the water." Now, Donny isn't quite the sharpest tool in the shed, but that was probably the smartest thing I've ever heard him say. We continue wading through the water, and Donny tells us what happened to his family.

"It was crazy, man. My dad changed so quickly and basically ate my mom as we sat down for dinner. I ran into the room and loaded my crossbow and shot him in the chest." Donny's the only kid I know who owns a crossbow. "He ripped the arrow out like it was nothing, man. He tore my brother and sister apart. I only escaped because he was busy eating them." He pauses but quickly recovers. It's the only time I've ever seen Donny show any emotion.

"Why didn't you go to Split Rock?" I ask.

Donny glares at me. "Of course I tried, stupid." I tighten from the words, and Craig grabs my shoulder. He knows Donny and I have never gotten along. "At first, I started towards my uncle's house. But as you guys know, this is happening everywhere. I saw so many of those monsters that it took me two days to get to the rocks. I hid in a car for a whole day. It was so hot with no AC, torture." Donny lowers his head and shakes it as he talks. More emotion, this doesn't seem like him at all. "The rocks were a bloodbath, man. There were guts everywhere." He holds his nose. "And the smell, it was awful." I notice Lauren almost looking relieved at this, knowing how badly she wanted to go back, wanted answers. "I didn't stay long. I slept in the woods under the leaves, anyway that I could hide from them, but they spotted me. I ran to the cliffs, hoping they would struggle as they did. That cliff saved my life, man." He looks up at the cliff and raises his hand to his forehead in salute. "I owe you one, brother."

We continue to trek down the beach and haven't talked since Donny's story. I think again about Donny's idea of living on a boat. Maybe we could find a sailboat and fill it with supplies. I bring it up and we discuss it. I don't think Donny's happy when we decide that maybe it isn't such a good idea. How would we get fresh water? What about food? How would we ever find out what's happening to everyone else? Our argument's becoming heated, and Donny's face gets so red it looks like he might explode.

"All right, enough arguing," Craig says, then points ahead. "There are the houses." Just like Craig said, they are right on the beach, only about twenty feet from the water. There are seven houses in a row, with a distance of about thirty feet between each one. We walk past them to see if the coast is clear and then make our way back to the first house. It has a huge deck that wraps to the other side.

"Be careful, guys. Don't make any noise," Craig says, looking at me. I feel rather small. Craig and Donny enter the house and come back out, signaling us to stop. "Don't look in there. Let's just move to the next one." I pass the glass door, and it's splattered with blood.

We hop a short fence and are on the deck of the next property. It's smaller than the first and is also one story. Craig and Donny go through the sliding glass door and, after a minute or so, signal us to come in. There's no blood in this house. Real estate cards are strewn all over the kitchen counter. It must be a summer rental.

"I don't think this was ever rented," I say as I hold up one of the cards. "Maybe this is safe." We move throughout the house, and it looks like no one has been here in a while. The beds are made, but the closets are empty. We check the refrigerator, not even a bottle of ketchup. The light in the refrigerator works, so I turn on the TV and sigh for a moment. Craig turns it off and smacks me in the head.

"Let's go into one of the bedrooms and leave the lights off," Lauren says. We move into what looks like the master bedroom, and Lauren and Summer lie on the floor and fall asleep, exhausted from the crazy day. The clock in the room says it's only 8:30 at night, but it seems much later. Craig and I help the girls into the bed and pull the covers over them. I take a pillow, yawn, and lean against the wall.

"Hey, guys. This might be a good place to stay for a few days," Craig says. "We have electricity, and the refrigerator works. In the morning, we can go over to the houses next door and search for food." Donny and I nod in agreement as my eyes feel overwhelmingly heavy. I hear Craig say, "I'll stay guard the first two hours, then..." but my head hits the pillow.

CHAPTER 13

PRESENT DAY

As I'm packing my bag, I look over to see Nightstar's doing the same. "It could take a day or two to get to the building, so pack for overnight." She likes to travel at night and underground as far as she can, although it takes more time. She says she moves fast, but smart.

Nightstar has blonde hair and pale skin. It looks like she hasn't been in the sun in a long time. Her eyes are blue, and her full lips remind me of Summer. She doesn't look like Summer at all, though. And although I'm usually not attracted to blondes, I find myself slightly attracted to her.

"Here's some water," she says. "Make sure you have enough food."

I throw the bag on my shoulder as she pushes the lever, and we crawl through the pipe. She hits the second lever, making the door pop up, pushing the water to the sides. I'm still impressed by that. Brute has to force himself through, his axes scraping the sides. I wonder how he ever fit. We swing to the other side, crawl through for a while, and come to the doorway that leads to the subway tunnels.

Nightstar holds up a hand. "Okay, listen. It'll be very dark in there. We'll only see light when we come to a terminal. I'm not going to crack one of the glow sticks unless it's necessary. We'll be traveling underground for a few hours. I know it's hard not to talk, but we need to be quiet. For some reason, they like the darkness of the subway. That's why we're traveling at night. They stay near the surface then."

"Whatever needs to be done," Brute says.

We follow her through the door, and she wasn't kidding. It's pitch black. I put my hand an inch in front of my face and see nothing. I even wiggle my fingers, nothing. We walk about ten feet, and I already struggle with not talking. This is going to be a long, boring trip. Nightstar and Brute's footsteps are the only sound in the tunnel. Nightstar's are light as a mouse, whereas Brute's sound like an overweight elephant. I figure he has to be three hundred pounds of mostly muscle.

It seems like we have walked forever. Aghh! Someone say something. Finally, Nightstar breaks the silence, whispering, "We have to find a subway terminal and check where we are. I haven't been down this way in a long time. Make sure you're alert. The terminals can be crawling with them at night." She leads us to the next subway exit where there's a very faint light shining down the stairs. I can't tell if it's the moon or some of the solar lights that light the city now. Nightstar pulls herself onto the platform and motions for us to get down. I look at Brute, and he smiles.

"Pretty cool chick, huh?"

I hit his arm. "Stop it, you big lug." Nightstar hops down from the platform and taps our shoulders to follow. We run down a tunnel, and it's pitch black again.

"We're close to Penn Station. We have just a few more hours to go. Remember, don't make a sound." We start walking, and again the silence is deafening. To pass the time, I think of Dad and Mom. I wish I could see them again. I miss the way Mom would take care of me when I was sick and how Dad would laugh at the stupidest jokes. A joke he used to tell makes me giggle, and Brute pushes me on the back. It's like getting hit by a grizzly. I've heard people say that time heals all wounds, but to me they never really heal; they just turn to scars. Yeah, it doesn't hurt as much—I don't cry every day like I used to—but I always think about them. Everyone I lost along the way will always be with me, in my heart. Thinking of them makes the time go by quickly, and I don't cry but smile, when Nightstar stops.

"The building's two blocks away from this station. We're going to set camp around here. We can't start any fires. We'll go up top in the morning when there are fewer Ragers." Nightstar looks for a place to camp and finds a door leading to a small room. It's damp and musty. I lie down, and my clothes are instantly soaked. The cold sends a shiver down my spine, curling my toes. If only I had my cover. I pull my hood over my face, hoping it will do, but it doesn't. I'm miserable. Breathing into my hands, the warm air comforts me slightly. Turning every which way, trying to get comfortable, I know this will be a very long night.

Nightstar shakes me, and I wake rubbing my head. Crust has built up in the corners of my eyes, so I pick it away with my finger. My head swims, and I feel dizzy from lack of sleep. It was a very uncomfortable night, to say the least. Brute looks like he didn't sleep well, either. He pulls his hand over his damp beard, shakes his head, and struggles to opens his eyes. "Come on, sleepyheads. Time to get up," Nightstar says. The grogginess finally dissipates, and I stand, ready to go.

"We're going up," she says. "Be prepared for anything."

Brute salutes her jokingly, and this time I slap *him* in the back. He doesn't budge. When we get to the stairs, Nightstar points up. Brute and I get low and move behind her. The sun blinds me and I try to use Nightstar's body to shield it, but I still can't see. She stops suddenly, her breath quickening. She pushes me to go the other way. "This is no good," she says. "There are too many of them. I didn't expect this many during the day. We'll have to go down one station."

Nightstar fidgets as she prepares to ascend the next set of stairs. She moves really slowly this time, dagger held in front. Peeking out into the street, she motions us to ascend. This time, a building blocks the sun and I can see the city as we emerge from the station. There aren't any creatures as I scan our surroundings. Nightstar points down the street and holds up three fingers. The building must be three blocks away. Straight ahead there's movement, and I know what that means. Manhattan used to be bustling, the city that never sleeps. Now the only thing that moves here is *them*. Nightstar takes out her dagger, and it drops to her side, turning and reflecting in the sun. I lift my hood over my head and ready my bow. Brute cracks his neck and wields both of his axes, forearms pumping. We're not heading back underground, not running. It's time to fight.

Four of the monsters turn and immediately tear towards us. We sprint towards them. It's the first time I've run at them and not away. I fire my bow and hit one right between the eyes. It falls, and its neck meets the sharp edge of Brute's axe. A creature, claws exposed, dives at Nightstar. She runs up the side of a car, slashing the creature in the neck as she flips over, landing in a perfect pose. The creature falls, blood gushing from the wound. Another lunges at Brute, and he quickly drops to a knee, chops off its leg with one axe, and its head with the other. I see the last one jump towards Nightstar and let loose an arrow. The beast reaches for her and falls, arrowhead pierced into its jugular. We stand over all four, breathing heavily.

The commotion has more of them converging on us. Nightstar runs towards the door of a building and Brute and I follow. "That's the one. Inside, quickly!" It's a revolving door, and Nightstar and I get in and start pushing, but it comes to a halting stop. I look back, and Brute has wedged himself against the door as monsters slam into the glass, cracks spreading from the force. "He won't be able to hold too long," Nightstar yells.

She kicks out the glass of the inner door and we hop through into a large lobby. "Check the elevators!" She finds one open and takes what looks like a grappling hook from her backpack. She grabs the cable of the elevator and tugs. "This'll do."

Loud squeaking fills the lobby. Brute's boots slide on the floor, his calf muscles bulge as he squats and holds the outer revolving door firm. The creatures slam into each other and bite at the glass, so close to their meal.

"Kid," Brute calls, "a little help."

Nightstar turns and throws a burning fuse towards Brute. A cloud of smoke billows, surrounding Brute and the door. The monsters are stunned, and the door starts to revolve the wrong way. I grab Brute, pulling him towards the elevator. Nightstar points up, and Brute and I dive onto the cable. I lose my grip, but Brute pulls himself up with such force that I grasp his shoulders and ride piggyback.

I look down, seeing nothing. "Nightstar!" No answer, just hungry screams. Suddenly, Nightstar's grappling hook shoots up and latches a cable. She swings in and quickly pushes off the wall to the side. Three of the beasts crash in, still reaching for her as they plummet. She seems part feline as she jumps from one ledge to the next on all fours.

"Come on, boys," she says as she leaps by. "Keep up."

"Show off," Brute says as he pulls. I let go of Brute and grip the cable. As we climb, the natural light dissipates and it's fairly dark. Nightstar breaks a glow stick and the green light fills the elevator shaft. We reach the next floor and Brute lies in the hallway, breathing heavily.

"Get up, lazy," Nightstar teases. "That was nothing."

Brute lets out a loud sigh and pushes himself up, fists pumping. "All right, what's next?"

Nightstar shakes the glow stick and it brightens. "This is the building that was broadcast on the radio. I guess we search for a room with light. I really don't know. Be careful, though. I'm sure they'll try the stairs soon."

The building's huge, at least fifty stories high, probably more. I wonder how we'll ever find what we're looking for. I'm not even sure what that is. We slowly walk through the halls and search for what seems like hours. We don't notice any monsters and figure they began hunting for their next meal.

Nightstar's glow stick starts to fade. "That's it. The rest must have fallen out of my pack. This is the last one. We'll be in the dark soon." It feels pretty hopeless.

"Hey, guys," Brute calls, "over here." He's staring at what looks like an arrow painted on the wall. "What's this?" Nightstar and I shrug our shoulders and we all follow it.

"Look, another one." Nightstar holds the glow stick up to the wall, showing another arrow pointing down the hall.

We follow, our eyes darting every which way, hoping to find the next arrow. At the end of the hall I vaguely see words, or numbers, on the wall when the green glow fades to darkness.

"Damn!" Nightstar shakes the glow stick. Nothing. "Does anyone have a light?"

"No," we both say.

"Hold on." I reach in my pocket. "What about my flint?"

Brute hits my shoulder again. "Good idea, kid."

I rub my arm and strike the flint. Sparks fly and a quick flash lights the wall. A word appears for a moment, not long enough to read.

Nightstar sounds urgent. "Try again." I strike the flint right next to the words and it reads "five".

"Did that say five?" Brute asks.

"Yeah," Nightstar says, nudging me. "Keep striking."

I strike again and the sparks illuminate "doors". I strike the flint one last time and the word "left" is revealed. "Five Doors Left," Nightstar says. "Let's go!"

We follow and feel for the doors. Nightstar stops in front of me. I guess that's five. I lost count. "This must be it," she says. "Be prepared for anything." She pushes the door and it creaks open. I look around her at a long hallway with another door at the end. A faint light shines through a tall, skinny window on the side. Nightstar crouches as she inches towards the door. I crawl and follow, Brute's breath warming my ankles. All three of us peek through the window. There are two bodies on the floor, lying in a pool of blood, their throats cut right at the jugular. A light flickers to the left, but I can't see its source. I strain, trying to catch a glimpse.

Brute whispers, "Can anyone see?"

"Shh," Nightstar hushes him. "I'm gonna open the door." I'm shaking from head to toe and take a deep breath, trying to calm my nerves. What's in there that did that? Nightstar carefully pushes the door. My head moves with it, but an intense stench of death makes me pause. Light flashes from a computer, and there's a man hunched over its screen. Is he alive? Nightstar stands and approaches him.

"Mister?" she says.

The man twists his head, his eyes wide. He slides his hands over his head and grips his hair in fists. "What are you doing here?" Before we can answer, he screams, "Leave me alone!" Turning back to the computer screen he punches keys on the keyboard, his shoulders heaving from deep breaths.

Nightstar steps towards him. "But, mister, we're here to—"

The man leaps, grabs Nightstar's neck, and lifts her, his muscle's bulging. "I said leave me alone!"

CHAPTER 14

FOUR YEARS EARLIER

"Wake up, loser!" Donny screams in my ear.

"What the hell? Don't do that!" I yell back. I sit up, my head now splitting with pain.

"Stop it, knuckleheads," Lauren says as she slaps us both. "This house is clear, but they could be close by."

"Where are Craig and Summer?" I ask as I try to clear out my ear with my finger.

"They went to look for food while you, lazybones, were sleeping," Donny says.

Summer alone with Craig? Oh, brother. "Where did they go?"

"I think they went to the house next door. Why, you jealous, lover boy?"

Oh, Donny. Gotta love him. He'll get under your skin faster than a splinter.

"No, I'm just wondering where they are; that's all." I walk away to escape the conversation and explore the house. I didn't notice last night, but it's very small. It has two bedrooms and must be a beach cottage. All the windows have long, dark curtains, and the rooms are covered in shadows and darkness even though the clock says 10:23 a.m. Man, I slept a long time. The house has old rugs throughout, except for the kitchen, which is discolored linoleum. I'm starting to see why this house wasn't rented.

"Hey, want some breakfast?" Craig says as he strolls in and puts a bag of groceries on the table. Summer follows and places a gallon of milk and a half-gallon of OJ on the counter. Donny high fives Craig, then searches through the food.

"Sweet," he says. "Bacon."

"Good job," Lauren says as she starts the stove. "I'm gonna make us a feast." She cooks scrambled eggs topped with cheese and bacon. It's the best meal I have ever had. Well, maybe not. Mom used to make really good spaghetti and meatballs, but breakfast tastes great.

"All of the houses are clear. I think we should stay here for a while," Craig says. "We have the safety of the water and there's enough food for a few weeks." I nod as I stuff a handful of bacon in my mouth.

"Can I watch TV?" I ask, bacon pieces spitting on the table.

"Yeah," Donny says, "Sesame Street." Summer giggles, and the blood rushes to my face. Stupid Donny.

"Real funny," I say as I push my chair out, squeeze my fists, and storm into the other room. I try to calm myself down, but it's close to impossible. Donny's making me look like an idiot in front of Summer, and I have real feelings for her now. The next chance I get, I won't back down. I'm gonna smash his head in.

Over the next few days, Craig realizes that Donny and I are about to go to blows. He squashes any arguments and deliberately keeps us away from each other, to the point where I don't feel the burning hatred towards him anymore. We are able to gather food from the other houses, and with the protection of the water, we begin to feel safe.

Lauren and Summer have been searching for clothes, and one of the houses must have had girls their age. For fun they decide to model some of the clothes, and Summer struts out wearing a bikini. I almost pass out. Girls develop at a younger age, but holy! She has curves in all the right places.

Later that night at dinner, we discuss the fact that we're beginning to run out of food—many of the houses didn't rent and were empty—and decide that we'll have to move on.

"We can travel the whole island by beach and then cross the Hudson to get upstate by boat," Craig says. "I think we should try to get to our cabin in Oneonta. It's right on the pond where we can hunt and plant vegetables."

"Why don't we stay on the island?" Lauren suggests. "It's surrounded by water."

"I've been thinking about that. The island seems safe now. The problem is that it's so close to the city," Craig says. "There has to be millions of them there. They'll be coming out here soon. I don't think they'll head upstate, because there are not as many people, not as much food."

"How do we know everyone has changed?" I ask.

"We don't," Craig says. "But I haven't seen an adult in a while. It's all kids our age now. I haven't seen a child, besides Katie. I think they've killed most of them." Summer begins to cry, and Donny comforts her. Damn it. I get up and stomp into the next room. With a deep breath, I try to control my emotions. I don't want her to know how I feel about her. I'm just not ready. The room's quiet when I walk back in.

"What if we can save them," I say, breaking the silence. "What if there's a cure. Maybe we can help Mom and Dad."

"Our parents are gone, stupid. Everyone's gone," Donny says. "And if you don't figure that out, you'll be next." He sticks his finger in my face, and I slap it away. I'm gonna kill him. I clench my fist and raise it, every muscle in my body tense. I step forward ready to crush him when Craig pushes me away.

"We're not fighting each other. Go outside and calm down." He shoves me, and I punch the screen door as I storm outside.

I hate Donny. What's his deal? I've never done anything to him. I pull at my hair, and my head feels like it's going to explode when I see three figures running towards the house. My eyes widen, and I'm frozen for a moment before I hustle inside. "Guys, get down. Someone's here."

"What do you mean *someone*?" Craig asks, looking past me.

I point down and put my finger to my lips. Everyone jumps on the floor and hides as I dive behind a recliner. Three large shadows cast onto the floor and slowly crawl towards us as the figures move. The wind blowing through the windows chills my skin. The silence is eerie. All you can hear is their breathing, quick and forceful. I peek over at Summer, hiding behind the couch. She's not moving an inch, her face pressed against the fabric. I reach behind me for my bow, but it's not there. We've gotten too comfortable. I look for Craig, knowing he's probably unarmed, too.

"Hey, is anyone in here?" a voice calls. "We need some help."

Lauren and Craig stand up, letting out loud breaths. "Rick," Lauren says, "thank God. You had us scared to death." I stand up from behind the couch to see three older boys in the living room. I recognize one, Rick Dickinson, a college kid who just graduated from high school last year. I don't know who the others are.

"We're so happy to see you guys," Rick says. "We've been running for days. This is Larry and Chris." They raise their hands hello. "They're my friends from college. We were lucky to escape. It's crazy as hell out there."

"Are you guys hungry?" Lauren asks. "We don't have much left, but you're welcome to it."

"Thanks so much. We're starving," Rick says. As they eat, they tell us how they came home from college and their parents started acting weird and turned. Rick's mom jumped into the pool after them and drowned. They found out their weakness quickly. They hid in their pool for a day, then headed over to Split Rock. When they got there, it looked like a massacre. Dead bodies were strewn all over the place.

Donny wasn't kidding when he told us the gore. Rick and his friends have been traveling by the water, also.

Rick points at me. "We saw you storm out onto the deck. Otherwise, we'd have kept going. We would've had no idea you guys were here."

Craig tells them our plans, and they decide to join. They're a few years older than we are, so at first it's weird, but I find them to be very nice. We stay one more night and head out in the morning.

We trudge along the beach, staying close to the water, ready to jump in at any sight of the monsters. We've been traveling a few hours when the sun, for the most part hidden behind the clouds, beats down, burning my shoulders. My mouth's as dry as a desert, and I struggle to swallow. I open my bag, hoping for water but forgot to pack any. Summer sneaks up next to me handing me her water bottle, and I smile. She smiles back. My heart seems to melt.

"Hey, guys!" Rick yells, killing the moment. "Up ahead is the marina. It may be a good time to get a boat."

"Don't you think we should wait until we get closer to the city?" Craig answers. "We need supplies, fresh water."

"Now's as good a time as any," Rick says. "We may never get another chance." Rick's friends agree, and we reluctantly say yes. Craig has been the leader since this all happened, and I'm not sure if I like following somebody else's orders.

The marina's full of boats, so we basically have our pick of the litter. Big boats. Small boats. Sail boats. Powerboats.

"Check this out," Donny says, jumping onto a tremendous yacht. It's huge, with a big deck and sliding doors leading to a beautiful cabin.

"Yeah, that's awesome," Larry says. I think that's his name, or is it Harry?

"We should take a sailboat," Craig says. "That way we don't have to rely on gas."

Donny jumps from the deck of the yacht. "Dude, you're becoming a party pooper."

Lauren steps in, face red. "Listen, this is crap. We've been doing well on our own. You guys can't come in here and boss us around."

"Shut up, you dumb broad," Rick yells so loud that a few seagulls fly from the sail of a boat. He doesn't seem so nice now. "I'm uh…" he runs his hand over his face, "sorry, Lauren. I don't know what came over me. Let's all relax. Maybe we should take two boats, considering how many people we have."

We nod, and I glance over at Craig. He has one eye raised as he stares at Rick. I wonder if he found Rick's yelling as strange as I did.

Rick and his friends decide to pick a powerboat that has a cabin underneath. Craig picks a sailboat that also has a cabin and looks very similar to the one Dad used to own. He loved that boat, and I think of the time we sailed to Sag Harbor.

"Hey, losers, I'm going with the powerboat crew," Donny says. "I hope you guys eat our wake."

"I don't know if that's a good idea," Craig says.

"I can make my own decisions," Donny snaps back. Craig shakes his head in frustration and walks away, saying something under his breath. Maybe he's starting to realize what a knucklehead Donny is. Donny looks at me and laughs before jumping onto the boat.

Craig barks out instructions as Lauren and I untie the boat from the dock. Craig steers with the tiller, navigating through the sea of boats. I breathe in the salty air and hear the screech of seagulls as I start to untie the main. Rick powers by the sailboat, water spraying our deck. He nails the throttle and does a circle around us before zooming ahead, the wake tilting our boat. Donny raises his arms and yells, something stupid I'm sure, and I can't help but hope he falls overboard.

Once we leave the harbor, Lauren and I set the sail and the main pops open with a gust of wind. The sudden thrust leans our boat to the side, and Summer gets thrown in her chair. She sits straight and gives a thumbs up as we leave a small wake behind. The hull splits a wave, sending foamy water flying into the air, spraying my face. I feel like I'm an eight-year-old on Dad's boat again, with no worries in the world.

We skim over the water, moving along the island quickly with a full northwestern wind. I know the creatures can't get us out here, so I put my legs up and lean back on the deck, soaking in the sun. The tall cliffs of the island look small in the distance. I notice the Harbor Hill mansion sitting in between two of them. Dad used to point it out whenever we came this way. It lets us know we aren't far from the city. Craig says we'll have to go under a few bridges to get to the Hudson. Then we can sail up the river and land in Jersey to head upstate. I wonder how he knows all this, then remember he went on a five-day sail with Dad when I was in baseball camp two summers ago.

Up ahead on the horizon is Throg's Neck Bridge. It's a tremendous mass of metal with long cables holding its weight, quite a sight to see. As we get closer, we're reminded of the horror of the last few weeks. Overturned cars litter the bridge and what looks like half-eaten bodies dangle over the edge.

"Look!" Lauren points up ahead. Rick's boat veers suddenly to the right and then quickly to the left. A body flies out of the boat, flipping head over heels through the air before smashing into the water. The boat turns sharply and zooms by us. I get a quick glimpse as it passes, and Rick has Donny pinned up against the wheel, tearing at his head. The boat goes left, then right, and collides with the bridge's pier, erupting in a tremendous fireball, the heat singing my face. The force of the explosion turns our boat, almost flipping us.

"Donny!" Craig yells as he let's go of the tiller. The boom of the boat swings wildly. I dive to the deck as it flies over me. My head smacks the cabin's roof, and I see flashes of lights as I close my eyes. I shake to try and clear my head, then push myself up. Water spills over the side and makes it impossible to get my footing. Craig dives and grabs the tiller, arms straining as he tries to right the vessel. The boom swings back over me when I see Summer raise her arms for protection. It hits her and sends her flying overboard. I feel the water smash my face as I dive in to save her.

CHAPTER 15

PRESENT DAY

I charge the man and grab his arm, but he elbows my face and I fall to the floor. Brute raises his axe over his head. "I suggest you put that little lady down, mister." The man loosens his grip, and Nightstar drops to the floor. She holds her neck, then draws her dagger. The man shakes his head. "I'm sorry. I... I can't help myself." His body jerks, and he staggers towards the computer. He pulls the chair and heaves it at Brute. Brute blocks it with his forearm as the man thrusts himself at Nightstar. Brute grabs his neck and puts him in a Full Nelson. He must have a hundred pounds on the guy, but his arms bulge as he struggles to keep hold. "You have to let me go," the man says as his breathing slows. "I have to find a cure."

Brute squeezes tighter. "You really think I'm letting go of you after all that?"

"You have to." His arms drop to his side, and he starts to breathe in and out in a slow rhythm. "I don't have much time. I'm about to turn."

I arm my bow and aim it straight at his jugular. "Brute, let him go. If he tries any funny stuff, we'll be ready."

"Kyle's right," Nightstar says, "but do it slowly."

Brute let's go and the man rushes to the computer, mumbling to himself as he types.

"Listen. Take this information. Use it to save humanity. Stop people from becoming," he points at himself, "this." He presses a button and pulls the memory stick out of the computer tower. His hands disappear behind his back, and he spins around. His eyes bulge as he leaps at us. Brute steps forward to block him. Before they collide, the man pulls a knife and swings his hand. It slashes straight through his own jugular. Blood shoots across Brute's chest as the man crashes into him, falling to the ground, clutching his wound. His body jerks wildly and quickly becomes motionless, lying in a pool of blood.

We stand frozen for a moment. No one says a word as Nightstar slides over to the computer and grabs the stick. She inspects it front and back. Stunned, Brute and I still haven't moved an inch. She inserts the stick into the computer and a screen appears. "Please enter password" flashes across it. "Seriously, this guy wants us to save the world and he doesn't give us a password? We're going to have to take this back to my place. I'll need time to figure this out."

"It's getting late. I think we should stay here one more night," I say. "Maybe not this room, though, these bodies creep me out."

"Good idea. They're attracted to the blood," Nightstar says. "I don't think we'd be safe."

We exit the room, and the hallway's pitch black. I'm not at all sure which way to go, but I turn left and head down the hall. I inch forward and slide my hand down the wall, hoping to eventually feel a door. Finally, my hand hits the metal of a door handle and I twist it open. "Guys, over here." I enter the room but am unable to see at all, so I strike my flint. The floor of the room is covered in paper. I gather a few pieces and scrunch a makeshift torch. It lights, but the paper burns through quickly. I bump into a chair and get an idea. The leg breaks off easily, and after a few tries at lighting the top, a bright flame fills the room.

There are desks strewn throughout. Office supplies are scattered amongst the paper, and a few vending machines stand in the corner. In the far left is a sign for a bathroom. Brute sprints past us, runs in, and shuts the door. Nightstar and I look at each other and laugh but quickly cover our mouths.

The windows in the room don't open, and with no power or air conditioning, the heat makes it difficult to breath. I plop down onto the papers and wrap my arms around my knees, trying to rest. "It looks like he killed those other two before he turned," I say. "Was that all there was? Three guys trying to figure out what's wrong with us?"

Nightstar sits next to me. "Well, we won't know until we go back and analyze this stick. Maybe they had outside communication with others. They somehow had that computer working. They could have had Internet. We'll leave for my place first thing in the morning."

Brute shuffles out of the bathroom. "Sorry about that. When a man's gotta go, he's gotta go." He points to my makeshift torch. "That won't last too long, kid. Looks like we'll be sittin' in the dark."

"It's probably for the best," Nightstar says. "We don't want to attract them while we sleep."

Brute places his axes on the floor and sits next to us. "That was crazy back there. I wonder how he controlled himself. Anyone I've seen turn went bonkers and quick."

"He seemed to control it with some sort of breathing technique," Nightstar says. "He lost it at the end there, though."

"Good thing he killed himself. I didn't want to have to save you guys..again." Brute winks at us then smiles ear to ear.

Nightstar kicks his shin. "I can handle myself. So Brute. I'm curious. Were you born that big?"

"Ha Ha. Very funny." Brute sticks out his palm and holds it close to the ground. "I was actually the shortest kid in my class."

"The shortest?" Nightstar says.

"I wouldn't kid around about that, little lady. Grew seven inches one summer. Had to get metal splints on my legs I shot up so fast.

I was picked on. Guess I'm a little shy and withdrawn cause of it. Especially around the ladies. What about you, kid?"

Nightstar shoves my shoulder. "Yea, I bet you were a little ladies man, right?"

I lower my head and it takes me a second to answer. "I'm just havin' fun listening."

"Come on, Kyle," Nightstar says. "You probably had tons of girlfriends."

"Not really. I was into reading when I was young. I guess the other kids didn't find that cool. Wasn't very popular with the girls either. But I'm good with it now. I'm just happy I met you guys. I was so close to giving up after Summer."

Brute wraps his arms around the two of us and pulls us into a bear hug. "I'm happy I met you guys too, kid."

We talk for a while until the light on the torch fades. We then tell stories in darkness, and it's weird not seeing Brute's facial expressions, which are always so animated. I'm glad I opened up. I feel comfortable around them. They don't care what I say or how I act. They're the closest thing to family I've had since Summer died.

**=

Brute's grunting as I wake, but it's not his usual snore. I search the room, and his big body's sprawled in front of one of the vending machines. He's jerking his arm and cursing.

"What's wrong, Brute?"

"Nothing." He tries to peek back but can't turn.

The vending machine's glass reflects the light of the morning sun, and it's hard to see inside. I squint for focus, and see Brute's big paw wrapped around a Twix candy bar. "I couldn't be more embarrassed, kid. Don't tell Nightstar."

"Too late." Nightstar leans over the vending machine and peeks in. "Did you try letting go of the candy bar?" Brute unwraps his fingers and forcefully tugs his arm, dragging the vending machine with him.

Finally, it pops out, and Brute stretches his long, fat fingers in front of him. Brute's face turns red, and he slouches his shoulders. They shake up and down, and he turns, face glowing, as he starts to laugh then covers his mouth.

Brute places his jacket on the floor under the vending machine. He then raises his arm and gives a light jab to the glass with the haft of his axe. It shatters a hole in the lower corner and the glass and candy bars spill onto his jacket. Brute is doing this as quietly as he can; it looks so comical that Nightstar can't help but giggle. Brute bends over and grabs a handful of the candy, unwraps it and stuffs it into his mouth. A satisfying grin covers his face. Nightstar and I grab a few and we all have a very unhealthy breakfast.

"We're gonna have to get going soon," Nightstar says. "I think we should take the stairs this time." We grab our gear, and I notice Brute stuff a few more candy bars into his bag. He looks at me, shrugs, and smiles.

Nightstar pushes the door open, and we timidly enter the hallway. Sunlight bleeds under the doors, allowing us to see, which is comforting. The door at the end of the hallway has no light. It must be the stairwell. When Nightstar opens it, I can't see but I feel the railing of the stairs. Sliding our hands along the railing, we move down about three flights when a door thrusts open from below.

"Kyle, try your flint," Nightstar says. I strike it in the middle of the stairwell. The specks of light explode, glowing as they float down, rising in a breeze from below, then descending again. The glow reveals many beasts, fangs exposed, shoving each other as they climb the stairs. "Go!" Nightstar screams. "Get to the roof."

I take two steps at a time as I climb the stairs. Brute's probably taking four, and his heavy breathing keeps getting farther away. A door opens about two flights above and light rushes in. I peek over the edge to see them, only three flights below, looking hungrier than ever. Sunlight blinds me as I jump through the door, and Brute slams it shut. He swings his axe and, with a harsh blow, jams it into the bottom of the door. "This won't hold for long."

Nightstar sprints around the roof, searching for an escape. I race to the edge, and it must be thirty, maybe forty feet across to the next building.

"What do we do?" I ask.

Nightstar looks side to side and points behind me. "The crane." I turn and there's a huge crane running parallel to the edge of the building. "We can use it as a bridge to that building next door. See if it has power."

I jump in the operator's chair and stare at the myriad of handles. I close my eyes and grasp one, pulling it down. Nothing. I try another. "I got nothing!"

I jump to the edge and push the boom of the crane. It won't budge. Brute leaps by me and smashes into the boom. It creaks before slowly turning. I back up and jump as high as I can, crashing into metal. The boom gains momentum. Brute pulls himself up and grabs my cloak, flinging me behind him. I turn and see Nightstar charging towards us as the door behind her flies open, creatures spilling onto the roof.

"Move!" she yells. I shuffle along, struggling with my balance. I haven't looked down yet, but can feel how high I am. I stay right behind Brute when he abruptly stops about twenty feet from the end.

I run into him, clutching his belt. "Why'd you stop?"

He points, moving his finger slowly with the crane. "We have to wait till the crane lines up with the building." The creatures' screams become louder. *Come on, Brute, move.* Finally, he runs, and his feet go airborne. I push with my legs and leap as high as I can, wind blinding me as I soar through the air. Brute crashes onto the edge of the building and hangs on. I land on his waist and hold for dear life. Something grabs my legs and holds tight. I hope it's Nightstar, but it feels much heavier. I look down, and she's clinging to me with one of the beasts attached to her. Brute's arms bulge as he slowly lifts us. We rise up about a foot and drop back down. "I can't hold on, kid."

Nightstar falls down to my ankle, her grip weakening. I hug Brute's leg with one arm and snatch her wrist with the other. My arm stretches violently and I struggle to hold on. Brute begins to slip, and I turn to Nightstar. She stares at me with desperation in her eyes, then smiles.

I squeeze tighter. "I won't let you go!"

"I know," she says. "I will." She loosens her grip, slips from mine, and falls.

CHAPTER 16

FOUR YEARS EARLIER

I search for Summer as I enter the water, my face still stinging from the dive. Her hand's just out of reach, and as I stretch to grab her, the wake from the boat thrusts her into the darkness. Swirling water lifts her into sight, her body spinning, arms lifeless. I wrap around her and pull for the surface. She must have been knocked out. She can't be dead. We emerge and a wave crashes over us, water filling my lungs. Craig whips the boat around as Summer's weight drags me under again. "Craig!" I lift Summer towards the surface as I go under. A life preserver lands next to me as I come up. I lunge for it, Summer still in my grip. If I can just reach it, Craig can pull me in. I grab hold and the preserver jerks, dragging us to the boat. Lauren grasps Summer's arm and lifts her in. She's safe now. I claw at the side of the boat, trying to pull myself over, but I fall back in. Sinking, I reach my hand towards Summer. I don't want to leave her. Not now. Craig's hand enters the water and grabs my wrist. He yanks me on board, and I tumble to the floor. I'm too tired to move.

I force myself onto my side and see Craig putting his ear to Summer's chest then shaking his head. He pushes his fingers into the side of her neck. "I don't feel anything." He checks again, this time pushing his fingers deeper. "Crap! Lauren we have to do CPR. I learned it in Boy Scouts. I'll push on her chest and you give her mouth to mouth."

Lauren runs over shaking her hands. "I've never done this before. What do I do?"

"Uh..I give ten thrusts. Or is it twenty? Crap! I don't remember. Then you blow air into her mouth. Make sure you tilt her head back and hold her chin up." Craig starts to push on her chest counting each thrust. "1, 2, 3, 4…10, now Lauren." Lauren wraps her mouth around Summer's. Her chest rises slightly. Craig checks her pulse again. He shakes his head and continues the thrusts. I crawl over to Summer and grasp her hand. It's ice cold. *Come on Summer, please.* Lauren blows again and Summer's chest rises. Her body convulses and water spits from her mouth. She pulls in a deep breath and coughs out more water. Lauren and Craig jump up and hug.

"I can't believe it!" Lauren yells. I sit up and pull Summer towards me and hold her. Her whole body shakes and shivers. She starts to cry. Thank God she's okay.

Summer sits on the bench of the sailboat with a towel wrapped around her, water dripping from her hair. She's still breathing deeply and shaking from the cold. I stare at her and when she looks up at me, I don't look away. Our eyes meet and she smiles. "Thank you," she whispers, and I smile back. I'm so happy that I haven't lost her, so proud I wasn't too scared to save her.

Craig and Lauren sit in the corner of the boat both breathing heavily. Lauren has a wide smile but Craig is holding his head in his hands. He must be upset over Donny. I can't muster the same feelings. I've lost so many that I loved that I have no emotion over losing him. I walk over to Craig and put my arm around him, but my only thought is Summer. She looks cold, so I offer her a blanket and sit next to her. I'm not touching her, but I can feel her. She slides over towards me and places her hand on my knee. Her touch sends shivers up my body, and I almost pull away. The sudden warmth from her hand calms me, and I place my hand over hers.

We must pass under a few more bridges, but I'm too busy staring at Summer to notice. Craig turns the tiller and we tilt right as we enter the Hudson River and sail a couple miles upstream.

The boom moves above us, and Summer shudders as it passes by. I look out over the water. Why are there no boats? Why would no one else be out here escaping them?

Summer interrupts my thoughts as she covers her nose. "What's that smell?" I sniff, and notice, but it's not too bad. As the boat moves closer, though, the terrible stench slaps me in the face. Something bumps into the side of the boat with a loud thud. I peer over, eyes half-closed, and there are dozens of bodies bobbing in the water, a floating graveyard. A girl passes by, her eyes bulged, face covered in a white residue. Her bloated tongue sticks out slightly, and her hands, rigor mortis having set in, clutch a Raggedy Ann doll. I can't help but wonder how old she was, what her family was like. Her made up memories flash through my mind as she slowly floats away. I look at Summer, and she's covering her eyes as the boat's hull pushes the bodies aside. She hugs me closely, pressing her face into my chest.

The boat inches towards the shore and comes to a stop as the keel scrapes the sand. The hull turns and tilts slightly from the tide, allowing us to see more bodies littering the beach. Craig grabs his stomach and vomits onto the deck. Seeing him throw up makes all three of us sick, and it takes a while to recover from the morbid scene.

We gather ourselves, then jump to the beach; there are corpses everywhere, as if the monsters couldn't eat everything. Every inch of each victim's swollen. Because of their size, I believe most of them were children. The thought of this and the stink in the air makes my stomach turn, but to my surprise I don't hurl again. I must be getting used to the smell and numb to the sight of death.

It's a short distance to the street, so we run up to escape the carnage. Bodies are scattered on the road but not nearly as many as the beach.

I imagine the children heading towards the city, trying to escape, then meeting water. Nowhere to go, and maybe not knowing the creatures' weakness, the monsters quickly converge on them. Their screams echo through my head as I grab Summer's hand and squeeze. She looks at me through tears.

Craig and Lauren shuffle, shoulders drooped as we move towards the woods. We cross a highway, not bothering to look both ways. We walk about a hundred yards into the forest and collapse.

Craig covers his face with his hands. He lifts his head and tears flow down his cheeks. "So many children." It's the first time I've seen him cry since our parents turned. We all lie down and don't say a word. I don't worry about the creatures finding us. I almost welcome it. This is pure hell.

I must have dozed off and wake to Craig making a fire. He doesn't even look up as he says, "Listen, we're not giving up. We have to pull ourselves together and get through this. Dad would want no less." He sticks out his hand, and I grab it with a strong grip. He pulls me up and punches me in the chest. "Now go find us some breakfast." I nod and collect my bow. Craig has helped show me that, yes, many have died, but we still have life.

The stillness of the woods calms me even more, and I feel a sense of hope return as a rabbit bounds by. I raise my bow and fire an arrow. The head pierces the rabbit's side. I know we can survive. Craig guts and skins the rabbit and sets it over the fire. Lauren and Summer wake to the smell of roasting meat.

Lauren sits up and looks at Craig. "What's our plan?"

"We're gonna get as far away from the city as we can," Craig says. "I mentioned Dad's cabin, and it's probably a few weeks away but I still think it's our best bet. We know the land and even in the winter we can survive."

"Whatever you think's best," I say. "You've been right to this point."

"Yeah, we trust you," Summer says.

You can tell Craig feels good from all the praise. We finish breakfast and check over our supplies. Not much is left. We had some things on the boat but after the crash, and the bodies on the beach, I guess it slipped our minds. We won't be able to survive very long with what we have, so we'll have to find a house or store as we move north. "Let's get as far away from the city as we can," Craig says.

The next few days, we travel through the woods. We've passed many houses but have yet to find one that we feel is far enough from the city to stay overnight. We haven't seen many bodies, but we've also stayed in the forest most of the time. We've been able to hunt some game and quickly run into houses to gather food. That has sustained us, but the constant threat of the beasts has made everyone very uncomfortable.

We come across a road and notice a few small stores. It reminds me of some of the towns we would pass on the way to our cabin, and I feel that maybe we're finally putting some distance between ourselves and the city. There's a rusted old sign up ahead that reads "Grocery" and Craig points at the store. A few abandoned cars and a pick-up truck are parked in front. Craig pulls open the door of the store, and it creaks as it swings. We don't see any bodies or any sign of damage. It smells of rotten food, and when Craig opens the large refrigerator doors, a sour milk stank fills the store. Craig covers his nose and slams the door closed. We decide to focus on the shelves. "Grab anything canned, and look for a can opener," he says.

"Hey, who's here!" someone yells.

We dive behind the shelves, and I look for where the voice came from. I smell an overwhelming scent of scotch. "Um, we're looking for food," I say.

"Get over here," someone mumbles.

I peek around the corner and spot a small bar with three stools and a man sitting on one of them. I see his reflection in the mirror, elbows on the counter, and he looks anything but coherent. His hands are planted in his cheeks, and his elbows balance his head as it sways side to side. His face slips from his hands and hits the bar with such force that I'm sure he's knocked himself out, but he surprisingly recovers. I can't help but chuckle.

"Hey, what are you laughing at? I know your… type. You come in here with your fancy clothes and your pretty girlfriend." I look down at my ragged clothes and twist around, but everyone else is still hidden. Man, this guy's drunk. "You know, I had a family once. I oughtta get up and kick your ass." He stands to come towards me, and I brace myself to catch him. He staggers a few feet and falls flat on his face before reaching me.

Craig hurries over and helps me lift the guy off the floor and lean him against the bar. "Go get some water," Craig says. "He looks like he's been here awhile." Craig slaps his face and tries to shake him awake. But he's not waking up. He's too drunk. "Let's gather up any supplies we think we'll need. This place looks clear. Maybe we'll stay here for the night and see if this guy sobers up."

We search the store and it's a survivor's paradise. There are weapons, ammunition, camping supplies, and although the refrigerated food's spoiled, there are a bunch of canned and boxed goods. Craig starts stuffing items in his bag. "Don't take too much or it'll weigh us down."

"Hey, guys," Summer says, "over here." She points off of the bar where there's a small kitchen with a gas stove. Craig turns it on, and Lauren lights it with a match. It fires up. "Look! There are pots and pans. We can have a nice little meal tonight." The girls prep the meal while Craig and I check on the drunken stranger.

Leaning against the bar, he starts to budge and slides slightly but doesn't fall. He has grey hair, and stubble's trying to stick out over dirt that's caked on his face. His stomach protrudes and hangs over a leather belt with one of those big, shiny buckles. Drool drips from his mouth, staining his jeans. I feel like throwing him in a shower and leaving him there for a week.

"This is the first adult I've seen since this happened," Craig says.

"Yeah, I was thinking that myself," I say. "Maybe not everyone older has turned."

All of a sudden, the man starts to move. His eyes open and they squint as he looks towards us. "Why… arg," he mumbles and then throws up on the floor. He slides down the side of the bar and passes out again.

"Better lie him on his stomach, bro, or he's bound to choke on his own vomit. He's gonna need some time to recover from this. I've never seen someone so drunk before." We lie him on the floor and place a towel under his head.

Lauren and Summer find some plates and silverware and set a small table next to the bar. They are able to make salmon from a can with a side of rice. The meal's great, and it's nice to sit down at a table instead of the dirt. We make our beds on the floor of the store and check that the man's still breathing. We sit him up briefly to try to give him some water, but he's still unconscious. We figure he won't recover until the next day.

***

"Get up! What are you guys doing here?" I wake up with the chill of metal touching my neck. The drunk man must have sobered up, and he has his arms wrapped around me, knife held to my throat. I gulp, and the sharpness bites my skin. I wonder if I'm bleeding, but don't feel any blood dripping down.

"Hey, mister, we just showed up last night looking for food," Craig says. "You were really drunk, so we didn't think you'd mind us staying the night."

"Yeah," Lauren says, "we're not here to hurt you."

I nod, and the blade digs deeper. This time it breaks through, and I can feel a trickle of blood flow down to my chest. The man drops the knife and starts to cry. I run behind Lauren, sliding my hands over my neck, but it's only a small cut. "I'm sorry. I'm not usually this way. I haven't seen anyone in a month, and I overreacted. I've lost my family. Everyone's gone." He covers his face and sobs. Lauren pats his back and he gathers himself. "Thank you. I'm actually happy you're here. I didn't think anyone had survived. So, where'd you guys come from? Are there others? Have you seen any of those monsters?"

"We're from Long Island. We've seen a lot of them," Craig says. "We think they're heading to the city, so we're going to head as far north as we can. What happened to your family?"

"My daughters." Tears start to fall from his eyes. "I find it so hard to talk about them. Those monsters got them. And when my beautiful wife, Jen, turned, I hid from her. She ran out of the store, searching for food, and hasn't returned. I've been hiding here since. No one or nothing has come, until you guys." He wipes his eyes then holds out his hand. "I never introduced myself. My name's Mike."

Craig shakes his hand. "I'm Craig. This is Lauren, Kyle, and Summer. It's very nice to meet you. You're the first adult we've seen in a month."

"I know. It seems like all the adults have turned. I was watching on the news. They broadcast for a few days after this all started. One of the newscasters actually turned on air. It was pretty crazy stuff. They had scientists trying to explain it all. They were thinking maybe a specific chromosome, theories on global warming, but no one had a real answer. It went blank a few weeks ago. After that, I was listening to radio broadcasts of survivors, but my radio stopped working and I've been in the dark ever since."

"How old are you?" I ask.

"I'm 38. I don't know why I haven't turned yet. Tell you what, if you see me starting to turn, shoot me right between the eyes. I don't want to become one of them."

We talk the rest of the night and I'm really starting to like him. I feel funny calling an adult by his first name so I start calling him Mr. Mike. He says it sounds too much like he's a teacher, but he agrees to the name. He shows us around the store and the apartment upstairs and says that's where his family used to live. He gives us a tour and chokes up when we pass his daughters' room. They were twins, only eleven years old. When Craig mentions we're twins, Mr. Mike smiles.

We spend the next two weeks in his house. It's nice to not have to hunt, and I feel safe being here. Mr. Mike tells us some great stories of his family and when he was a kid. He drinks a few beers every night, and Lauren sneaks a few, too. When he drinks, he's really funny. I bet he was the life of the party before all this. He becomes very animated and has fallen a few times, telling us the story of when he threw his wife in the pool, chair and all. "Ironically, she wouldn't let me drink before all this," he says. "Here's to my wife and daughters." He raises his glass, then falls over and passes out on the couch. Summer grabs a cover and tucks it around him. We all eventually fall asleep after reminiscing.

The next day while Lauren and I are cleaning the dishes from breakfast, Craig yells, "Hey, guys, come here! I got the radio working. You have to listen to this." We all run over to the radio. "All right be quiet. Someone's broadcasting something."

"We won't let them win," a young voice demands. "We need to fight this plague. We won't let the beasts eat us like pigs."

"It sounds like he's a teenager," I say. "Mr. Mike, is this the broadcast you heard?" He shakes his head no.

"Quiet and listen," Craig says.

"All able bodied come to Aster Park. Join the revolution. Reclaim our right to live." The broadcast then repeats itself.

"It must be on a loop," Craig says. "Mr. Mike, is Aster Park close to here?"

"It's only a few miles away, but if it's on a loop, how do you know they're still alive?"

"I don't, but I think we should take a chance," Craig says. "Maybe there are more adults. Maybe they have some answers."

"But I feel so safe here," Summer says.

"I do, too," I say, "but I agree with Craig. We need to find reasons for this and see if more people are trying to figure out what's happened."

Mr. Mike talks us into staying for another week so we can gather our strength. We are finally set to go when he calls us into his living room. "I've decided that I'm not going to go. I've been in this house for twenty odd years and I'm going to die here."

"We need you," Craig says. "You're the only one who knows how to get to the park."

"You make us feel safe," Summer says.

He sighs and rubs his forehead. "Okay, I'll take you there, but as soon I see that you're okay, I'm coming home." We're all so relieved that he's going to guide us that we give him a group hug. We gather our supplies and head on our way.

Aster Park's even closer than Mr. Mike said. The entrance to the park's a giant wrought iron gate with its name in big iron letters. As soon as we get close, I hear someone speaking over a bullhorn and spot a large group of teenagers in the park square. "That building behind them is an old radio station," Mr. Mike says as he points. "They must be broadcasting from there. I don't know how smart it is to be making so much noise."

The crowd of teens surround a stage where there are about twenty figures standing. There's a tall teen in the center that appears to be their leader. "Gather round everyone," he announces over the bullhorn. "We now number close to a hundred, and we have the power." Whoever this guy is, he has a good presence. Besides his height, he's good looking and has a powerful voice. "This is our time. We..." He stops and looks right at us. He moves his mouth away from the bullhorn and points towards us.

About fifteen large thugs start running our way. I look at Craig, and he raises his fists prepared to fight. I raise mine, but before I can throw one punch, my arms are grabbed and thrust behind my back. About ten of them drag us to the stage. "Who are you?" the tall teen asks. I open my mouth to answer him, but a hand covers it instantly. "Why did you come here? Why do you have him with you?" He points to Mr. Mike and grabs him by the neck. I try to kick my legs to escape, but every move's met with the thugs holding me tighter. Craig almost gets loose before another thug runs over to contain him. "Don't you realize he could turn any minute. Prepare the rope." What? What does he mean by rope? What the hell is this guy talking about?

"Let him free!" Craig yells and elbows one of his captors. He let's go in pain as Craig punches the other in the head. He's free, but the bullhorn comes down with a thud, leaving Craig to fall to the ground unconscious.

"You bastard!" I yell. I'm able to punch one thug in the stomach, and as he bends, I kick him to the ground. The tall skinny teen's running towards me when I look up, bullhorn about to crush my skull, but he stops it inches from my head.

"Does anyone else have anything to say? Do you see what happens when you challenge authority?" I'm again grabbed, my arms forced up into my back so violently that I fall to my knees. The thugs turn me towards a large oak and in front are the tall teen and Mr. Mike, his hands being held behind his back by two of them. A rope's thrown over one of the tree's large limbs, and the noose dangles on the other side. Is this what I think it is? This can't be happening.

Mr. Mike tries to break free, but they stop his escape. Summer's crying and screaming. Lauren yells profanities, and her neck bulges with madness. Everything seems to be moving in slow motion. Mr. Mike's eyes are wide open, his legs shaking uncontrollably, as sweat pours down his face. How did it come to this? Two thugs step up to the end of the rope. The tall teen talks into the bullhorn, pumping his fist. I can't hear anything he's saying. I just watch Mr. Mike's eyes, and I mouth to him that I'm sorry. I can't help but think that he wanted to stay home. We begged him to come. Suddenly, the rope becomes taut and his legs dangle and kick. His body convulses for a moment and then becomes motionless, slowly swaying side to side.

CHAPTER 17

PRESENT DAY

My eyes are closed as Nightstar falls. I can't watch. Brute pulls himself over the ledge and throws me onto the roof. I sit up, hands shaking, and clutch my hair. She let go to save us, and now she's gone. "Hey, kid, look!" Brute's pointing over the side. I quickly race to the edge of the building hoping a miracle has happened. Nightstar's dangling by a rope, her grappling hook attached to the inside of a shattered window, shards of glass still raining down. On the ground below is the creature. Its legs are pushed up through its shoulders and its head's smashed like a pumpkin, brains oozing out of the side. I guess that's another way to kill one—drop it off a skyscraper.

"Stay where you are," Nightstar yells as she climbs the rope.

I haven't known Nightstar very long but I'm jumping up and down knowing she's alive. Brute must be happy too as he grabs me in a big bear hug and squeezes.

"Brute," I say as he lifts me off the ground, "I can't breathe."

"Oh, sorry, kid."

Nightstar jumps over the edge, and we run into a hug.

"Thank God you're alive," I say.

"I know. That was a close one. But no time to celebrate. We have to figure out a way to get back in the tunnels." She points to the roof of a building adjacent to us. "That building has direct access. If we can get to the elevator shaft, maybe we can get down to the basement and into the subway." Good idea, but how do we get over there? There's a crane on the other side, but the distance between the two buildings must leave at least a twenty-foot jump. Even Brute would struggle with that.

"I have an idea," Nightstar says. "Brute, exactly how strong are you?" Brute smiles and flexes his huge biceps. "This is going to sound crazy, but I don't see any other option. These buildings are crawling with Ragers, and the streets are even worse. We have to get into the subways and that building's our only chance. There's a crane on that side. It should be long enough to reach over here to create a makeshift bridge."

"But how do we get from here to there?" I ask, glancing over the edge, getting lightheaded again.

"That's where the muscle comes in." She hits Brute on the back, and he poses again. "Have you ever tried the hammer throw?"

"I was captain of the track team."

"That'll work," she says. "I'll need you to throw me."

"What? Hold on." I step in between them. "If you have to, throw me."

"I'm a hundred twenty pounds. That's probably sixty less than you. I can handle myself." She's right. I saw how she saved herself, and her catlike movements make me think she can land on her feet in any situation.

"Okay," I say, "but please be careful."

Nightstar and Brute walk to the edge of the building. I peek over, and the distance from them to the ground seems like miles. Brute grabs both of Nightstar's hands and grips them tightly. "Spin me until you get momentum and then throw me at just the right time," Nightstar says, her teeth clenched as she squeezes tight. "Okay, I'm ready when you are."

Brute's shoulders and biceps bulge as he starts to swing her in a circle. I wince as she gains speed, and I pray this won't end the way I expect it to. Nightstar's hair whips behind her. Brute flings her and drops forward, catching himself before he tumbles over the edge. Nightstar flies across, soaring like an eagle, into a perfect dive. She flips midair and lands, feet skidding across the gravel roof. "Amazing!" I yell, pumping my fists. Brute raises his arms to the imaginary crowd. Nightstar marches to the edge, takes a bow, and blows kisses as we clap and hoot. Brute runs over to me and we high five.

"Okay, guys, enough," she scolds. "Be ready for the crane."

Nightstar runs over to the end of the crane and gets on her tiptoes. She pushes as hard as she can, but it doesn't budge. She's not tall enough to put any strength into it. I hear her cursing and see gravel fly across the roof.

"She can't reach." I step over to Brute and grab his arm. "You're gonna have to throw me. I know I'm heavier. You think you can do it?"

Brute punches his fist into his palm. "Don't worry about me, kid."

I get to the edge and look down. Bad idea. I feel like I just got off a ride at the carnival. The one where the floor drops and you're spinning so fast that you get sucked against the wall. The one where I puked up so much cotton candy that the grass was probably pink for a week. I stare ahead and swear I won't look down again.

Brute grips my hand and looks at me, stoic. "You'll be all right, kid. Just hold on tight!" He starts to spin me, and my legs lift off the ground. I expect the dizziness to take over, but I feel fine. It's actually kind of fun. One of my hands slips from Brute's and panic sets in, but I know I have to do this. I snatch his hand and Brute adjusts his grip. I close my eyes and feel the weightlessness. Brute screams as he lets go, and I'm airborne. Gliding through the air, I open my eyes to see the roof a foot away and crash in a heap, rolling across the gravel. I stand, face bloodied, and spit out a few small pieces of stone as I bow. Nightstar runs over and hugs me.

"You did it, Kyle," she says as she steps back and claps. I don't know if I should be proud or embarrassed, but I bow again. We run to the crane and push it so it creates a bridge with the other building. Brute balances across.

"Good job, kid. Not the best landing, but I'm impressed."

"That was all you Brute, thanks."

Nightstar points to a door at the end of the roof. "Okay, let's go to the elevator and work our way down. Once we get to the garage, there's an entrance to the subway tunnels." We push open the door and find the elevator right down the hall. The shaft's empty and all we see is the elevator's cable hanging in front of us.

My arms feel like they'll explode, and my legs are basically eaten raw from the metal cable, but I'm able to hold myself as we descend about five stories. We finally reach the roof of the elevator, open the latch, and climb in. Brute rubs his forearms. "Let's rest here for a while."

"Yeah, but not very long," Nightstar says. "We're going to have to leave the elevator and move down one floor to get back on." We sit and pull in deep breaths. Between Brute throwing me and the long climb, the fact that I'm even breathing surprises me.

Brute stands and grabs his axe. "All right, enough sittin' around." He jabs the blade into the elevator door, forcing it open. He bows to Nightstar. "Ladies first."

She pushes him aside and takes one step out into the hallway, then freezes. She raises her hand and steps back in. "Close the door, Brute. Now!"

Brute puts his palms on the door to slide it shut and the sound of skin sliding against metal, like fingernails against a chalkboard, fills the elevator. A razor sharp claw flashes through the opening, ripping into Brute's arm. He pulls it back, wincing as he grasps the wound. I let go an arrow, and it pierces the creature's hand, sticking it into the wall. It screams and yanks its arm. Brute kicks the creature square in the chest, and it smashes against the wall. Nightstar leaps towards it and slashes at its jugular but hits its head. It grabs Nightstar and hisses, fangs exposed.

"Get off her!" I yell as I plunge my knife deep into its back. I hang on to its veiny skin, slipping as I push the knife deeper. The beast jerks in pain, and I'm thrown against the wall before falling onto Nightstar.

The monster looks at us, then lunges, its jaw extending, saliva spraying my face. A flash of metal slices through its neck and blood splatters the floor. Its head rolls down the hall like a bowling ball as Brute jerks his axe from the wall.

Nightstar jumps up and points. "More are coming."

I scramble to my feet and hurdle the creature's headless body. We push the elevator doors, hoping they'll close. Brute slams his hand into the door and shoves so hard that the metal starts to bend, but they won't budge. "Back away," he says. He raises his axe and, with two quick blows, chops a gaping hole in the elevator floor. "Get in!" He pushes us down through the hole. I grab the cable and look up as he faces the beast. Before meeting Brute, I had never heard the sound before, but his axe severing flesh is now all too familiar. Blood showers down as Nightstar and I lower ourselves.

My grip begins to loosen when Brute jumps in through the hole and grabs on. "There's one more. Move!" We descend as quickly as we can when the creature lowers its head into the hole and lets out a piercing scream. Brute's axe whips through the air and cuts its head clean off, silencing the beast. The head falls, bouncing off the sides of the shaft. Its body slowly slips through the hole and follows, hitting my shoulder as it passes. The taste of blood sickens me as it pours over my head and body. The cable becomes slick from the fluid, and we struggle to climb down. I finally get to the bottom when I hear a loud crash. Brute must have slipped and is lying face down on the floor.

Brute grabs his back. "I'm hurt, kid." He turns over and there's a huge slash from his deltoid down to the middle of his back, just short of his spine. It's a deep cut, but not much blood. His muscle and fat are exposed, but no bone.

"We have to get him back," Nightstar says. "We need to stitch that cut before it gets infected. Can you walk, Brute?" Brute nods his head slowly and winces. Nightstar and I put his huge arms around our shoulders and begin the long journey through the tunnels. Luckily, we don't see any creatures along the way, and after a few hours, we arrive at Nightstar's entrance. Brute's on the verge of passing out when we drag him through. We get to the gap in the tunnel, and Nightstar hits the lever.

"How are we gonna get him across that?" I ask.

Nightstar ponders for a moment, then runs off and comes back holding a long piece of wood. She places it over the gap, and we are able to pull him through. We drag him onto the bed, face down, and Nightstar inspects his wound. Brute better be okay. He's become like a big brother to me.

"He's dehydrated. Pull that crate from beside the bed and bring it over here." I drag the crate and notice it's filled with medical supplies. "Hand me the IV bag." She taps a syringe and sticks it into one of Brute's veins on his forearm. I want to ask her where she learned to do this, but I keep quiet so she can concentrate.

She raises and squeezes the bag, hanging it over a lamp. She then searches through the crate and takes out all different tools and syringes. She dumps some kind of liquid on the wound and it bubbles. Brute's body convulses, but then he's motionless again. At least I know he's alive. Nightstar takes out a long, hooked needle with what looks like string attached. "Hold him down. This is gonna hurt."

I place my knees over Brute's waist and push on his shoulders with my elbows. The needle enters the top of his wound, and he jerks violently back and forth. I feel like I'm riding a mechanical bull as I get thrown around. Nightstar places a wet towel over his forehead, and he calms down slightly. She stitches the rest of the wound, plus the one on his arm, and covers them both with large sterile pads. "He's gonna be okay, but it may take him a while to wake."

Brute's snoring as I dab the wet towel to his sweaty face. I crouch down next to him as his chest takes in deep breaths of air. The big lug saved me again. He's done it so many times, and I swear to myself that I will one day do the same.

"Hey, Kyle," Nightstar says as she waves the memory stick back and forth, "we almost forgot." The memory stick, that's right. I walk over to her to grab it, and she teasingly hides it behind her back.

"Come on. Don't be silly." I reach behind her, but she spins away and dangles it in front of me. This is ridiculous. We have to figure out what's on that thing and she's playing a game. I reach again, and she jumps into my arms and kisses me. I'm caught off guard. It's the first time I've kissed anyone besides Summer, and I push her away. "I can't do anything in front of Brute."

"He doesn't know what's going on," she says. I look over at Brute, and he has a goofy smile on his face, caught in a dream.

I drop my head and shake it. "I'm sorry. I'm just not ready for this."

"Oh. Don't worry about it," she says. "Maybe next time."

Looking at Nightstar I'm slightly attracted to her and I want to approach her, but I again think of Summer. It's only been two months since I lost her, and it would feel like cheating to me, even though I know she's gone.

Nightstar holds up the memory stick. "Let's take a look," she says, obviously trying to change the subject. She inserts it into her laptop and a "please provide password" sign appears. "I forgot all about this. This could take me some time. Go tend to Brute. Make sure the IV's still dripping." Brute seems to be doing well. He's breathing normally now, and the IV bag's still half full.

"Kid?" Brute whispers. He's awake, thank God. "I'm pretty beat up, huh?"

"You have a bad cut on your back, but you'll be fine."

He grabs my forearm. "Thanks for looking after me."

"Anytime, Brute, anytime." He looks like he wants to say something but his head slumps back onto the pillow and he falls fast asleep. I sit next to him for a few hours and begin to doze off. I'm wakened by Nightstar.

"Kyle, I'm finally in. He had some info about the Yankees on there. It took me forever but it was Yankees7."

"Good thinking. So whadya find?'

"Come look at this. A lot of it's science gobbledygook that I don't understand. But if you read here," she points at the screen, "it looks like a log of some sort. He's been keeping a journal of his research. This is his last log. It's from yesterday."

August 21, 2018:

I've made real progress in my research. I have isolated the chromosome in the human cell that's responsible for the change. The deformity has caused an adenoma to develop in most humans' pituitary glands. The neoplasm has caused rapid distension in the gland resulting in extreme levels of testosterone. I believe it's environmental in nature, but have yet to prove my theory. An antidote is not probable, but possible. I have run out of subjects to test, as they have all turned. There's been no luck in finding subjects that are immune; I feel this would have furthered my research. The inevitable has happened. I believe I'm succumbing. My pituitary gland has doubled in size, and my thoughts have become extremely aggressive. I wish I could have done more.

Non Omnis Moriar.

"We'll need a dictionary for some of these words," Nightstar says.

"I wonder what that last line means," I say. "It's not in English."

"I'm not really sure."

Brute leans in behind us. "It's Latin. It means not all of me shall die."

CHAPTER 18

FOUR YEARS EARLIER

"He didn't need to die!" I yell at the top of my lungs. I struggle with the guards, wanting to kill this kid.

"Shut up or you'll be next," the tall skinny teen commands.

They let the rope loose, and Mr. Mike's body collapses to the ground. He's just lying there, alive two minutes ago, now motionless, deprived of a future. My face reddens, and I clench my fist. I'm about to scream when Craig finally comes to. He opens his eyes, and Mr. Mike's body is the first thing he sees.

"You bastards! Why'd you kill him?"

"He'd have eaten us," the tall skinny teen says. "It's either us or them."

Lauren steps forward. "But he wasn't one of them."

"He'd have become one of them!" he yells. "Then what? We let him devour us."

"We came here to help you. To help you fight against them," Summer says. "What about the revolution?" I already know the answer. It's all a lie.

"The revolution? You actually thought that was real?" He rolls his eyes and saunters around us. "Idiots. We're not gonna fight them. Have you seen them? They're monsters. They'll tear us limb from limb."

"So you send out false hope?" I say, feeling stupid for asking. He's not the type of kid that's gonna help anyone, let alone us.

"Hope? Don't you guys get it? There is no hope. We're all going to turn. I have maybe six months, if I'm lucky, a year. Then I become one of those sick creatures. I'm not just gonna sit back and wait."

"So then fight them, you coward," Craig says.

"It's not about being a coward. It's about being smart. If this is it for me, I'm at least gonna have fun before I go. Right, boys?"

"Yeah!" the crowd yells, raising their arms.

"Throw them in the cages!" he commands. Cages? What does he mean by that?

The thugs drag us, and I find my answer. Behind the stage are huge animal cages. This park must have been a zoo years ago. Tall wrought iron bars surround a huge fake tree, branches jutting from the stump, reaching to the outer edge of the cage. There are five or six different cages, but the crazy thing is they're filled with kids, trapped like animals. They seem to be boys around my age. They're wearing next to nothing and look gaunt.

A teen throws the door open, and the prisoners scatter like cockroaches. By their reaction, I can't imagine what the thugs have put them through. They toss us in and slam the cage shut.

The tall teen walks up to the bars and sticks his head in slightly. "You guys belong to me now. You follow my rules or you'll end up like him." He points to Mr. Mike's lifeless body and then addresses the prisoners. "Everyone in these cages is years away from turning. You have the equivalent of a lifetime. But, this life will be cut short," he pulls the bullhorn across his neck, "terminated, if you try anything against us. We are your parents now. We set the rules. We have the power, and don't you forget it!" He walks away, high fiving his friends as they go.

Craig stares after them and grasps the bars of the cage. "Oh, he'll get his."

"I wouldn't mess with him," a tiny voice says. "He's crazy." I turn to see who spoke and a prisoner, a young boy, maybe 12, moves from behind the stump.

"Who are you?" Lauren asks.

"I'm sorry. My name's Chris. I was thrown in here a few weeks ago. The leader of those freaks is Dylan."

"Why's he such a jerk?" I ask.

"He's always been that way. He was a high school senior in my town. His parents were super wealthy, and he's a spoiled brat. But now, I guess he's on a power trip. He has those guys listening to his every word."

Summer gazes at the prisoners. "So, he cages all the younger kids?"

"Yeah, anyone younger than seventeen. He thinks if you have more than a year, you have too much to live for, and he doesn't trust that you'll obey him. A boy lied, saying he was seventeen, and then tried to escape. He went to get help. They caught him and hung him, just like your friend." Even the mention of Mr. Mike makes my blood boil.

I look around the cage at the other prisoners as Chris talks and notice that there are only boys, no girls. "Where are all the girls?" I ask.

Chris turns, shaking his head. "Oh... I don't want to know the unspeakable things they're doing to them. Girls seem to change later. Dylan keeps them knowing they won't turn for a while. I've seen a few battered and bruised and then usually they're gone. My friend, Sara, was taken, and I never saw her again."

"How long do we have?" Summer asks. "I don't want to be taken by those creeps."

"Don't worry," I say. "We won't let them put a hand on you."

"Yeah. They'd have to kill us first." Craig points to a corner in the cage. "But let's keep you towards the back. Out of sight out of mind. Hey Chris, what do you guys do during the day? Do they keep you in the cages?"

"Thank God, no. I couldn't stay in here all day. They put the boys to work." Chris points towards a hill in the distance. "Over that hill there's a farm that we've been tending to. Don't try to escape, though. He has the place surrounded. Each of them has a rifle, and it's like target practice to them. They've all gone mad."

Craig straightens up when Chris mentions the guns. "Where do they keep the weapons?"

"I've seen them come out of that shed over there. They have all kinds. Not far in town there was a pawnshop; I used to go there with my friends. They had every weapon you could think of, but Dylan and his cronies stole everything, so they're heavily armed."

"Yeah, and ironically they use it against us and not the creatures," Craig says. "They have the weapons to fight them, but they cage and kill humans instead."

"Have you guys seen the monsters?" Chris asks. "Luckily, we haven't seen them here in a couple of weeks In the beginning, they used to come a lot. Dylan thinks they've all gone to the city. But I don't know who the real monsters are anymore. The creatures," he points to the crowd of teens, "or them."

Craig nods his head at Chris' statement, then stares at the prisoners. "Hey, Chris, you think these guys can fight?"

"I don't know. We're pretty weak, physically and emotionally."

A few boys must have been listening in and shuffle over to us. "I think if someone can lead us, we're willing to fight," one boy says. "Nobody here wants to live like this anymore. Plus, we're thinking that they're close to turning. Once that happens, and we're in these cages, it'll be a bloodbath."

"Well," Craig says in a strong voice, "if you're willing to fight, I'm willing to lead."

***

For the next couple of days, Craig doesn't talk to us very much. He just plans. Chris says that they usually let the girls get comfortable and then take them. He figures we have maybe a week before Lauren and Summer are gone.

Craig drills Chris with questions, and he seems happy to help. Craig's focus is the weapons, and he asks me to look for ways to escape. I check over every inch of the cage and notice one of the bars in the back's almost rusted straight through.

"Hey, Craig, look here," I say as I poke at the rust. It flakes and feels soft.

"What did you find?" he asks.

"This bar can probably be removed with a swift kick." I fake kick at the bar. "One of us could squeeze through."

"Good. We're going to go out together and try to take down those guards." He points to three guards standing in front of the cages. "I've noticed that the middle guard has the keys. We'll do it during one of Dylan's stupid speeches. They'll be distracted."

During the day, a few teens escort us through the forest to a small farm. Young boys in ripped clothing shuffle through huge cornfields, picking corn and throwing it into piles. Then more prisoners drag the piles with nets back towards the zoo. A few teens sit on horseback, guarding the workers, barking orders every few seconds. One of them notices us. "Bring them over here." A few guards usher us over and push us down into a puddle of mud. "What's up, newbie's? It looks like you enjoy being dirty. Make them clean up after the cows." I don't like the sound of that. The guards shove us into a pen, and the smell is awful. After a few hours of shoveling, we're covered head to toe in manure.

The whole time we work, Craig is scanning his surroundings. He notices some haystacks. "Maybe we can hide there." He points at a barn in the corner of the field. "That might make a good stronghold." I wish I could be as observant as he is.

On the way back from the fields, Craig motions to the shed that houses the weapons. "We have to figure out a way to get in there. If Chris is right, they're our way to escape. We have to sneak out one of the next two nights and hide the weapons in the woods. But we have to make it look like it hasn't been tampered with."

"What if we break in through the back and only take the weapons from there?" I suggest. "This way when they open the door, they won't notice."

He slaps me on the back. "Now you're thinking." Ha, ha. I knew I could help, just have to think like Craig, always looking, always planning.

As the sun's setting, I start to get nervous from what's about to unfold. I know I've been confident the whole time, but I'm worried I'll screw up, do something wrong, and botch our plan. As I rub my head nervously I feel someone touch my back. It's Summer. "Are you ready for tonight?"

"If I can be honest," I say, "I'm a little scared. I trust Craig though, with all my heart."

"Yeah, your brother's pretty amazing."

I kick the dirt. "I know he is."

"Well, I think you're pretty amazing, too," she whispers and kisses me on the cheek.

My whole body feels warm as she walks away, looking at me with those hazel eyes. I can't even remember what I was thinking about when Craig startles me with a punch to the arm.

"Hey, bro, you finally have a girlfriend."

"Ha, ha. Real funny." Oh, how I wish it were true. "Hey, Craig, if tonight doesn't go as planned, I just want you to know that I respect what you've done and that I love you." I know it sounds mushy, but what if one of us dies during the escape? I didn't get a chance to say goodbye to Dad and it haunts me every day.

"That means a lot," he says as he hugs me. "I love you, too."

The sun falls, and the moon rises. It's half full, which makes the conditions perfect for escape. Just dark enough to not be seen from a distance, but light enough to see in front of us. You can hear Dylan's voice over the loudspeaker as Craig says, "Okay, bro, it's time." My stomach drops slightly, and my palms start to sweat. I rub my legs, then smack my head. *Concentrate. Don't screw this up.*

A few of the prisoners stand in front of us to try and block the guards' view. I follow Craig as he sneaks to the back of the cage and kicks the bar. It goes flying into the woods. I knew it was rusted through and feel a sudden surge of adrenaline. We squeeze through the hole and quickly dart into the woods.

"Follow me," Craig says. I crawl behind him, trying not to rustle too many leaves, then realize that Dylan's voice is so loud I can barely hear myself think, so I don't worry about being too quiet. The guards have moved closer to the stage to watch Dylan, so the shed's not guarded at all. We run to the back of the building and Craig rubs his hand around until he feels a loose board. He pries it off, and then the two next to it. "You go in and hand me what you can. I know where to hide it."

I squeeze through the hole and it's close to pitch black. There's a little light coming through a small window on the door, and when my eyes adjust, I can see the shadow of a huge pile of weapons. I grab whatever's in front of me and hand it out to Craig. Each object I touch feels like cold metal, and I can tell that most of the weapons are either rifles or guns. After Craig takes a few, I hear him run to hide them. I lean down and don't make a noise. My breathing's calm. I was ready for this all along. Craig's hands appear again, and I realize I don't have a weapon to give him. There's some sort of crate in front of me and I reach in but can tell right away it's not a gun. My hand scoops up what feels like oversized golf balls. Grenades. I laugh slightly as I hand them out, knowing how Craig's face will light up when he sees them.

"All right bro, let's go."

I start to leave but stop. I'm forgetting something. My bow. I push weapons aside as I head to the front of the shed. I can't leave this behind. It's the only item I have that reminds me of Dad. I get to the front, trying not to disturb the other weapons. It needs to look like we've never been here. My bow's in the very front of the pile. I grab it and throw it and the quiver around my shoulder. I somehow feel whole again. Hopping over a pile of weapons, my foot hits something big. I reach down and feel metal. Whatever it is, it's huge. I can barely lift it, let alone fit it through the hole.

"Really? A bazooka?" Craig says, smiling as he replaces the boards. "You don't think that's overkill?" I carry the bazooka on my shoulder and it's so heavy that I lose balance and feel like I'm going to topple over. I imagine myself falling, it going off, a rocket exploding in the middle of the forest. Dylan might even hear that over his loud, annoying voice.

Craig gets to a spot in the woods behind a huge fallen oak tree. The weapons are stuffed in a hole behind it, very well hidden. He grabs a bag and stuffs a few things in before we run back to the cage. We slip in and everyone surrounds us.

"That was amazing," Lauren says.

"Yeah, I can't believe it," a few prisoners say.

"Thanks, guys," Craig says. "But now everyone needs to focus and prepare. For months they've treated you like slaves." He takes out his bag and empties the contents. Handguns and grenades spill onto the ground as he raises his fist. "But tomorrow's our revolution."

The next day, Craig shows me and a few prisoners from each cage exactly what needs to be done, and where to be at every moment for it to work. He shows us how to cock the handguns—I'm so used to my bow that I've never shot one—and where the best place to shoot a human is, the head. He picks a few to show how to pull the pins on a grenade and how long to count before throwing. "But don't wait too long, if you know what I mean." He gets a few chuckles, but mainly scared stares.

Dusk begins to settle in when Craig gathers us to go over the full details of his escape plan. "All right, listen and make sure you follow these plans word for word. We can't have any mistakes. Once Dylan starts his nightly speech, Kyle, Chris, and I will sneak out and take out the guards. We'll wait for the precise moment, when Dylan's at his loudest, to fire." He grabs Chris and sticks the gun in his back. "This is how you deaden the sound. Stick it up into their back as far as you can before pulling the trigger." He lets go of Chris, who walks towards us, slightly shaken. "Once the guards are down, we'll grab the keys and let everyone out. The weapons are hidden, but I've told two prisoners from each cage exactly where they are. As soon as we arm ourselves, we have to fight. We can show no fear." He looks at us with such determination. "I'll fire the bazooka and take out the shed. They'll retreat if they have no weapons. I've told a few of the prisoners to fall back to the barn and use that as protection if the bazooka doesn't work. Are we ready to do this?"

We all nod our heads.

"All right." He stands and punches his fist into his palm. "We escape tonight!"

***

It's about time for Dylan's speech so Craig gathers everyone in a circle. Most of the prisoners look scared and apprehensive.

One prisoner, his legs shaking uncontrollably, asks, "After we escape, can we just flee?"

"What? Didn't we just talk about this? No!" Craig shakes his head. "We can't run. We must fight. They'll hunt us down. We have to stand our ground."

"But there are many more of them, then us."

"Yeah, but we'll have the element of surprise," I say. "They won't expect us to have any weapons. You can't chicken out now."

"I'm scared," a small voice says.

"I know you're scared," Craig says. "You have every right to be. But we need to turn that into anger. Anger over what they have done to you. Anger because they cage you and barely feed you. Look what you've become." Craig points around. "You deserve better than this. You are a human, not an animal. Take back your right to enjoy life. Your right to live!"

Everyone starts to get excited, when Dylan's voice silences us. "Hey, ladies, I've noticed the beautiful girls you have here and was hoping you'd share."

Craig's eyes bulge. "Don't touch them."

"You don't tell me what to do." He points for the guards to open the cage. Two come in with shotguns raised, reaching for Summer and Lauren.

Craig looks straight into my eyes then down towards his belt and nods. He lifts his shirt to reveal two handguns. I carefully remove one, making sure the guards can't see. Oh, man. I wasn't ready for this. I hold the gun, hands shaking, and take a deep breath, waiting for Craig's next move.

Craig turns and raises his pistol. He takes out two armed guards with perfect shots to the head. I hold the gun one handed and don't expect the kick as I fire. The bullet misses the target I intended but grazes the guard in the shoulder, bending him over in pain. My next shot hits him right on the top of the head, and I look away as blood spurts from the wound. Chris picks up one of the dead guard's guns and shoots another in the stomach, then finishes him off with a shot to his chest.

Dylan yells something then pulls his gun and fires. It strikes a prisoner's head next to me, and he falls into my legs. I drop in pain, head smashing into the ground. My gun flies out of my hand and fires, just missing Craig. I crawl and search for the weapon, but it's gone. I look up to see a guard holding my gun, pointing it at my head. I close my eyes, squeezing them, waiting. A shot rings out, but I don't feel a thing. Is this what death feels like? Nothing? Something falls next to me, and I open my eyes. The guard's sprawled on the ground, a bullet hole placed between his eyes. I turn and Craig stands in front of me, smoke rising from his gun.

Dylan fires a shot then turns to run. "Get the weapons from the shed!"

"Bro," Craig yells to me, "get the keys. Release the other prisoners." I scramble to my feet, and Lauren helps me wrestle the keys from the lifeless guard's belt. Prisoners from our cage push to get out and flee into the woods. Lauren and I are able to squeeze through the crowd and open the doors to the other cages. As the prisoners escape, I look for Summer. Where is she? I haven't seen her since the gunshots. I turn and see Craig helping her into the woods.

I sprint towards Craig, and he's handing weapons to the prisoners. Some of them take the guns but most keep retreating to the fields. "Don't run you cowards. Fight!" Craig yells. Some return, but most don't even look back. Dylan must have made it to the shed as bullets whiz by my head. Prisoners fall dead around me as I drop to the ground and twist towards my brother. He's screaming something at me but I can't hear him. I turn my head slightly left and see Lauren and Summer huddled behind a tree, bullets piercing the bark. Craig's words suddenly become clear. "The bazooka!"

Craig points to a spot in the woods. There are raised leaves in the ground, and I race over to pull it out. I push the leaves aside and pick up the huge weapon. I don't even know where to begin. There are different levers or triggers, not really sure. It's hard to lift, but I place it on my shoulder and see what I think's the sight. I close my left eye and peer through with my right. A tiny "X" is aimed at the shed. I pull the trigger and get immediately thrown back, sliding on the leaves as the bazooka flips to my side. I look up to see the shed explode. The weapons inside erupt into a fireworks show. Teens scatter, hair and clothes covered in flames.

Craig grabs me by the shoulder. "You did it, bro." I turn to celebrate but bullets ricochet off the ground at our feet.

"Guys, this way!" Lauren yells as we sprint towards the barn. Most of the prisoners that stayed to fight have been killed. A boy next to me is hit and falls. We dive behind some logs and continue to shoot. Summer even has a rifle, looking clumsy as she fires. I fire my gun but quickly run out of ammo. I shake it and squeeze the trigger again. Empty. Everyone else fires their last shots, and we look at each other, puzzled. "What do we do?" Lauren says. Not really knowing the answer, I peak over the log and see Dylan approaching with about five guards, guns raised. They are the only ones left.

"You thought you could defeat me?" he yells. "Surrender or be killed!"

Craig gets up, hands behind his back. What the hell's he doing? "I surrender," he says as he approaches Dylan. "Just don't hurt them."

"Let me see your hands."

Craig throws his hands forward. "See? I'm not armed." On his finger spins a metal ring. Dylan looks down as a grenade rolls between his legs. His eyes widen as he raises his gun and fires a shot. The grenade detonates, sending body parts flying everywhere.

We huddle under the logs and a plume of smoke floats past us. I jump from behind the log as Lauren and Summer embrace. "That was awesome," I yell, surrounded by a wall of smoke. The smoke begins to clear, and I wonder why Craig hasn't joined the celebration. I look for him, and notice he's lying on the ground, holding his stomach and writhing in pain.

I can't move from the shock. Summer rushes over and kneels at his side afraid to touch him. "He's hurt, bad."

Lauren falls to her knees and screams. I sob as I run to Craig's side. Summer gathers herself and applies pressure to his wound. Blood spurts in between her fingers as she pushes as hard as she can. The bullet has ripped open his stomach. I help Summer push against the wound, trying to stop the blood. "Craig, don't leave me," I beg.

"I'm sorry, bro." His voice is beginning to fade.

"I can't do this without you," I say, holding his hand.

"Yes, you can." He struggles to speak, blood pouring from his mouth. "You always could." Craig tries to sit up but his body slumps down into a fetal position. "I thought my plan would work, bro."

"It did Craig. They're all dead." I pull his head towards me and look deep into his eyes. "You saved us." I lower his head and cradle it in my arms. He coughs up more blood and closes his eyes. I'm losing him and there's nothing I can do. Utter sadness sweeps over me. My mom, my dad, now my brother.

Craig opens his eyes and squeezes my hand. "Kyle." His voice lowers to a whisper. "I love you. Keep Lauren and Summer safe. I'll say hi to Mom and Dad." He takes one last breath and dies in my arms. My twin brother. A true hero. I hug him, and my head sinks into his chest as I cry.

CHAPTER 19

PRESENT DAY

"So he figured out what's wrong with us?" I say.

"It looks that way, kid." Brute grabs his wound, grimaces, and falls back on the bed. He lands on his cut and screams. Nightstar and I hurry over and turn him on his stomach.

"Brute, you need to rest," Nightstar says as she holds her palm against his forehead. "No more getting up. Promise me."

"Yeah, I promise." He winces and lays his head down.

Nightstar pulls a cover over Brute. "He'll be okay. His fever spiked a little." She logs back onto the computer. "If you look at some of his old notes, it keeps mentioning a lab in Philadelphia. See here?" She points to a log dated August 7. It reads Specialty Labs, 28 Hawthorne St. Philadelphia, Pennsylvania. "I think he meant for us to get this data there. He must have thought that whoever's there would be able to use it to find a cure."

Suddenly, the computer powers down. "Damn, I thought this might happen." She smacks the side of it. Still blank. "Quick, write that address down." I grab a pencil and jot the address on a piece of paper. "There's not enough power. The solar energy doesn't sustain the computer for long," Nightstar says. "We need to bring this memory stick to that lab."

"Philadelphia. That's a long trip. Must be a week away."

"It's our only option. What lies on this stick could very well be the answer."

I hop up. "I agree. Let's go!"

"Whoa, settle down. Brute won't be able to travel for a few weeks with that injury. And knowing what's out there, we're gonna need his muscle."

"What do we do till then?"

"Well, you've gotten really good with the bow. One of the best shots I've seen. But you need to learn how to fight during close combat. I need to teach you to handle a sword." Nightstar walks to her bed, bends down, and reaches underneath. She pulls out a long, black leather box and slides it to the middle of the room. I peek over her shoulder as she unlatches the locks and pushes it open. Inside is the most beautiful sword I've ever seen. Its handle is a shiny white, might be ivory, and its blade is so smooth and polished that even the small amount of light that spills into the room reflects off it and blinds me. She squeezes the handle and holds it with both hands in front of her nose. She lifts the blade, then slices it in front of her so fast that it makes a cool whooshing sound. She freezes, arms extended, and holds the pose.

"How'd you learn to do that?" I ask.

"It's a long story," she says.

I point to Brute, who's snoring loudly. "We have plenty of time."

Nightstar sits in her recliner and leans towards me. "Okay." She takes a deep breath. "But expect me to cry. My parents died when I was about five. They were in a car accident, I think. I only remember a few things about them, small memories or dreams. When they passed, no one from my family wanted me. Imagine that pain, so young. Why would nobody want me?" My stomach drops. How awful. Five years old and no family.

"My uncle left me at the orphanage. I remember how big and dreary it looked. Everyone there was so mean. From day one, all the girls picked on me relentlessly. I remember this especially awful girl." Nightstar pauses and shudders. "Beth. She was the worst of the worst. I was sitting alone one day, eating my lunch when she stomped over." Nightstar lifts her legs and pounds them into the floor with a mean growl on her face. She swipes her arm through the air. "She swatted my food right into my lap. Everyone laughed. I stood up and squeezed my fist so hard I think my knuckles bled. I was going to take the anger of losing my parents, nobody loving me, everything, out on her big, fat puss. I lunged for her, but she punched me so hard I was bedridden for weeks. As soon as I healed, I escaped from that place. I couldn't take the hatred, the lack of love anymore."

Nightstar covers her face, and I pull her in close. "The orphanage was terrible, but the streets were worse. I'd curl up every night from hunger pains. I searched the alleyways for food, anything I could scrounge. Luckily, I found a restaurant that threw their scraps onto the street. I picked through it like a mangy stray."

A smile beams across Nightstar's face, and she suddenly seems happy. "I took a different route to that restaurant one night. I don't know why, maybe fate. I passed a small building and looked into the window. A short, old man was teaching people to fight. He moved so smoothly," Nightstar performs what looks like martial arts moves, "that he seemed to float through the air. I watched for over an hour. He peeked over at me and our eyes met. I ran away too scared to stay."

"Did you go back?"

"Yeah, the very next night. Kyle, I swear he didn't peek over on purpose. He didn't want to scare me away. The following night the pickings were slim at the restaurant and I was weak from hunger. I dragged myself to the dojo and collapsed in front. On the step was a small, beautiful basket. I reached over and carefully lifted the lid.

Inside there was a warm loaf of bread and a delicious smelling bowl of soup. I looked into the dojo, and the old man gave me a wink. He motioned for me to come in. I opened the door, and he said, 'Konnichiwa' in such a soft voice. He took my hand and sat me down. I watched him teach as I ate, and he would look over and smile. That was the first time I felt loved since my parents died."

"He seemed like such a sweet man." I grasp her hand, and Nightstar nods. She doesn't speak and just looks up for a moment.

"He was my sensei for the next five years. He left a basket of food every night, and I always went in to eat and watch. After eating, I'd practice with him and his students, and as I got older, he'd teach me how to use the sword. He eventually became old and sick. He gave this sword to me the day before he died. Lying in pain on his bed he called me his little otome."

"What does *otome* mean?"

"It's Japanese for girl." Nightstar covers her face and cries. She lifts her head, her eyes soaked with tears. "He was like a father to me, Kyle. I don't know what I'd have done without him."

Her story makes me think of Dad, and I feel like crying too. I grab her and hug her. She puts her head on my shoulder and her tears fall, soaked up by the cement below.

Nightstar wipes her eyes, looks at me, and smiles. She clears her throat. "Okay. Where do we start?" I stick out my chest and stand at attention. "The first thing we need to work on is getting you some muscles." Ouch. "Don't be fooled, though. Yes, you need power, but with a sword it's all finesse. Use the over aggressiveness of the Ragers against them. But before we even begin, I want you to carry this sword with you everywhere. It has to become an extension of your hand. Sleep with it. Eat with it. Breathe with it." She hands me the sword. It feels clumsy in my grip. I raise it up, trying to copy her move, and smack myself right in the nose. Good start. She grabs my wrist and straightens it. "Today it feels weak. Tomorrow we begin your training."

For the next few weeks I train, while Brute sleeps. Nightstar makes me lift anything I can get my hands on, while Brute lifts a fork to his mouth. He teases me relentlessly, like a big brother would, but I feel stronger every day. I develop muscles that I didn't know existed, and standing back-to-back to Brute I'd say I was now close to 6'2". I feel like a man.

Nightstar takes me to the tunnels every morning to teach me to use the sword. We find an area of the tunnel that has light and she feels is safe. "There are many different moves, called katas, but because we don't have much time," she raises two fingers, "I'm gonna show you two of them. The first," she raises the sword to my side, "is called Yoko Giri. Bring the blade straight in a strike across your body, all the way through your target. Remember to always drive through, like swinging a bat in baseball. The next is Kesa Giri. It's a similar move, except you start the blade at the side of your head and drive diagonally through your target." She takes the blade and shows me the moves. "Now, do these over and over, thousands of times. You can't think of the kata; you just do it."

I practice until my muscles burn. "You're doing great," Nightstar says. "Take a break." I rub my arms, and Nightstar takes the blade and practices. Her movements are fluid and precise.

"Watch this." She steps back, sprints, and leaps against the wall. Her legs push off, she flips, and lands on the floor, blade raised. She smiles and winks. "You'll get here one day." I beg her to teach me that move. She promises to, but only if I work hard. I practice with my sword every day, so each night she teaches me the flip, and each night I fall on my face.

Over the next few days, Brute starts getting his strength back and he comes to watch me practice. "You're gettin' good, kid."

Soon Brute's strong enough to spar. We face each other and bow.

"Don't be easy on him, Brute," Nightstar says. "He needs to feel defeat."

Brute nods. "That shouldn't be a problem."

Brute wields his axe and stomps towards me at full force. He raises the weapon, and it descends with a powerful blow. I quickly step to the side and swing my blade. Brute blocks it with the heft of his axe and dropkicks me into the wall. He grips my neck and holds the axe to my throat. "Not quite ready, kid."

This scenario happens over the next few days. Me fighting my hardest but Brute always coming out on top. Each successive match I get closer and almost beat him. One spar I duck Brute's axe and throw a punch but miss. Brute puts me in a headlock until I say "uncle".

I throw my blade down in disgust. "I'll never be ready!"

Nightstar barrels into me, knocking me to the ground. She holds me down and looks me straight in the eyes. "You never throw your blade. To be a warrior, you need to keep your mind clear, even in the face of death. Use Brute's strength, his aggression, against him. Get up, wield your weapon, and fight."

I stand and halfheartedly raise my blade. I look at Brute and just see my friend. This is stupid. How do I fight him? I put my head down and think of Craig. How strong he was in the face of battle. How he never backed down. I now have focus. My mind's clear. I'm ready.

Brute again raises his axe and chops down. This time I slide to the side and kick his knee. He grimaces and swings his axe, but I block it with my sword. He throws his paw forward to grab me, but I duck and elbow his face. Brute snarls and lunges at me, axe swinging from his side. I jump against the wall, flip and land right behind him. I place my blade against his neck. Brute drops his axe and raises his arms, a smile crossing his face.

"Good job, kid."

"Kyle," Nightstar says as she runs over and hugs me, "now you're ready."

I back away and bow. "Thank you, sensei."

CHAPTER 20

FOUR YEARS EARLIER

I hold Craig and can't feel a heartbeat. I press my hand against his back to search for one. When I was younger, I had trouble sleeping and Mom would have me lay next to him for comfort. I'd hear the beat as I rested my ear to his back. The rhythm would soothe and lull me to sleep. Now, nothing. Please, just beat. Please. Still nothing.

"No!"

Summer reaches out to me.

"Get away!" I yell, the anger boiling inside me. I turn to the prisoners and point at Craig's lifeless body. "Look what you cowards did to him. If you didn't run away, he'd still be alive!" I grab a boy and slam him into the ground. I twist and raise my fist at another, but it's pointless. Craig's not coming back, no matter who I blame.

My mind races. Lauren throws her arms around me, and we hug and cry for what seems like an eternity. Summer covers Craig's wound and closes his eyes. I kneel beside him, his face so calm. He's fought so hard to keep us safe. His hands are clenched in a fist and feel ice cold. I pry them open and place them on his chest. "You don't have to fight anymore, brother."

I stay awake most of the night, knowing that we will bury Craig tomorrow. My grandfather passed away when I was young, and Dad wrote a poem for him and read it at his funeral. I never saw Dad as the sentimental type, but I, and everyone who attended, thought it was very moving. I find a pencil in our supplies and try to write a poem for Craig. I want the last words I say to him to be special, but I struggle with what to write. I finally finish and read it aloud to myself, hoping I've found the right words.

The next morning Lauren and I search for Craig's final resting place. He loved nature, so we fortunately find a hill filled with wildflowers, overlooking a stream. I dig Craig's grave and lower him in. I construct a cross out of two solid branches and stick it in the ground behind him. Lauren, Summer, and I kneel next to his grave.

"I love you, Craig, and I will miss you," Lauren says. She starts to cry and can't say anymore. Summer can't speak at all and lowers her head in prayer.

I take out my poem but have a hard time starting. I finally read it, pausing to gather myself throughout.

"Oh, dear Lord in heaven,
My brother comes to you.
He fought for us, protected us,
And helped to see us through.
The world has turned to darkness,
He was our guiding light.
When we thought that all was lost,
He taught us how to fight.
No matter how tough he seems,
He may cry for a while.
Take him to my mom and dad,
For it will make him smile.
And when my time has come,
And you're looking for another.
Bring me up to heaven,

To be closer to my brother."

I place the poem on top of his grave and cover it with a large, flat rock. Thoughts of Craig race inside my head. The fun we had together and all the good times. Then I think of how I'll never see him again. Never be able to talk to him. Knowing he's gone forever.

"I'm so sorry this happened," Summer says as she wipes tears from her eyes.

"Thank you, Summer," Lauren says, giving her a hug.

I'm too distraught to show any emotion. Without saying a word, I bolt towards the woods.

"Kyle!" Summer yells as she trails after me.

"Let him be," I hear Lauren say. "He needs some time alone."

I stumble through the trees and think about Craig and everyone else I've lost. All that I see, everything I hear, reminds me of them. I gaze up into the clouds. "How could you take them from me?" It's all too much, and I collapse to the ground, crying. I sob so loud and hard that I feel like I can't breathe. Sometimes after I cry over something or someone, I feel better, a sense of relief, but that never seems to come. The hurt, the pain, the loss flows endlessly out of me. By the time I'm dried up, I'm physically and emotionally exhausted. I try to stand, but can't, and fall asleep lying in the leaves, deep in the forest.

Water splashes me in the face, and I dig with my oar, struggling to steer clear of the large rock that my raft seems destined to slam into. "Pull harder, Kyle," Dad yells. "We have to get around that boulder." Craig is next to me. He turns and smiles, whitewater kicking into his face. He squeezes his oar tight and drives it into the water. The front end of the raft turns and it slips by the boulder as we are whisked down the river.

The rapids calm so I lay down my oar and put my feet over the edge of the raft. Relaxed, I recline and soak up the sun.

"Hey, Kyle!" Dad yells. I look up to see a rush of water. He got me again. Dad's king of the bucket soak. He can lift a full five-gallon bucket over his head and soak you in about three seconds flat. Craig and I grasp our oars, and a water fight ensues. This is always my favorite part of our Boy Scout trip, and we continue the battle for a while, laughing the whole time.

Out of nowhere, black clouds roll in and the sky becomes dark and ominous. Wind begins to whip, and large waves kick up. We're pushed sideways and rushed downstream. We pass a huge rock and are sucked into a funnel of water. A liquid tornado. Our raft spins and I'm thrown to the side. Dad yells, "Hang on, son!" The raft bucks, and I'm tossed head over heels into the river. Sucked into a vacuum of water, I reach towards the surface. Craig and Dad reach for me, but I sink lower. "Kyle! Kyle!"

"Kyle! Kyle," Lauren calls, "where are you?" I sit up dazed. "Oh, thank God I found you. I've been looking for a few hours, and it's starting to get dark. Let's head back. We set up a shelter in the barn." She lifts me off the ground, but I'm still exhausted. I heave my arm over her shoulder, and she carries most of my weight as we trek through the woods.

"Who's with you at the barn?" I ask. "Is Summer okay?"

"Yeah, she's fine. How you holding up?"

"Not so good. I can't stop thinking about them. It seems so pointless to go on. What's there to live for?"

"Me and Summer." Lauren's tone is suddenly very serious. "Craig asked you to protect us before he passed. He wants us to survive. He wants us to continue to fight. He saw in you what you don't see, a leader who can protect us, can guide us through the evil this world has become."

Lauren's right. Craig would want me to move on. With the beasts pursuing us and other teens trying to kill us, there's no time to sulk, no time to cry. I have to grow up quickly and become the leader we need to survive.

We approach the barn and a flickering light becomes visible through the cracks in the wood. I walk in, expecting to see many people surrounding the fire, but it's only Summer and Chris. "Where is everyone?"

"They all left," Chris says. "I think they feel terrible for what happened to your brother."

Sadness surfaces again. This'll be harder than I thought. "Where'd they go?"

"Not really sure," Chris answers. "Maybe back to their houses. I appreciate what you did for me, but I think I'm going home, too. I feel safest there. You're more than welcome to come."

I shake my head. "Thanks, but we're gonna try to make it to my dad's cabin. Craig thought that would be the best place for us."

"I totally understand," Chris says

We sit for about an hour, and then Chris says his goodbyes. I thank him again for helping with the escape, and he shakes my hand firmly before leaving. Summer, Lauren, and I warm our hands by the fire and don't speak. I stare at the flames dancing and can't help but wonder what lies ahead. And I wonder if I can be strong enough to fight, no matter what it is.

Summer slides in closer to me and places her hand on my knee. "I loved your poem. I thought it was so moving." I smile, and she smiles back.

She cuddles into my chest, and the warmth of her and the fire comforts me. I'm about to fall asleep when Summer shakes me. "Do you want to take a walk?"

"Sure," I answer, wondering why she would want to leave the barn so late at night.

I look over at Lauren, and she's sound asleep. I hesitate leaving her for a moment, but figure she'll be fine. Summer pushes the barn door open, and we head towards the cornfield.

"I'm sorry I woke you, Kyle. I know you just lost your brother, and I feel such sorrow, but it's made me think about my family and I just needed somebody to talk to."

"Don't feel sorry. We've all lost so much. You've never really spoken about your family. What were your parents like?"

"I don't remember my dad very much. My parents separated when I was very young. I try to think of a happy time with them, but I don't remember ever seeing them together. My mom told stories about him. I know he was very young when I was born, maybe eighteen. My mom was even younger, like sixteen I think."

"Wow, that's only three years older than we are." I couldn't imagine having to care for a baby at that age.

"I know. Way too young. My dad went through a lot. He was in the Portugal infantry when they were in a war with Africa. During a firefight, one of his best friends was badly hurt. The wound was too deep for my dad to mend. Nobody came to help, and my dad sat with him for days as he slowly died in his arms. My mom said it scarred him forever. He'd wake up in the middle of the night screaming. I was born a year after he came home from war, and my parents divorced shortly after. He moved to the United States and started another family. I've rarely talked to him." I can see the pain she feels from this. My dad meant everything to me.

"My grandpa stepped into my dad's shoes, and he was the most loving man. He would take me on long strolls along the canal, and to this day I remember how he held my hand so gently." She squeezes my hand and closes her eyes.

"Times were tough in Portugal. My mom was so young I don't think she knew what to do. She sent me to America. I guess she felt that I needed a more stable life. I was maybe five. She sent me to stay with my dad's mom. I was devastated. The day I left I cried for my family and fought to not get on that plane. I felt such hatred towards my mom for removing me from the life I knew. I moved in with my grandmother and never really felt loved by her. She was mean and would hit me if I didn't listen. You know, after that I never really had much of a birthday. It's in September, and my grandmother would rarely throw me a party. I was too afraid to tell my mom in fear of my grandmother hitting me if she found out.

Nevertheless, during the summer I'd go back to Portugal and feel such love. My real name's Sandra, but my family nicknamed me Summer, because that's when I'd visit. My grandpa would say it was the best time of the year, and my mom and I got along so well when I was home. She talked about moving here, and I'd have stayed with her, but all this chaos happened. I don't even know if my family in Portugal is still alive."

She's crying, and I hug her. We embrace for what seems like forever and the warmth of her body calms me. I gaze into her eyes and wipe away the tears. She leans in and kisses me, and I don't pull away. I've never kissed a girl and I feel clumsy, but the softness of her lips makes me want to kiss her forever. She pulls away slightly and places her head on my chest.

"I really care for you, Kyle. Promise that you'll never leave me."

"I promise," I say as we embrace, and for the first time since this all began, I feel at peace.

CHAPTER 21

PRESENT DAY

We decide to stay a few more days before traveling to the lab. Brute and I continue to spar, and I notice his frustration when I defeat him, although he still kicks my butt most of the time. I workout, practicing most of the day, and am gaining strength and building confidence in my abilities.

"I think it's time we get ready to go," Nightstar says. "It'll be a long trip, so make sure to bring a good amount of water, but not so much that you'll slow yourself. We have to watch for the Ragers."

I start to pack and put the remaining arrows into my quiver. I'm down to six and because of a lack of wood and feathers in the city, I haven't been able to make anymore. I'm so grateful to Nightstar for teaching me how to use the sword. I now know that I can fight in close combat.

A metallic grating sound fills the room, and I glance over to see Nightstar sharpening the blade of her sword with a whetstone.

"Kyle." She slides the sword into the scabbard and holds it out in front of her. "I want you to have this."

I shake my head. "I can't take your sword, Nightstar. Your sensei gave it to you, and I know how important it is."

"It means the world to me, and I treasure it," she says, "but it would mean even more if you'd use it. You've been a great friend, and I know my sensei would be proud of you."

She tosses me the scabbard, and I remove the sword and slice it through the air. I want to give her something but the only possessions that matter to me are my cloak and bow, and I know she won't take either, so I kiss her cheek. She blushes, and because of her fair skin, it's a really bright red. I've never seen her embarrassed before, and she turns quickly to continue packing, shielding her face.

We grab our gear and begin to climb through the pipe. As we leave, Nightstar stops and looks back. Tears roll down her cheek, and she wipes them clear. "This has been my home since I can remember." She pushes the lever and water spills over the opening, hiding the pipe. "I hope I see her again."

We enter the subway and follow as far as we can go. "I think after your bridge experience," Nightstar says, "it's best if we take the Holland Tunnel under the Hudson to get to New Jersey. Then we'll head south from there." Brute and I nod in agreement. If I never see another bridge again, it'll be too soon. We climb the stairs and walk out onto the street. No Ragers; that's good. I smell the saltwater as we overlook the Hudson.

Nightstar begins to jog, and Brute and I follow. We get a few blocks, always keeping our guard. I think the monsters have gathered more in the center of the city because we don't notice any. We turn the corner of a building and see the entrance to the Holland Tunnel. I expected it to be much bigger. As we get closer, I notice that it's extremely dark, like a bat cave. As a matter of fact, I half expect hundreds of bats to fly out as we enter, and I duck, even though I know there aren't any.

We're only about a hundred feet in when the sunlight disappears and walls of darkness envelop us. The coldness constricts my lungs, and I find it hard to breathe. This is even worse than the subway, if that's possible. "Nightstar, can you break a glow stick?" I whisper, not knowing if I can stay in the tunnel much longer.

"I'm not gonna waste one. Just walk straight ahead and follow the sounds of my footsteps. We shouldn't encounter any Ragers in here. The tunnel's about a mile and a half long, so we should get through pretty quickly. Once we get to the other side, we'll hit the highway."

I listen to her footsteps and the rhythmic beat calms me. After about a half hour, light appears at the end. I've never been so happy to be able to see. We exit and start to make our way to the highway, when Brute stops abruptly and points. I pull an arrow and ready my bow. He starts sprinting, a huge smile spanning ear to ear, and I see what he's so happy about. It's a big sign that reads, "Hank's Harley Dealership". Nightstar and I look at each other, start to laugh, and follow.

Brute's like a kid in a candy shop as he points to all the different motorcycles. "This is an Electraglide, and this is a Road King, but this is my bike of choice." He pats the seat and beams at the beauty of a bike. "The Fat Boy." It's tough looking, all black, except for very shiny chrome on the handlebars, engine, and muffler. Brute straddles the motorcycle and pretends that he's cruising down the highway. "What I'd do to ride this."

"You just might be able to," Nightstar says. She points out a huge glass window. "There's a gas pump in the back."

"Do you think the gas is still good?" I ask.

"There's only one way to find out," Brute says. He stomps out the side door and sprints towards the pump.

The pump's surrounded by a chain link fence that's not locked. Brute grabs the nozzle and squeezes. Nothing spews out but a strong gas odor. Brute pulls in a long sniff. "Smells like it's still good. Look for a hose, kid. I'll try to siphon some." I notice a hose hanging from the fence and hand it to Brute. He lifts the lid to the tank and snakes it down. Nightstar finds a five-gallon can. Brute lets out a deep breath then puts his mouth over the hose and sucks in until his stomach looks like it may touch his spine. The gas must come up quickly because Brute spits about a gallon of it onto the ground. He sticks the hose in the can and seems to cough up a lung. I have to step away because each cough smells continuously worse.

"Ugh, I hate that taste," Brute says as he gags even more.

The can quickly fills, and he dumps it into the tank of the Fat Boy.

Brute straddles the motorcycle and tilts his head towards the sky with his eyes closed. If there's a motorcycle god, he's praying to him right now. He turns the key but nothing happens. His head drops. Brute then looks up to the sky again and puts his palms together in prayer. He turns the key and again nothing. He whacks the engine in disgust. Brute stands, cracks his neck, and then rubs his hands together. I've never seen anyone look so determined.

Nightstar grabs him by the arm. "Hey, Brute, we have to rethink this. I know we're outside the city and haven't seen any Ragers, but if you start that thing, they'll be here and quick."

Brute looks at the engine of the Fatboy and rubs the chrome. "I'll take that chance, little lady." He pulls out the kick start and places his boot on top then pauses. "Maybe you're right. I don't want to put you guys in harm's way."

I can tell Brute's really upset. I look around the yard of the motorcycle dealership and notice a large garage attached to the showroom. "Hey guys, what about that."

"That might work, kid. Good job. Let's check it out."

The garage doors are open about half way and Brute is able to push the motorcycle inside. He grabs the bottom of the door and pushes it down to close it. The garage is huge and, except for a few motorcycles in a corner, it's empty. It'll be the perfect place to test drive the Fatboy.

Brute pushes the motorcycle to the middle of the garage floor. He looks as happy as I've ever seen him. He rubs his hands and his smile turns to a determined look. "Okay. The battery must be dead. I'll try the kick start." He steps on the lever and gives it a strong kick. The motorcycle roars for a second, then stops. Brute's eyes light up. He kicks again, and the engine comes to a full roar. He closes his eyes and listens to the loud purr of the engine. It's music to his ears.

Brute turns the handle and revs the engine. Nightstar covers her ears and looks around. "Don't worry," Brute yells. "These walls are soundproof. The Ragers won't hear a thing." She smiles and gives a thumbs up.

Brute revs the engine again. The motor's roar is deafening, and he takes off and does a circle around the garage. "You gotta try this, kid," Brute yells as he flies by, beard whipping behind him. He skids to a stop, and Nightstar hops on the back. They zoom around for a few minutes, Nightstar's smile almost as wide as Brute's.

"This is a great way to get to Philadelphia!" she yells as they pass again. "Find yourself a bike."

I hustle through a door into the dealership and scan the different motorcycles. I've driven two in my life. One of them I was hoping to never be reminded of again.

It was two days before Christmas when Craig and I were seven. I'd been hoping for a basketball hoop, and Craig wanted a mini bike. Dad placed a huge present under the tree and covered it with a sheet. "You can't look until Christmas morning," he said. He knew he'd have to guard it with his life.

Despite my and Craig's best efforts, including Craig pretending to break his leg to divert Dad's attention, we weren't able to peek under the sheet.

On Christmas Eve, I prayed for the basketball hoop, while Craig simultaneously prayed for his mini bike. We woke the next morning before sunrise and darted into the living room. Mom and Dad were sitting on the couch, waiting. "Can we open it? Can we open it?" Craig and I both yelled, the anticipation killing us.

"You'll have to wait till after your sister wakes," Dad said. What? Lauren was a notorious late sleeper. This was torture. "Just kidding. You can open it now."

"Yay!" We both grabbed the sheet and yanked it off. Craig let out a squeal of joy as I tried to hide my disappointment. No basketball hoop. Just a shiny, new mini bike. Craig jumped up and down for about twenty minutes. I think I may have cried, but I don't remember. He sat on the mini bike and pretended to rev the engine. Dad rolled it outside, and Craig started it up. He ripped through the backyard, feeling on top of the world.

Craig pulled over and leaned the bike towards me. "You have to try this." I remember wanting to throw it to the ground, but I didn't want to make Dad feel bad, so I reluctantly hopped on. Now, I don't know if a mini bike is even considered a motorcycle. This one didn't even have a clutch or any gears, you just turn the handle to accelerate, but I found out it's fast.

I squeezed the handle, and it jutted forward. Almost right away, my pant leg got stuck in the chain and I was tugged back. I should've let go of the handle. That's what anyone else would have done, but I decided I would hold onto it for dear life. Not the best idea. I ended up speeding through the backyard and ramming into a tree. My ego was more bruised than my body. Needless to say, I never touched that mini bike again.

Years later, maybe six months before everything happened, I went to Mark's house and his brother had just gotten a dirt bike. It was an Endororacer. It had gears, which took a while to get used to, but I became a pretty good rider. That's the extent of my experience, so I hope I can handle a Harley.

I walk through the showroom staring at the different motorcycles. There are a few of Brute's Fat Boys, but smaller and lighter would probably be easier for me. One catches my eye. It's about half the size of Brute's, and when I hop on it, I can tell it shouldn't be too much weight for me. It's black, just like the Fat Boy, and the chrome shines brightly. I roll it out to the lot and fill it up with gas. I then push it back into the showroom, through the door and into the garage.

Brute's tires squeal as he brakes and skids in next to me. "Good choice, kid! That's a Harley Sportster. I had an older version when I was a teen." That's all he says as he nails the gas and speeds away, Nightstar still on the back, spreading her arms, laughing.

I convince myself I'm ready and mount the bike. I kick start it, but nothing. I kick a few more times and still nothing. So far, not so good. Finally, I get a sputter. One more kick and the engine roars. I rev the engine and every inch of me vibrates with the roar. I have to admit it feels good.

I pull in the clutch and put it into gear. Now, if I remember correctly, first gear is down and the rest up. I let go of the clutch, and the bike jumps forward and stalls. I look up, hoping nobody saw that. Brute and Nightstar are still riding, not paying attention. It takes a few times, but I get the bike going. At first it's incredibly wobbly to the point where I'm sure I'll be crashing into one of the walls. Once I pick up speed though, it's much easier to balance and it feels natural. Maybe I have a little of Craig in me after all.

Brute finally pulls over, and I do the same. "I can now die in peace," he says with a huge smile.

"Let's fill these bikes with some gas. We'll get to that lab much quicker now," Nightstar says. "Did you notice any helmets in the showroom?"

"I don't wear a helmet," Brute says. "Never have, never will."

"I don't think they have one for that melon head anyway, but Kyle and I should wear them." We search the showroom and can't find any full-faced helmets, but we do find two helmets that just cover the head, not the face. "That's called a shorty," Brute says. There's a mirror on the wall, and I get a glimpse of myself with the helmet on. I don't care what it's called; I look ridiculous, but Nightstar bugs me so I reluctantly agree to wear it.

We jump back on our motorcycles and open the garage doors. Nightstar puts on her helmet and tightens the strap. "We won't have to worry about the noise now. We can outrun the Ragers if they hear us." She jumps on the back of Brute's Fatboy, and we head out onto the highway.

The wind whips my face at the higher speed, and it reminds me of the fun I used to have in Dad's Jeep when we would drive on a hot summer day. I pull up next to Brute, and by the look on his face, he's loving it, too.

The highway is littered with cars, but for some reason they're pushed to the side, which seems strange to me. Because of this we're able to ride down the middle, cruising between the cars, at about 60 mph.

We travel roughly five miles when Nightstar twists around and points frantically. I turn and see the grill of a truck bearing down on me. I shift down, pop the clutch, and pull out of the way just in time. I turn to see Brute's done the same, and the truck locks its brakes, skids, and does a 180, heading back towards us. Three men stand in the bed of the truck, wearing bandanas over their faces, armed with rifles.

"Follow me!" Brute yells as his tires spin, smoke flying in the air.

One of the masked men fires a shot. Sparks fly where the bullet hits the pavement, just missing Brute's tire. I nail the gas and actually shoot ahead of Brute. He must be weighed down by Nightstar. My speedometer reads 90 mph, and I feel like I might lose control, when another rifle shot rings out. A loud, metallic thump comes from my engine, and the smell of fumes hits me first, followed by blinding smoke that spews from below me. My motorcycle slows, and I hear Brute's engine pass me. Brute heads towards the forest, and Nightstar waves me on. Rifle fire continues to ring, ricocheting off trees as I sputter into the woods behind them.

I dodge the trees as well as I can and turn slightly to see the truck stop at the forest's edge, men screaming and horns blazing. A loud shot fires, and I feel something sting my back. I reach around to feel what it is. My hand touches a hole and pain rips through my body. Have I been shot? I look down and the bottom of my shirt's soaked in blood. My head starts to swim, and my bike tilts to the side. I try to right myself, but it's hopeless. The dizziness has taken over, and I have no control. My front tire smacks into something solid, and I feel weightless as I'm hurled through the air. Leaves consume me as I slide. A loud thud and I'm stopped. Above me a huge, towering oak's leaves explode, their shadows dancing as they float to the ground. No pain, leaves floating, calmness surrounds me when Nightstar rudely interrupts, "Kyle, get up. We have to move. They're coming!" Then darkness.

CHAPTER 22

FOUR YEARS EARLIER

Summer and I walk hand in hand back to the barn. Lauren's still asleep, and I'm relieved she's safe. I was worried something might happen to her, and I'd have felt guilty if anything did.

Summer and I settle down in front of the fire still holding hands. We watch the flames dance; I love how they flicker off the ceiling and then hide in the shadows. Summer asks questions about my brother and sister and what they were like when they were younger. I ask her about her family and what it was like growing up in another country.

"How did your parents meet?" Summer asks, leaning against me. "I was never really told how mine met."

I lean my head against hers and let out a loud yawn. "I'm sorry."

"No, don't be sorry," she says as she raises her hand and yawns, also. "You can tell me in the morning."

She reaches over to rub my arm. Her touch jolts my senses, and I'm suddenly wide-awake. "No, I'm fine. I love to tell the story. My dad loved to tell it, too. He'd have a few drinks beforehand, though. My dad had just returned from Vietnam, and my grandma set him up on a date. He never remembered the girl's name because he said the date was awful. They went to the movies, and my dad took her home right after. It was still early though, so he decided to go to the local bar and have a few drinks. He noticed my mom right away. 'Love at first sight' he'd say. I remember him reminiscing about how beautiful my mom was, and she'd always blush a bright red as he hugged her. I think she loved the story, too."

Summer cuddles in closer. "That's so cute."

"I know. They loved each other so much. My dad was really shy so he couldn't get the courage, even after a few drinks, to approach my mom. She said she noticed him and introduced herself. They talked for a few hours, and he eventually asked her to dance. My dad would say it was like dancing with an oven, she felt so warm. He knew she was the one he wanted to marry, and he proposed two months later." I begin to tear but don't feel embarrassed in front of her. "I loved them both very much."

"They sound like wonderful people. I wish I had met them." She hugs me, and I kiss her forehead. I've never felt so comfortable around a girl before. We eventually fall asleep to the warmth of the fire.

I wake to the smell of rabbit, and I start to salivate. Lauren must have gone hunting this morning. Considering my body's reaction, I must not have eaten last night.

"Hey, Kyle, long night, huh?" Lauren says, winking at me.

I smile back, then peek over at Summer. She's curled up next to the fire. I can't help but stare at her.

"Kyle, over here," Lauren says. I shake my head and turn towards her. "I know you have feelings for her, but remember what we talked about yesterday. You need to step up and take the leadership role. You may have to put those feelings aside for now. Don't let your brain get muddled by this. You need to be able to think straight, be able to react at any moment."

I agree but know that I can't stop these feelings. I'll just have to try to concentrate on surviving for now.

***

We stay at the barn for a few weeks, and Lauren and I teach Summer how to shoot a rifle. Craig showed her the basics before we left the power plant, but she needs practice. I have to admit, she picks it up quickly. She's become a good enough shot to hunt once in a while. I practice with the rifle also, but still prefer the bow. I like how quiet it is and that it won't attract any of the creatures, even though we haven't seen any since we've been here.

We look out for the teenagers that escaped from the battle but, without Dylan as their leader, I have a feeling they separated and won't return. Lauren still thinks we should travel to Dad's cabin, and although it's at least a two-week's walk, we decide we'll head north.

The heat of summer has started to turn to the chill of fall, and the nights are becoming cold. We travel through the forest for safety, but every once in a while we have to cross over a road or highway. After two days, we come across a small town. One of the stores here is similar to a Salvation Army we used to visit with Mom.

"We can definitely find some warmer clothes in there," I say. "Let's look for jackets, gloves, anything that'll keep us warm."

We approach the store and push the door open, weapons raised, but everything is clear. The store's been ransacked—I'm sure looting occurred everywhere—and clothes are strewn over the floor. As we sift through, most of the leftover stuff is beyond old. Bell-bottoms, parachute pants, shirts with huge collars, and leg warmers. I could care less about fashion, but even I wouldn't be caught dead in most of them.

We finally find some jackets that we can wear, along with scarves and gloves. Lauren even finds some blankets, and although not the most comfortable, I can feel myself curling my toes up in one of them already.

"Kyle, come look at this," Summer calls from across the store, holding up something black. "My favorite movie was Lord of the Rings. This looks like the cloak that Legolas wore." She tosses it to me, and I try it on. Although a little long, it fits very well. I lift the hood over my head and picture myself looking quite menacing.

"It looks awesome," Lauren says, "but no time for a fashion show. We have to get moving. We need to set camp before it gets dark."

"Why don't we stay here for the night?" Summer suggests. "There are a few mattresses and covers to keep us warm. We won't even need a fire."

"That's a good idea. We just need to search for some food," I say. "Summer, you set up here. Lauren and I will find food in one of the stores in town."

Lauren and I find a few stores stocked with canned goods and come back with our supplies.

"I said we didn't have time," Lauren says before we even put the food down, "but now we do. We need to laugh and have some fun. Let's have a fashion show."

Summer starts clapping and then winks at me.

"What?" I say, already feeling my face turn warm in anticipation of the embarrassment. Lauren looks me up and down and pretends to take my picture.

"I think we'll use a male model for this one," she says.

"Oh, no, no. I'm not dressing up in this junk. No way!"

"Come on, Kyle. It'll be fun," Summer says. After much coaxing, and a promise that they'll model also, I reluctantly agree.

I hate to try on clothes. I used to run the other way when Mom would ask me to put on the sweater my grandma got me for Christmas, but this might be fun.

Summer tosses me the first outfit, a lime green jogging suit from the eighties, I guess. I slip it on, and it's like the material sucks into my skin it's so tight. I walk like a penguin as the pants ride up my butt and have to pinch it out every few steps I take. Lauren and Summer roll on the floor as I spin at the end. A loud rip emanates from my pants. I immediately cover myself and run to the back, while their roars of laughter fill the store.

I couldn't be more embarrassed, but I grab the next outfit nonetheless, knowing that we're having fun for the first time in a long time. An awful looking tuxedo's laid out on the floor in front of me. It's white with a huge—so huge I wonder what they were thinking back then—pink collar. I pick it up, and it slips out of my hand, must be made of polyester, definitely seventies. I can tell this is Lauren's pick because it looks similar to the one Dad wore at his prom. The pictures of him in the suit, with a huge mustache across his lip, would make the whole family laugh for hours.

I walk out and strut my stuff.

"Woo hoo, sexy," Summer says.

The girls hum disco tunes as I spin and do my best dance moves. At first embarrassed, I now love showing off. I try on a few more outfits, each one worse than the last. The sound of Lauren's laughter brings me back to much better times. It reminds me how much fun she used to be prior to her teen years and before all the hell that's happened. She claps as I continue dancing, and I can see in her eyes how much she's loving tonight.

Although the girls don't come through on their promise to model, it was so much fun that I don't mind. Lauren yawns and gets her bed ready.

"Thanks so much for tonight, Kyle. For the first time in so long I felt normal." She tosses me a cover. "Get a good night's sleep. You need it after all that dancing. Tomorrow we have to get back to reality."

I lie down on the mattress, my toes curled under the covers. I dream of all the wonderful times I have had with Lauren and my family. It's the best dream I've had since this nightmare began, and I sleep soundly through the night.

We wake the next morning and pack all the supplies from the store before leaving. I now feel comfortable that we'll have enough clothing to survive the winter. We leave the store, and after a few minutes of walking, I spot a convenience store just up the road.

"Hey, girls, I have to go to the bathroom."

"Why didn't you go before?" Lauren asks.

Why do people ask that? If I needed to go before, wouldn't I have gone? But she's partially right; I don't really have to go. I have another motive. "Don't make a big deal of it." I jump on my tiptoes to make it look urgent. "I just have to go."

"Just go already," Lauren says, obviously annoyed.

I run into the store and search for what I need. I throw the supplies in my bag and run out. "Ahhh, much better," I say.

We continue north. I have to say I'm loving my cloak, and I keep pulling my hood up over my head, then taking it off to see how each way feels.

"Quit it, Kyle. You're driving me crazy!" Lauren hits me after doing it for about the twentieth time. I don't stop, though. Half because I like it, and half to drive my sister crazy, which I suppose all brothers do. As a matter of fact, Craig and I became experts at it when we were younger. We'd purposely leave the light on in our room and call out her name. She'd yell back at us, "Shut up!"

"Lauren, Lauren," we'd continue calling slowly, getting louder each time. "Lauren, Lauren!" Finally, out of frustration, she'd storm into the room.

"What do you want?" she'd yell.

"Can you turn off the lights?" we'd both say as we giggled wildly. Oh, I miss those nights.

We walk for most of the day into the dark of the night. "Let's stop here before it gets too dark," I say. "Lauren, let's have Summer set up camp, and we'll go hunting."

Lauren raises her eyebrows. "In the middle of the night?"

"Yeah. The raccoon hunting's great now," I lie.

"That seems silly," she says.

"Would you just come with me?" I say through clenched teeth. Summer seems to be getting suspicious or just thinks I'm crazy at this point. Lauren and I go into the woods, and I tell her my plan. We return about two hours later to Summer setting up the beds. "Where have you guys been?" Summer asks. "I was worried sick about you."

"Well um, um, well," I stutter.

Lauren steps in, elbowing me aside. "We had no luck hunting raccoon. Sorry we made you worry." That was a close call. I suck at lying.

We make a fire and cook some of the canned food Lauren and I took from the stores. The glow of the fire hits Summer, and she looks so beautiful. I walk over, sit down next to her, and she places her head on my shoulder. I'm dying to show her my surprise, but I know I need to wait.

"Kyle," she says softly, "do you know what tomorrow is?"

"No," I lie again.

"It's my birthday," she says.

"I'm so sorry, Summer. With everything going on I forgot."

"It's okay." Her smile turns to a frown. "I understand."

* × *

We wake up the next morning and eat breakfast. "Let's stay here a few hours," Lauren says. "Summer, I'm going to teach you how to fish. I noticed a stream over the hill yesterday. Kyle, you collect firewood."

"Aye aye, captain." I salute. Summer laughs and leaves with Lauren. I'm so thankful for my sister. She just bought me another hour to prepare.

Lauren and Summer return. We mull around for the rest of the day until we start preparing dinner and the sun begins to set. Lauren steals a glance at me and mouths, "Is it ready?" I nod. I know she wants me to start, but for some reason I'm nervous. I take a deep breath and grab Summer's hand.

"Summer, come with me. We have a surprise for you." I walk her over a hill to a part of the woods that's covered in pines. She breathes deeply and closes her eyes as if the smell evokes a cherished memory.

When I was here earlier, the smell made me think of Christmas. It's funny how different scents can bring you back in time.

We navigate our way through the pointy branches. "Cover your eyes," I say, "and don't peek." She puts her hands over her eyes, and I wave my hand, checking to see if she's cheating. I hold her shoulder, and she's shaking as I guide her to a small clearing within the pines. "Okay, open your eyes."

"Surprise," Lauren and I both yell. "Happy birthday!"

In the clearing is a small table that I've made from a large piece of bark and a few chairs from stumps I found around the forest. Multi-colored streamers and balloons, they were in abundance at the store, adorn the trees. A radio that I found with a tape cassette (yeah, that old) sits on the ground with new batteries from the store. Three plates filled with rice and beans are on the table, each with a rolled up napkin and plastic cutlery.

Summer actually seems to faint slightly from the surprise, and I have to stop her from falling. She immediately cries and hugs me. She cries some more, tears of joy I hope, and runs over and hugs Lauren. "I can't thank you enough for this."

I saunter over to her and stick my arm out. She stands up straight, wrapping her arm around mine. I escort her to her seat and pull out the stump. She sits down as I push it underneath her. I do the same for Lauren, and when I go to sit, the stump tilts and I fall right on my butt. I stand and take a bow. Lauren and Summer laugh so loudly that a few animals scurry away in the trees.

We eat and talk. It's as if there are no problems in the world. When we're finished, Lauren excuses herself and I follow. I peek back at Summer, and she has the biggest smile I've ever seen. I can't help but smile, also, knowing she's so happy.

Lauren and I return with three hostess cupcakes, one with a lit candle in the middle.

"Happy birthday to you. Happy birthday to you. Happy birthday dear, Summer. Happy birthday to you," Lauren and I sing. Summer covers her face, trying to conceal her joy.

"All right, make a wish," I say.

Summer closes her eyes and blows out the candles. Lauren hugs her and says, "Happy birthday" again, then heads back to camp.

"Kyle, you have no idea what this means to me," Summer says as she grabs my hand and places it over her heart. We hug, then I hold her hands up.

"I have a surprise for you. I couldn't think of a present special enough, but I wanted to be the first to have a birthday dance with you. It'd mean so much to me." I pick up the radio and push the play button. I pull her close to me as the beautiful lyrics fill the small space in the forest. I hug her tightly and feel the soft beat of her heart. Its rhythm calms me as we dance in the moonlight.

CHAPTER 23

PRESENT DAY

My eyes open to bright white and pain eating at my stomach. They close to streaks of wobbly light. I want to sleep, to desperately sleep, but the throbbing keeps me awake. "He's been shot, Brute. We have to get him out of here." My arm's stretched as I'm pulled over a bulky shoulder. I'm thrown on rubber and metal, and the deafening roar and heat overwhelm me. My hands brush leaves one second, then slap my face the next.

"We have to get him to a hospital. I need supplies. Go deeper into the woods so they can't see us, then try to run parallel to the highway. There's an old hospital off the next exit." Hospital. Has someone been hurt? Thoughts return with pain. I've been shot. I reach down and hold my stomach. The ache burns from my back and zips down into my legs.

"Hold on, kid," Brute yells as the trees whoosh by.

I don't notice whose chasing us or why. All I can really hear besides the engine is Nightstar and Brute barking instructions at one another. The back tire locks with a squeal, and the bike skids to a stop.

I can't lift my head but hear water rushing by and see its reflection off the bright chrome.

"The hospital's close. Brute, push the motorcycle into the creek. We can't let them track us."

"Nightstar, not the Fat Boy." Brute's pleas are followed by a loud splash. I'm lifted again, and the dizziness returns with a rush. My head bounces, but I can make out a building approaching, when everything goes black.

***

I don't know how long I've been out. I open my eyes and can tell I'm in some kind of bed. There's a white sheet over me and a pillow pushed behind my head. An IV's hooked up to my arm with liquid dripping one drop at a time. My vision's blurry, but it seems like a hospital room.

"I have to go search for medical supplies. The IV'll help, but we need more. It looks like the bullet went straight through, but he lost a lot of blood before I stitched him up. What blood type are you, Brute?"

"Type O positive, I think," Brute says shrugging, "but not sure."

"I'm AB which is rare," Nightstar says. She walks over to me and lifts my head. "Kyle, what type of blood are you? Kyle?"

I find it hard to speak and shrug, which tugs at my stomach causing me to grimace. I know I'm the same as Craig, but that doesn't help.

"Well, we're just gonna have to take a chance, otherwise he won't make it. Brute, stay here and watch over him. I have to find some needles to start pulling your blood. He doesn't have much time."

Nightstar turns to leave. "Get down, quick." She points out a window. "It's the pick-up truck." I slunk down in my bed, but its set high so I can see the truck pull into the parking lot, drive around, and then speed away. "They're looking for us. Stay low and be safe." Nightstar hurries to the door. "I have to find supplies. We don't have much time."

Brute plops down in a chair next to me and puts his hand on my shoulder. The weight tilts me to the side. "How you doing, kid?"

"Okay." I feel a little better and try to sit up slightly, but lose my energy almost instantly and slide back down. I can feel myself trailing off when I look at Brute. His head's lowered, and he's wringing his hands.

I'm cold so I pull the sheet up to my neck. "Brute, can you tell me more about June?"

"Sure, kid. Anything you want." He pauses for a second. Brute looks funny when he's deep in thought. "I'm gonna tell you the reason why I loved her so much, just how special she was."

I nod and close my eyes.

"She took care of me at the rehab center, and I began to recover from my addiction. One day, we went out to this beautiful courtyard on the grounds. It was filled with flowers and trees, a very peaceful place. It had this old wooden swing that we loved to sit on, but that I was sure I'd break." I laugh slightly at that, which sends a sharp pain stabbing into my stomach.

"You okay, kid?" I nod. Brute checks my temperature by placing his hand on my forehead. "Don't worry. The swing didn't break. Well, one day we noticed a little nest built into one of those planters you hang in a tree. I found it so weird that the mother would pick that for her nest, but when we looked inside, there were three little eggs. She must have built the nest the day before, and there were already eggs. Even I thought it was the most amazing thing, but June was so elated I thought she was going to cry. We went out every day to look into the nest. It was so cute when the mother would fly back and nestle against her eggs. Well, not two weeks later, they hatched. Kid, they were the ugliest little things you've ever seen. No feathers, just little bits of what looked like hair, like a scrawny rat. But she thought they were the cutest things on this earth. We'd sneak a peek, but mainly watched from the swing as the mother and father would come back with worms or bugs to feed the babies."

"That's nice," I mutter as I begin to feel weaker. "Go on."

"One day the parents didn't return. I don't know if they'd been killed or what. The babies began to get weak. June was distraught. She wouldn't let them die, kid. She researched what they ate. Ends up canned dog food is best. Weird right? She hand fed the birds throughout the day. She was so nurturing. One of them would even perch on her finger. That's when I knew how caring she was. That's when I knew I wanted to be with her forever. She got sick a few months after that, and I've never been the same. How someone that beautiful, inside and out, could be taken... I keep telling myself they needed another angel in heaven."

"She sounds so nice," I say. "I wish I had met her."

"I wish you had met her, too, kid. She'd have liked you."

I smile, and Brute grabs my hand and squeezes.

"Hey," Brute says his voice raising, "you've mentioned Summer but you've never told me about her."

"I loved her, Brute," I say, my mind starting to wander. "I'll never find anyone like her again." I start to lose consciousness and can feel Brute's huge hands lift my head.

"Kyle! Kyle! Come on. Stay with me, kid." I can barely see him run to the door. It looks like he rips it off its hinges. "Nightstar! I think we're losing him! Nightstar! Hurry!"

Brute's voice trails off and sparkles illuminate in front of me. Rapid bursts of bright light. It's so peaceful and calming, but it's interrupted by loud bangs. The lights disappear and something pushes on my chest.

"Get out of the way, you big lug. You're gonna break his chest plate." A burst of air enters my windpipe, and I feel a cough coming. The pain shoots back into my abdomen. I open my eyes, and Nightstar is kissing me. I cough wildly then start to breath normally.

"You did it, Nightstar!" Brute screams. He lifts her into the air and spins her in a circle.

"Kyle," she says on the first rotation. "Are you okay?" as she whips around again.

"Thank you," is all I can muster.

"Brute, let's hook you up straight into his veins and hope you're a match. You're through the worst part, Kyle. You just lie back and relax. We'll take care of ya."

***

I see Brute's mug when I open my eyes. "How long have I been sleeping?"

"About a week. You've been in and out, though. It's been scary, but seems like you're good. By the way, we have the same blood type, pretty lucky, huh?" I nod and fall asleep again, too weak to speak.

Again I don't know how long I've been out and can't open my eyes, but I clearly hear Nightstar's voice. She speaks with a touch of urgency. "We have to keep everything in here as clean as possible. Before you feed him, rub this antibacterial lotion onto your hands. Don't cough around him. We have to be really safe. If he catches any type of infection, he's a goner. I combed through this whole hospital. There's not one antibiotic."

"Anything that needs to be done," Brute says. Finally my eyes open, and I can see the concern on their faces. This time I feel stronger and am able to speak.

"Hey, guys, I'm gonna be okay."

Nightstar runs over. "I'm so happy you can talk. How do you feel?"

"Pretty good." As a matter of fact, I don't feel faint at all.

"Great, kid. I knew you were a fighter." For the next few days, Brute or Nightstar stands guard while the other goes to find food. The pickup truck doesn't return, but we always keep an eye out for it.

I get to the point where I can stand up on my own, although the stitches hurt whenever I move. A few more days pass, and I'm finally feeling well enough to travel. I've been getting out of bed and lifting anything I can get my hands on. My muscles atrophied, but because they have memory, I quickly gain back what I lost.

One night I wake up after a short nap and notice that Brute and Nightstar aren't watching guard. "Brute? Nightstar?" No answer. I look down at the chair next to my bed. There's a long plastic bag with a note that says, "Wear this." I pick it up and sticking out of the top of the bag is a coat hanger. It must be some kind of suit. I tear it open, and it's not just a suit, but a perfectly ironed tuxedo. I look around the room but realize that Brute and Nightstar must have something planned. It takes me awhile to put it on and the cufflinks prove especially difficult. I'm finally done and stare at myself in the mirror. My hair needs some work, so I go into the bathroom and, with some water, slick it back. I've always been the modest type, but I look pretty good. There's a loud knock on the door, and Brute throws it open.

"May I come in, sir?" he asks. I laugh right away at the sight of him. "Hey, be nice, kid." He's also wearing a tuxedo, but let's just say they didn't have his size. His chest's so big that it looks like it'll break through at any moment. The arms and legs of the tuxedo are about six inches short, and his toes stick out of cut-open dress shoes. He looks like a penguin on steroids.

"Brute, you look great," I say as I cover my mouth.

"All right, quit it." He stands up straight with a serious look on his face and says in a regal voice, "You are cordially invited to a ball hosted by yours truly. Your date for this evening will be the lovely Nightstar." Nightstar walks in the room, wearing a beautiful gown. It's dark blue, skin hugging at the top and flowing at the bottom. Her hair's up, and she's wearing makeup. She looks gorgeous.

"Wow, Nightstar. You look amazing." She blushes slightly at this and takes my hand. "Where'd you guys get all this?" Nightstar points out the window and right next to a convenience store is a big sign that reads "Tuxedo Rental". "This is so cool, guys. Thank you."

"Okay, guests, follow me," Brute says, and he escorts us to a room a few doors down. As we enter, I see the flickering light of a candle.

Inside the room, there's a small table set up with silverware, cups with what smells like wine, and a plate filled with food. Brute walks over, pulls out Nightstar's chair, and does the same for me. "Enjoy," he says, and then he marches out of the room, head held high. As he exits, I laugh again. He looks even funnier from behind.

"Nightstar, this is so nice. Thank you."

"You're welcome. Brute suggested it. I've never been to prom before, and he knows we've missed being normal teenagers. He wishes we didn't have to deal with all this death, all the heartache of losing our loved ones. He's such a wonderful guy."

"I know. He looks so tough, but he's just a big teddy bear."

As we eat dinner I occasionally peek over at Nightstar, she's stunning.

"Nightstar, can I tell you something?"

She puts down her fork. "Sure."

"You've meant so much to Brute and me these last few weeks, and I just want to say thank you."

"You're welcome. You and Brute are like family to me. I was so scared when I almost lost you and am just so happy you're okay."

Brute stomps back in and removes the plates, fumbling most of them. He must have found a CD player and puts on a disk that's from the eighties. It's scratched pretty badly and most of the songs skip. Brute curses while jabbing at the forward button. Finally, a song plays. Brute again stands, chest up like a butler, and excuses himself from the room. I walk over and grab Nightstar's hand to dance. She places her head on my chest.

Nightstar peers up at me. Her blue eyes sparkle. "Brute told me about Summer, Kyle. I totally understand. We can just be good friends." She squeezes my backside and I jump. "Let me know if you change your mind, though." We both start to laugh when Brute walks back in. Nightstar let's go and runs over to him, and they start dancing. We play that song over and over about twenty times, all three of us dancing. No worries in the world.

CHAPTER 24

SIX MONTHS EARLIER

Over three years have passed since my brother died and it will be four years this summer since my parents turned. We decided to give up on making it to my father's cabin. It's way too far of a walk, and it's impossible to travel during the colder months. The last few weeks, we have been staying at an old farmhouse in what I think is the Rockland area, but I'm not one hundred percent sure.

Lauren, Summer, and I have done well adjusting to life without Craig and have our little niches. Summer and I have become the hunters. She's quite the sharpshooter and can take down a deer with one shot (if we're lucky enough to see one). I myself have practiced each day and can snatch an arrow from my quiver and hit a moving target with extreme accuracy, in under a few seconds.

"Kyle." Summer points to the right of a large boulder coated in ice. "Is that what I think it is?" I peer around the rock and there, scraping the ice with its pointed tusks, is a big, fat warthog. We haven't had much besides rabbit meat and the occasional venison. Pork would be wonderful, and I salivate just imagining the succulent meat. I pierce its rib cage, and it drops immediately. We find two long branches and tie the warthog to the middle of it. Dragging it slowly back to the house, a trail of blood stains the pearl white snow.

The deepness of it—it probably snows everyday here—has made it quite difficult to travel. Luckily, I was able to make snowshoes out of old tennis rackets I found in the basement of the farmhouse. They look incredibly stupid, but work surprisingly well. But because it just snowed last night, my legs still sink close to a foot. I have to rest about every ten steps, which makes trekking through the snow mind-numbingly slow. I look over at Summer; her heavy breathing crystallizes around her. She struggles just as much as I do, if not more so. Her short legs sink passed the knee, and she has to grab the back of each one with her free hand to force them out. I take more of the weight with my shoulders, and she smiles, her cheeks as red as a freshly cut rose.

We finally get to the house and push through the solid, wooden door that's covered in ice. I use the last of my strength to jar the door open and my last few breaths to speak, trying to seem excited in spite of the exhaustion. "Lauren," I breathe in deeply, "look what we found."

Her face beams as we drop the warthog to the floor. "Finally," she says, smacking her lips, "something besides rabbit." We drag the carcass into the kitchen, and I use the skills Craig taught me to gut and clean the animal.

Lauren whistles as she sets the spit over the fire. She bangs two pots together, and a smile widens as she rubs her belly. "We're gonna have a feast tonight." It makes me feel so good to see her happy. She hasn't smiled in a while. Everything we've been through has hardened her. She was such the party girl growing up, but now she has matured well beyond her years. I don't know what Summer and I'd do without her, but the reality is that she's close to turning. She's almost 19, and she too realizes it could be soon. She's talked to me a few times about what to do if I notice the signs. The over aggressiveness. The rising tone. The eyes. "I don't want to live that way, Kyle," she's said. "You've gotta be strong enough to kill me." I tell her that I'll do whatever needs to be done, but hope that day never comes.

Lauren tends to the fire, and I notice that the pile of wood has gotten dangerously low. It's our only source of heat so collecting firewood has become a full-time job, and one of the most tedious. "Summer," I say, hoping she'll join me. "I'm gonna gather some wood. Wanna go?"

"No, that's okay. I think I'll sit by the fire for a little while," she says under her breath. "I caught a bad chill this morning." It's so obviously a lie. But I don't blame her. This job sucks.

"Lauren, how 'bout you?" I ask, knowing the answer.

"You're on your own buddy." She doesn't hide the fact that she doesn't want to go. "Bring your bow in case you see any game." I'm bummed no one will help me, but I tie on my tennis rackets and trudge out into the snow anyway.

The winters are gorgeous in upstate New York. Everything is covered in white. All different size icicles hang from the barn, with the sunlight shooting rainbows like a prism into the white canvas below. I jump up and break one off a tree to lick and suck in the refreshing coldness. Snow escapes from atop the towering pine, splashing into the fluffy powder surrounding me.

I plod through the snow and tire quickly. There's nothing to hunt, so I don't bother arming my bow. We, I should really say I, have gathered every piece of wood in the area. I'll scale the next hill and hope the heavy snow has toppled a sapling.

Walking up the hill makes it even harder, and I have to go over a few hills before I finally see some fallen dead trees. Their branches barely peek out of the snow. I break off a few pieces of wood and start to make a pile when there's a flash to the left. What was that? Could it be one of them way out here? It can't be. I haven't seen a creature since the first winter storm. My heart beats rapidly at the thought of a beast. My worry quickly resolves as the flash scurries by again, bounding amongst the base of the pines. A winter rabbit. White as snow. Winter's chameleon.

I aim my bow and fire quickly, hitting it in the neck as it runs. It's hard to spot the rabbit as I approach, and if not for the colored feathers of the arrow, I'd probably lose the kill. The rabbit's lean. There's not much meat, but it will add a different taste than the pig at the house. I pull my arrow and wipe it clean, leaving streaks of bright red blood in the perfect white.

I look around the trees again, still frightened. I've seen a few of the creatures far off in the forest. They must have been mostly teens who just turned. The beasts don't seem to venture this far from the city. They kill, eat, and then take off, bent for a larger food source.

I've heard really loud screams during the night sometimes, and it's definitely them, not human. It makes me wonder if they're somehow communicating and heading to the city. I'm sure it's crawling with them. You'd think people would flee those areas and not be the creature's prey. Maybe they're trapped, hunkered down, hiding in the sewers. Who knows? I hope to never find out.

I tie the rabbit's feet together and throw it over my shoulder. I'll just take a few pieces of wood and clean the rabbit when I get home. Summer and Lauren can start making the stew and then I'll collect the rest. It's still relatively early, and I'm already dead tired.

Snow starts to fall, and I catch a few flakes, the taste tickling my tongue. Before I know it, the small flakes have turned to large cotton balls and I can barely make out the landscape in front of me. I search for my tracks from before, but they are quickly covered.

My legs burn, and my tennis rackets sink even deeper into the newly fallen snow. I lean up against a tree, and the ice hard bark pokes into my skin. Turning my back slightly lessens the pain, but resting here is impossible.

There's a path in the woods, and I'm pretty sure the house is back that way, but I can't say for sure. It's probably right over this hill. I get to the top and squint, snow stinging my eyes. Wind whips the snow into small tornadoes, making it hard to tell which way is home. I just have to trust my instincts and keep moving.

It has to have been an hour since I started. Shouldn't I have noticed the house by now? "Lauren! Summer!" I have to rest for a moment to try to catch my breath. The wetness seeps through my pants, making me instantly numb. My toes have had no feeling for a while, and I wiggle them, hoping they'll wake. I should have dressed in more layers, but I didn't think it would snow. It always snows here in the winter. How stupid and careless of me.

"Lauren! Summer! Anyone!" My body shakes uncontrollably and every blink leads to a temporarily frozen eyelid. Maybe I should strip off my clothes and start a fire. Where's my flint? I search my pockets. "Here it is," but my clumsy fingers immediately drop it in the snow. I push the snow aside and luckily retrieve it. My wood's in a pile next to the bloody rabbit. I strike the flint and nothing. The wood's too wet. "Come here, bunny," I slur. "I'll start your fur." I laugh at how silly that sounds and think I may be slightly delirious. The fact that it looks like the bunny just winked at me solidifies the thought. "Lauren! Summer! Somebody!"

That's the last I can yell as I fall face first into the snow. It feels so soft, like a fluffed up pillow. I curl my arms in and sleep.

"Kyle?" Lauren yells, jarring me awake. "Summer, he's over here. Bring the cover!" Lauren wraps me up and holds my head with her hands. "Kyle, the house is just ahead. Can you stand?" I nod, and Lauren and Summer help me to my feet. I have no feeling below my waist and collapse immediately. "Crap," Lauren says. "We'll have to carry him. Take his legs." It takes a while, and they drop me a few times, but they eventually reach the front door of the farmhouse. They drag me in and place me in front of the fire.

Lauren carefully takes out my legs from under the cover and removes my boots and socks. She cups my feet with her hands and blows gently. After a few minutes, I get feeling back into my toes and

Lauren's breath tickles to the point of me laughing and pulling them away.

"Stop it, Kyle," she says annoyed. "I'm trying to help." After a few times she starts to giggle, realizing I'll be okay.

Summer walks in with soup, and I devour it. I'm feeling better so Lauren, Summer, and I sit around the fire, telling stories and laughing. I realize how close I came to death and stare at Lauren as she tells her story. She's become the responsible, older sister my parents always knew she could be, and I know they'd be proud of her. "I love you, Lauren," I blurt out.

"Thanks, buddy," she says, stopping mid story. "I love you, too."

The next day I feel like I was never trapped in the snowstorm. I'm gathering wood and trying to hunt, this time leaving cloth tied to a few trees to get back to the house. Summer accompanies me. We think it's better to go with a partner from now on. She shoots a squirrel, and we head back to the house to skin it. When we arrive, Lauren's sitting on the couch, shivering.

"I think I may have caught a cold," she says, her head falling back onto the couch. Her face is flush, and sweat pours from her temple.

Summer puts her hand against Lauren's forehead. "She's burning up, Kyle. Go get a towel and wet it with snow." I run and wet the towel, and Summer places it on her head.

"Thanks, guys," Lauren says, trying to sit up. She looks exhausted. "I'll be fine."

Over the next few days, Lauren's pretty sick and is agitated very easily. "Put out the fire. It's way too hot!" She screams so loudly that my ears ring. Her fever's abating, but she can't seem to calm down.

"Kyle!" she yells, "get over here." When I approach, she's breathing very heavily and her eyes are wide. She grabs my hand and pulls me next to her. "It's happening."

"What do you mean? Your fever's coming down," I say, but I know exactly what she means.

"Kyle." She looks at me and nods, red veins forming in the corners of her eyes. I nod back and start to cry. "You need to be strong. You can't leave me this way. I love you, and I'm gonna miss you, but you need to do this."

"Lauren," I say between sobs, "I don't know if I can."

"You can," she says, grabbing my face and looking deep into my eyes, "and you must." Lauren takes out her hunting knife and lays her head onto my lap. Tears begin to stream down her cheek, and I wipe them away. "Kyle." She suddenly sounds so gentle. "What's that song Mom used to sing to us when she tucked us in. The one about sunshine."

"You are my sunshine," I say, memories flooding my mind.

"Can you sing it to me, buddy? I used to love when Mom sang it."

"Sure." I rub Lauren's head, just like Mom used to do, as I sing.

"You are my sunshine,
My only sunshine
You make me happy
When skies are gray"

I can feel Lauren crying as her arms begins to jerk. I grab her by the shoulders and push gently at first, but strain as her whole body begins to convulse. Summer runs in and her eyes widen. "Kyle, what's happening? What do I do?"

"Hold her legs down! She's turning!" Summer puts her knees on Lauren's lower body, and I do the same to her shoulders. I look into her eyes, and the veins start to pulsate.

"Lauren?" I shake her but no answer. I have to kill her before she fully turns. I place her knife on her neck and quietly continue the song, whispering it towards her.

"You'll never know dear
How much I love you
Please don't take
My sunshine away"

I push my knife in, and blood spurts out. Her body shakes wildly and then seizes. The pulsing red veins in her eyes start to recede, and her body goes limp. I carefully remove the matted hair from her face and brush my hand over her eyes to close them. My beautiful sister, who matured beyond her years. Who saved me so many times. Who I love and care for is gone.

CHAPTER 25

PRESENT DAY

I'm regaining my strength and have begun to spar Brute and occasionally Nightstar, who's so fast that I have yet to beat her. We discovered an old basement in the hospital, and it's the perfect place to practice. The musty smell and darkness make it seem like we're in some kind of horror film trying to fight our way to safety. Although, I guess we kind of are.

I've become adept with my sword, and the blade is now an extension of my hand, just like Nightstar said it would be. I'm beginning to like it more than the bow, but realize how deadly the bow can be from a distance and how important that can be against the Ragers.

Last week's prom really lifted our spirits. But knowing we have to deliver the memory stick to the lab in Philadelphia, we ready ourselves to go. We'll spend one more night in the hospital, then be on our way.

"Philadelphia must be another few days on foot. We have to watch out for the Bandanas." Nightstar has a cool name for everything. "They may be more dangerous than the Ragers. The beasts kill for food. The Bandanas kill for fun."

"Let's hope we don't see them again," I say.

"That's wishful thinking," she says. Suddenly, a squeal from tires blasts through the window, and Brute jumps to look.

"They're back!" He's already reaching for his axe. "And they're chasing someone." The pickup truck has torn into the parking lot in pursuit of a teen that looks maybe seventeen years old. There are five or six hostages sitting in the back of the truck, blindfolded and hands tied together.

I arm my bow and bolt to the door. "We have to help them." We sprint to the entrance of the hospital, and the prisoner flees towards us. The pickup truck slams its brakes, and two masked figures leap from the back in pursuit. As soon as their feet hit the pavement, my arrow lodges into the neck of one, and Nightstar's dagger pierces through the other's chest. The driver's stunned. He turns the wheel of the truck sharply and nails the gas, rubber burning as he speeds away.

"Hey, over here," Nightstar yells.

The teen freezes and stutters, "Are.. you.. guys.. friendly?"

"Nothing but friendly here," Brute says. He ducks to exit the hospital's front door, and you can tell the guy is in awe of Brute's size because he cowers at the sight of him.

Nightstar stops Brute with her arm. "Don't scare him, big fella. They'll be coming back for us. Let's get inside before they do."

As soon as we get to the room the guy looks around and asks, "Who are you?"

"We're just some friends trying to help," Nightstar says. "What happened with the Bandanas?"

"The who?" he asks. He must realize who she meant. "Oh, yeah. They came out of nowhere. We were traveling towards Philadelphia when they captured us. They took six of us and killed two. It happened so quickly. I can't even remember how I escaped."

"Well, we don't have much time," I say. "When they find out that you're with us, your friends are toast."

"What's your name?" Brute asks.

"I'm John."

"Nice to meet you, John," we all say.

"Can I ask a question?" John says. We all nod. "How are the four of us gonna take on all those Bandanas?"

"Don't worry, John," I say. Brute stands up, cracks his neck, and wields his axe, fists pumping. Nightstar throws her dagger at the wall, and it sticks with a thud. I stand and pull my hood over my head, slide my sword from its scabbard, and execute a perfect slice through the air. "They'll have no idea what hit 'em."

We immediately begin to prepare for the rescue when Nightstar says, "We have to figure out where their camp is located. John, do you know?"

"I don't think it's far. When I escaped I noticed that taller building," he points out the window to the town hall, "so it must be close."

"We'll have to try to free the prisoners at night," Nightstar suggests. "Hit them when they're off guard. Do you know how they're contained?"

"Not really sure," John says. "I didn't get a very good look at the camp."

"Kyle, you and I are gonna go scout their camp tonight to devise a strategy. Do you know how to shoot, John?" He gives a thumbs up. "Good. Then we save your friends tomorrow night."

John seems like a nice guy. We gather supplies, and he helps me load the rifles.

"So, how many prisoners are there?" I ask as I'm checking a ten gauge for ammunition.

"There are four left. Two girls and two boys." He begins to choke up, but he raises his hand and continues. "I'm sorry. We had just started to enjoy whatever semblance of life we had, then this."

"You don't have to be sorry. We've all lost so many."

"I know. It's just that they took me in after my family died. I'm so grateful for everything they've done for me."

I pat him on the shoulder. "Don't worry. We'll get them out."

Nightstar and I are ready to go, and with my black cloak and her black hoodie we're virtually invisible at night. It's my first time seeing the town from outside the hospital, and it's actually quite nice. There aren't many cars in the street, and it looks like none of this has ever happened. It's late October, I think, and I almost expect children dressed in costume to start walking onto the streets from their homes, trick-or-treating with their families. It's a nice feeling.

Nightstar notices me dreaming and slaps my back. "Snap out of it. That building John was talking about is up ahead. He says the Bandanas are just past it. Keep an eye out. I wouldn't doubt they're patrolling the area." We get past the building and don't see a camp, but can see lights beyond some trees, maybe two streets over.

"Lights? How's that possible?"

"Listen." Nightstar puts her hand on my shoulder. I hear a slight humming. "It must be gas generators," she whispers. "We'll have to take those out when we execute the escape."

We sneak behind cars and see a large brick building. Two armed guards lean against a brick wall; cigarette embers glowing their faces bright red. Above them is a sign with the word "PRISON" in block letters and then the word "KENTUCKY" crudely spray-painted to the left of it.

"I'm going to assume they're from the South," Nightstar says.

"What are they doing all the way up here?"

"I don't know, but we're gonna find out soon enough. Let's go check out the back."

We sneak to the side, and the back of the prison has a huge yard that's surrounded by chain link fence. The fence is topped with barbed wire and must be twenty feet high.

"Remember a bolt cutter for that. I noticed a hardware store in town. I'm sure it'll have one," Nightstar says. "I wonder how John didn't notice the lights, or the fence, or the building for that matter."

"Maybe he was blindfolded."

"Yeah, maybe," she says, then pauses. "Let's head to that hardware store and hurry back to the hospital. We'll need a good night's sleep. This's gonna be a tough prison break."

We find bolt cutters at the store and head back. John and Brute are already asleep.

"Good night, Kyle," Nightstar says as she hops into bed. "We'll talk strategy tomorrow."

I climb into bed and lay my head down on the pillow. In the past I'd have a hard time sleeping thinking about tomorrow, but for the first time I'm not afraid. I'm excited. I fall asleep proud of myself, and ready.

We wake, have breakfast, and Nightstar goes straight into how we'll pull off the escape. "We'll go late tonight. Kyle and I noticed two guards in the front. There were also guard towers in the back, but they were empty. If we cut a big enough hole in the fence, we should be able to sneak through. Even you, Brute." She winks at him. Brute winks back with a silly grin.

"We couldn't see inside the prison, but I assume they're holding the prisoners in the cells. Although, they may be using them as sleeping quarters. John, any idea on how many of them we may face?"

"Sorry. It happened so fast I don't remember much."

"There may be many, so we have to hope we don't wake them. We'll go in through the back to not disturb the guards in front. Kyle and Brute, you'll take out the guards in the towers, if there are any. I'll sneak in to find the keys to the cells, and escort the prisoners out. Everyone good?" She gives us a thumbs up, and we all nod.

It's dark as we head towards the prison. Cigarette smoke swirls past the lights out front, and three guards are there this time. We easily get by them as they argue over their favorite football team in a distinct southern accent. We sneak to the back gate, and for some reason the lights are off. It's hard to see, but the towers look empty. It's smooth sailing so far. Brute squeezes the bolt cutters and cuts a hole big enough that I think two of him can fit. We easily walk through and enter the yard.

"Hey, guys, over here," John says. "There's a shed on the side we can hide behind." I can't see the shed but find it odd that he knows where it is. I hear him reach behind it and grab something. Chhhh. "Hey, Brendan," he says into a walkie talkie. "Turn on the lights. I got these northerners."

CHAPTER 26

SIX MONTHS EARLIER

My sister has passed and I can't even bury her. The ground's so frozen that even after many strong blows with an axe, I've done nothing but dent the ice. I vaguely remember her saying that she'd like to be cremated, so I decide I'll set a fire and incinerate her body. Summer and I gather as much wood as we can, and I set up one of the beds from upstairs in the field. I know this may attract a creature, but I need to have a proper burial for my sister. I need to mourn.

We stuff sticks under the bed, and after struggling to carry her, we place Lauren on the mattress. I stare at her, lying there so peacefully, so beautiful, so strong. My whole body's numb as I think how everyone in my family's now gone. It's so hard to believe that I'll never see any of them again.

Summer and I kneel next to the bed and say a prayer. I cover Lauren with more sticks to make sure she burns to ashes. I strike my flint, and the wood ignites. We back away as the flames engulf the bed. As Lauren burns, I keep adding wood, and as I toss every piece, I'm besieged with memories. The wonderful times with her. The loving moments. After about an hour, all that's left of my beautiful sister are embers.

I gather as much as I can and put the ashes into a small box I found in the house. Summer and I carry the box to the top of the tallest hill we can find and throw Lauren's ashes into the wind. A grey cloud fills the air and gently floats away. My sister, who began to soar so high in life, will do the same in death. "I love you, Lauren," I say, "and I'll miss you."

***

We stay at the house for a few months, and winter turns to spring. I've been depressed and find it hard to do anything. Summer tries to help, but I can't seem to shake it. It's all too much. Every time I feel like I'm recovering from the sadness, somebody else dies. What's the point really? I'll turn soon, then Summer, and it'll all be over.

"Kyle," Summer says, "can I talk to you?" I nod, finding it hard to even speak. "I know you've been through so much, but I've been through a lot as well. I have no idea where my family is. At least you were able to spend time with your wonderful brother and sister. At least you had those moments. I didn't get the chance to say goodbye. You should be grateful that you did."

She begins to cry, so I take her in my arms and hug her. I can be so self-centered sometimes. I forgot how much loss she has had to suffer through. Her family. Her friends. She also loved Craig and Lauren, and I'm sure she misses them dearly.

"I'm sorry Summer," I say as her tears flow down my neck. "I've been very selfish. I know you've suffered, also."

"You know, Kyle, in Portugal we light a candle for anyone who has passed. We do that to remember their spirit. Can we go into town to find a church and light a candle for them?"

"Of course we can. That would be wonderful."

The next day we pack and head into town. We've only been there one other time for supplies. It's nice, and although the streets are littered with cars and garbage, it looks rather peaceful. We saw the church the last time we were here but have never been inside. It's a tall Catholic church. White wood outlines grey brick and large colored glass windows have pictures of bible scenes. It's beautiful and majestic.

We walk inside, and it looks like it hasn't been touched by the chaos. It's spotless and the pews all sit straight towards the alter. On the right are the confessionals, and on the left are the candles. There's a large match next to them, and I grab it to strike.

"Hold on, Kyle, not yet." Summer takes the match. "You have to say something about each person before you light their candle. A certain quality that you found very special about them." Summer's quiet for a moment and then lights her match. She pauses, and I'm sure she's thinking of someone she loves, before she lights the first candle.

I look down at the candles and find it hard to think of anything to say. I've been so upset about my family lately. Any memory of them has put me into a deeper depression, and I've tried to suppress any good thoughts.

Summer nudges me. "Go ahead, Kyle. Start lighting your candles."

As I reach for the match, my hand shakes. I strike it, and it lights. I look at the first candle and think of Dad. He was so special to me, not just because of who he was, but how he was. He never made anyone feel bad about themselves. He was always kind and lighthearted. His friends would tell me that I reminded them of him and I would pretend that it meant nothing to me, but it meant the world. I was so proud that people would think I was like him. You were my world, Daddy, and I miss everything about you. I will never forget you and I can't wait to see you again. I light his candle and the flame starts to flicker. I immediately feel a rush through my body, like I've set him free. I look at Summer and want to tell her what I just felt, but she'll think I'm crazy.

The second candle is for Mom, and I immediately think of her tucking me in at night. How she would rub my head and sing to me when I would have a hard time sleeping. She was so loving to all of us and took such good care of us. Yes, she had her illness, but it wasn't her fault. When she was well you couldn't find a better mom. I love you, Mommy, and I'll miss you. I light her candle and get the same chills as before.

I look at the third candle and start to choke up. What can I say about my twin brother that will justify what he meant to me? We were so close, doing everything together. Yes, we weren't as close when we went through our preteen years, but that happens to all twins. He became such an amazing person after our parents passed. He led us and encouraged us to fight, and I respect him so much. I love you, brother. I light his candle.

The fourth candle is for my sister, and her death is so recent that I don't know if I can think about her, but I know I must. She grew so much in such a short time because she knew she had to protect us. When she was younger, she had her rough times, but I knew she always loved us with all her heart. I was so proud of the person she became and know my parents would have been proud also. I love you, sis. I light her candle.

Summer finishes and lays her head against my shoulder. "Did you feel their spirits?" she asks. I break down and cry, and so does Summer. I finally feel like I can let them go. Let their spirits be free and pray that I'll see them again someday. We stay in the church most of the day, saying prayers for our loved ones.

"Thank you so much for suggesting we come, Summer. That was so special. We'd better start heading back to the house before it gets dark." We push the door open, and I notice movement outside. I grab Summer's shoulder and pull her back into the church. "There's someone or something out there," I say. I peek through the opening of the door and see six figures walking down the street. They're moving slowly, and I realize that they're human, not beasts.

"What should we do?" Summer asks. "Do you think they're friendly?"

"I don't know. Let's watch them for a minute."

They walk through the town, looking inside stores. There are three girls and three boys, probably around our age. They're carrying a different assortment of weapons, and I guess they're searching for food. Summer starts to push the door open. "I think we should approach them."

I'm apprehensive and stop the door, but Summer has good instincts and I'll trust her. I let go, and the door swings open. We walk out of the church towards them and they turn, surprised, and immediately draw their weapons.

"Hey, freeze right there!" one of the boys yells. "Who are you guys?"

"We're friendly," I say, putting my hands in the air. "We have a house just a short distance away. We have food that we can share."

"Okay, how do we know you're friendly?" the same boy asks.

"How do we know you're friendly?" Summer says.

"Feisty, I like that. Okay disarm guys," the boy says as he motions to lower the weapons and gives a quick wave. "I'm Jake. We've been traveling for some time, from Connecticut. This is Brian, Justin, Carol, Sara, and Robin." They all wave. "We're starving and will take you up on your offer."

As we walk it's obvious that Jake's their leader. He's tall, good-looking, but seems a little cocky. Not sure if I like him.

We get back to the house and prepare some soup. They're all very grateful and scarf it down. We sit around the fire as they tell us a little bit about themselves. They're from the same town and traveled to Manhattan to see if they could find some answers. They saw that it was overrun with the creatures, so they have been traveling town to town searching for food and shelter. They've lost a few along the way to the creatures, starvation, and the cold. They seem friendly, except for Jake. He was probably a jock growing up, the star quarterback or something. I hated his type in school. In spite of that, I'm glad we have some company.

They decide to stick around for a while, and with the extra mouths to feed, I end up hunting most of the day. Brian and Sara seem like the hunters for their group, and they join me. We're able to shoot two rabbits and a skunk. Although the skunk was a bad idea and the forest stinks for days.

Jake's been talking to Summer a lot, and I'm feeling jealousy creep in. I know she loves me though, and I can trust her. But, regardless, I keep my eyes on Jake for the next few weeks.

***

It's now May, and Jake and his friends have been here for close to a month. We're sitting, having breakfast, when Jake stands.

"Hey, guys. I'm getting bored just sitting around here all day. We saw a beautiful lake but a few hours from here. What do you say we go there and have some fun?"

"I don't know how safe that is," Summer says.

"I think it's a good idea," I say. Summer gives me a cross look. "We need to live a little. It'll be a good break from the monotony." Everyone agrees, so we prepare to go to the lake.

Early morning, we leave. It's a beautiful day. The weather's unseasonably warm, close to 85 degrees, and not a cloud in the sky. It takes a few hours to get to the lake. Summer talks to the other girls and smiles the whole time. I think she's happy talking to someone besides me. "Hey, Kyle." Jake taps me on the shoulder and slides in next to me. "Summer's a really cool girl, huh?"

"Yeah, she is."

"Are you guys an item or something?"

"I guess you could call it that."

Jake sticks out his chest. "I was the captain of the football team." I knew it. "I dated all the cheerleaders, and I gotta say, they have nothing on Summer. You're a lucky guy."

I don't really know how to respond to that but am instantly jealous. "Um, thanks, I guess."

"No problem. Just let me know if you're ever out of the picture." He elbows me a little harder than I expected and laughs as he struts ahead.

The lake appears on the horizon, and it's beautiful. It's surrounded by forest, except for a long stretch of what must be man-made beach. I take off my boots and socks, and the sand feels so soft on my feet. I haven't felt that sensation in a long time. The last memory I have of being at the beach was the day my parents turned and everything went to crap. The memory jars me and I don't enjoy the feeling so much anymore.

I jump into the water, and Summer follows in her bikini. I catch Jake staring at her, and I think I like him even less now. The water's always a comfort to me. I know the creatures aren't around here, but it's like a security blanket.

It's great swimming with Summer, and she seems to love it, also. She floats on her back and sighs. "It feels like everything's normal."

I swim next to her and take her hand. "I feel the same way." We float for the next few minutes, enjoying the serenity.

Summer grabs my hand and pulls me closer. "I'm so happy we came." She turns her head and kisses me. It's such a wonderful kiss that I lose a little feeling in my legs and start to sink. We both go under still lip locked, and we float there, kissing, lost in the moment. Summer, obviously needing air, let's go and swims to the top. I follow, and when I break through the water, she kisses me again.

"Get a room," Jake yells. That's actually funny, and I giggle slightly. Summer stops and blushes, and now I'm angry he said anything. Stupid Jake.

We swim to the shore, and I can't take my eyes off Summer. Her hair's slicked from the water, and it reaches the small of her back. With her hair removed from her face, I can see just how beautiful she is. Her petite nose, her high cheeks, her lush lips, all complimented by her big hazel eyes. She turns and I continue staring. She looks around to see if anyone's looking and does a sexy pose for me. I collapse onto the sand

and sit up shaking my head. Summer smiles and then runs and dives into the water.

She continues to swim, and I lay on the beach, stretching my legs and relaxing for the first time in a long time. No hunting today, no gathering wood, no worries about the monsters. Just staring into the big, blue sky, thinking of my family. Knowing they're up there looking over me. I say a prayer to let them know I'm fine.

I must have fallen asleep in the sun because I'm awakened by yelling. "Hey, guys!" Jake gestures towards the edge of the forest that outlines the lake. "Look what I found." A few hundred feet to the right of the beach is a tall oak tree with a rope tied to one of its branches. Jake jumps and latches his legs onto the rope. He swings through the air and lets go, spinning before he hits the water with a big splash. All the girls clap, including Summer. Show off.

Everyone else gives it a try and really loves it. It's finally my turn, and I grasp onto the rope. It's so old that it must have been tied to this tree during the Jurassic period. I pick up my legs and start to swing. I don't wrap my legs tightly enough so I start to slide down. The rope burns my hands, and I kick out my legs in pain. The momentum of the kick carries my legs over me, and I do a perfect flip into the lake. When I pop out of the water, everyone's clapping. Jake rolls his eyes. "Pretty impressive, Kyle." Summer's jumping up and down and clapping, and I raise my arms, pretending I meant to do it.

The day at the lake has been perfect. It's such a nice break from our life, and we act like normal teenagers for the first time in a long time. We talk and laugh—Jake's even nice— as we sit around a small fire on the beach. It's beginning to get dark, and we realize it's time to head back to the house. We gather our weapons and start the walk home.

"I had so much fun," Summer says. "Thanks, Jake, for suggesting it."

"You're welcome. It really was a great day." He points back towards the lake. "And look at that view." We all turn around. The hill we're walking up overlooks the lake. It's quite a sight.

"Check out this cliff guys," Brian says as he looks over the edge. I walk over and peek down. It must be fifty feet high. It reminds me of the cliffs of Long Island, but it looks like it's more dirt than sand. Without the trees in the way, you can really see the beauty of the lake. The setting sun and the orange sky reflect off the perfectly still water. Trees overlook the cliffs as if they're guarding the lake below, not allowing the ugliness of the world to disturb its beauty.

Suddenly, there's a piercing scream, definitely not human. I know what that is. I turn and search for Summer. "Get down!" I yell. She's already on the ground, whipping her head around, searching for the source of the scream. I stand to run to her when I notice them coming. Three of the beasts are tearing towards us. I grab Summer and push her behind me. I arm my bow and let loose an arrow. It pierces a beast's stomach, but it continues its pursuit.

Gunfire rings out. "Get up one of those trees." Summer scrambles up an oak that's hanging over the cliff, half of its roots sticking over the edge. I twist to fire again and see Sara and Robin taken down by two of them. The creatures rip at their flesh and blood sprays across my face. I'm blinded for a second but fire another arrow. It misses, and the beast catapults over me and digs its claws into the bark of the oak.

Summer climbs and the beast swipes at her leg. "Kyle!"

I leap onto its back and jam my knife into its side. It shrieks and twists to reveal sharp fangs. We plummet and crash into the cliff. The tree's roots dig into my side as I tumble down. I'm able to right myself and run down most of the hill. The creature's at the bottom, bloodied from the fall but ready to eat. I sprint right by it into the water. It chases me and when the beast gets close, I grab its head and submerge it. I don't have time for it to drown. I have to get back to Summer.

I charge out of the water, make my way around the cliff and sprint back up the hill. It's a long way and my legs burn, but I won't stop. "Summer!" I yell, but there's no reply. She has to be okay.

I finally get close to the spot but don't hear any screaming or gunfire. When I get there, all I see is death. There are body parts everywhere, blood splattered on trees and guts strewn all over the ground. It's hard to tell whose body is whose. I look at each one, but they're so mangled and bloodied I can't distinguish between boy or girl. There were seven of us right, or was it eight? I can't even tell how many bodies there are.

I kneel down and sob into my hands. "No, not Summer." I check the tree once again and look over the cliff. Maybe she fell, but there are no signs of her. "Summer!" I walk through the woods, searching and yelling. My first love is gone. I must have searched the woods for hours and don't even know which way the house is. I collapse in the leaves and cry, wishing I could find her, hoping when there's no hope.

The next day, I trudge through the forest, crying with every step. I look up to the sky. "Why couldn't you leave me one thing that I love? Why did you have to take everyone?" I have no strength to go on and think of ways that I can end my life. I know Summer wouldn't want this, but I want this. I rub my face and realize I should live. I should exact revenge on these creatures who have taken everything from me.

Day turns to night, and thirst and hunger confuse me. As I stagger, one persistent thought runs through my muddled mind. Everyone I've ever loved is gone. A small cabin forms in the distance. Shelter. I push open the crooked door, and the smell of mouse droppings gags me. I search the cabin but am so exhausted that I collapse on something soft. Dust fills the room, then darkness.

CHAPTER 27

PRESENT DAY

Floodlights power on and John aims a gun straight between my eyes. We're surrounded by at least twenty armed guards wearing bandanas over their faces. I can hear Nightstar's sigh as she realizes it's a trap. "I knew it."

"The bastard tricked us," I say, clenching my fists, wanting to smash his face.

A few guards march over to us, snatch the weapons, and tie our hands behind our backs. Another man approaches, and with a deep accent says, "Good job, John. Throw these pigs into the cell."

Guards escort us into the prison, and I notice the other prisoners as we're ushered by their cell. There are four of them, sprawled on mattresses. It's very dark so I can't see their faces, but their shoulders are slouched forward and they barely lift their heads as we pass. We walk down a long hallway and are thrown into the front cell. I spot keys hanging on the wall, and I'm sure Nightstar has also noticed; she's probably plotting our escape already.

"Take off your hood, boy, and show some respect," Brendan says. He pulls my cloak down and slaps me in the face. "You northerners think you're better than everybody." He walks over to Nightstar and grabs her shoulder. "Who's the little lady?"

"You touch her," Brute says as he steps towards him, "and you're as good as dead."

"Calm down, big fella. Holy, we don't get men as big as you down south. Whatcha doing with these little weasels? Don't you know they're gonna turn soon? Gotta dispose of them before it happens, you know. Why don't you join our posse here? We could use some muscle."

"Never," Brute says with a sneer. "So, your idea of fun is killing innocent kids?"

"No, I kill eventual monsters." He stands on his tiptoes to try to reach Brute's face. He's not even close. "We're the new law here. You better start following our rules, all of you, or you're gonna end up like the others we've sacrificed for our cause."

"What exactly is your cause?" Nightstar asks.

"I love it when little ladies think they can speak when a man talks," he says, slapping her across the face. Brute kicks him into the wall, and it takes about five guards to take him down. I punch one of them but two guards tackle and restrain me. Brendan gets up, wipes blood off his mouth, and gets in Nightstar's face. "Don't you see? Everyone here's older. We're immune. We're gonna kill everyone before they turn. This is the new world order, honey. Get used to it." He raises his hand to slap her again, then stops. "You're not worth it. You'll be dead by tomorrow."

They leave the cell, and Brendan locks the door behind him. Brute stands, his face bloodied. I grab his shoulder. "Are you all right, big guy?"

"Yeah, kid." He sits on the bed and rubs his head. "I've had much worse." The cell's small and damp. There are two mattresses on iron bedposts. They must have those metal springs because Brute's weight pushes the mattress almost all the way to the floor.

"That stupid, John. I had a funny feeling about him," Nightstar says. I had a feeling about him, too, but for some reason I didn't act on it. "It's gonna be tough getting out of here. There's no way to reach those keys and that's our only hope. Brendan seems like a serious guy, and I don't think he'll let his guard down. We have a day to figure this out."

"You'll think of something, Nightstar," I say. "You always do."

The sound of Brute's snores reverberate through the room, and this time I'm dumbfounded that he can fall asleep after everything that just happened.

"Hey, guys," Nightstar calls out to the other prisoners. "How many you have?"

Before they can answer, the guard from down the hall yells, "Shut the hell up, before I come in there and knock your teeth in!"

I look at Nightstar, and she raises a finger to her lips. I shrug and nod. We won't be able to plan until he falls asleep. I peer around the cell, and it doesn't look good. This isn't like the cages at the zoo. There won't be any bars that are rusted through. Our only hope is the key, or maybe wrestling one of the guards. That would be tough though, because they're heavily armed. We need an element of surprise.

I offer Nightstar the bed, but she insists on me trying to get some sleep. I lie down and stare at her, and she looks deep in thought. She seems to get an idea, then shakes her head no. How will we ever get out of here? Will tomorrow be the last time I see Nightstar and Brute? I've lost so many that I loved. I can't lose them now. It seems pretty hopeless, and tonight I fall asleep not so sure of myself, hoping a miracle happens.

Nightstar's sitting in a corner, still planning our escape, when I wake. Brute's snores still fill the tiny cell. "Nightstar, did you sleep at all?" I ask.

She bites her nails and doesn't look up. "A few hours."

"So, what do you think? Any chance of escape?"

"Is Brute up yet? I really need to talk to both of you."

I shake Brute, and he pushes me away. "Wake up, you big lug," I say pushing my shoulder into his side. "Nightstar wants to talk to us, and it seems serious."

He finally sits up. His beard and hair point every which way. His morning breath pushes me back, and I wave my hand in front of my nose. "What's the matter?" he asks, rubbing his eyes.

Nightstar puts her finger to her lips, grabs both of our hands, and sits us in a circle on the cold floor. "Talk quietly so they can't hear us, okay?" We both nod. "I've been trying to figure out what to do. I checked all the cell bars last night, hoping maybe one was rusted through, but they're all solid. The keys to the cell are hanging on the wall across the hall." She points to the keys dangling from the hook. "There's nothing in here to reach them. I've run out of ideas, guys. I just can't think of a way out of here. I feel like I've failed you."

"You've done everything you can, Nightstar," I say. "None of this is your fault."

Nightstar squeezes our hands tightly and pulls us even closer. She runs her hands through Brute's hair, trying to straighten it. "Can I say something?"

"Sure, anything," we both say.

"I just want to tell you guys how much your friendship has meant to me. I lost my parents at a very young age." She covers her face with both hands. Nightstar has such a tough exterior, and I realize now how vulnerable she can be. "I've never really had any friends. You two have been like family to me. We laugh together and cry together. I love you guys, and if a miracle doesn't happen, I'll miss you with all my heart."

I look at Brute. He has his big paws covering his face, and his shoulders start to jerk up and down. He removes his hands, and his eyes are welled up in tears.

"I want you guys to know how much you've meant to me, also. After June died, I contemplated suicide so many times. I couldn't find a reason to live. Then when I lost my friends, it seemed too much." He pauses for a minute, wipes his eyes, pulls in a big sniff, and looks over at me. "Kid, you've been like a little brother to me. As soon as I walked out of the woods and met you, I knew there was a reason to live." He looks at Nightstar and grabs her hand. "You, little lady, are one of the most caring people I've ever met. You took us in and never questioned once why you should put your life on the line for us." He stops and looks towards the sky. "Just like June took care of those baby birds, I wanted to take care of you guys. You two are my reason for living."

I want to say something. The two of them have meant so much to me, but I find it hard to speak. "I just... want to... say—"

"Hey, it's time for breakfast, love birds," a guard interrupts as he slides a tray under the door. He doesn't look like the others. He can't be more than 20 years old. He peeks down at the tray and motions us towards it, then winks. "Now start eating, scum." He walks away, and the three of us look at each other and shrug. Nightstar wipes her eyes clean and picks up the tray. Underneath one of the plates is a neatly folded piece of paper. She opens it and reads it to herself.

"We got our miracle, guys," she says as she shakes the paper in front of her. "Be ready to escape."

Nightstar tosses the letter to Brute, and he reads it to me very quietly.

"I don't agree with what the bandits are planning to do with you or what they have done to others. I want to help you escape. They're going to hang you tonight, about an hour after the sun sets. They usually party and may be drunk. This could aid in your escape. I'll hide the keys on your dinner tray. The door to the right of your cell holds your weapons. I'll turn off the generator as soon as it's dark. I wish to come with you, if you don't mind. I've never believed what they preach, and never will. God speed, Kevin."

It truly is a miracle. I'm skeptical and hope this isn't another trap, but it looks to be legit. If Kevin comes through as he's promised, we should have a chance to escape.

We eat breakfast, and Nightstar continues to plan. A different guard brings us lunch, and she shakes her head and grinds her teeth as he serves us. She was hoping to get assurance from Kevin that the plan was still on.

The rest of the day's spent waiting. I chew my fingernails to the bone and pray that it isn't a scam, a way to crush our spirits even more. But I'm also bouncing around the cell, hoping that it might be real and we could be free by tonight.

It's a few hours before dinner when Nightstar calls us over to discuss her plan. "Kevin says he'll hide the key on one of our trays. Let's pray he comes through. Once we get the keys, we'll have to wait to escape at dusk. He said that he'd turn off the generator as soon as the sun sets. It was hard to see in the prison last night, so we want to open the cell before it's pitch black. There's usually one guard. Brute, you use your muscle to take him out. I'll run down and release the prisoners." She points at me. "I'll then get you the keys. You open that door and find our weapons. Once we have them, we escape through the front, take out the two guards, and run." It sounds great, planned as only Nightstar can.

It's just around dinnertime when we hear the hallway door open and footsteps of who we hope is Kevin. Whoever it is plods down the hall, and it feels like forever before he pops into our view. Thank God, it's him. He places the tray down on the floor and slides it through, then scoots away without saying a word. I find that strange, but hope he's just nervous. Our freedom rides on him, someone we barely know.

Nightstar picks up the tray and hesitates, maybe saying a prayer. I peer across the hall where the keys still hang from the hook. My stomach drops. He chickened out. Nightstar lifts the bowl and holds up the keys, duplicates. A smile crosses her face. "He did it. We owe him our lives."

Nightstar hides the keys under the mattress, and we sit down to eat dinner. As we're eating, we again hear footsteps, definitely louder than Kevin's. "Are you Yankees enjoying your last meal?" Brendan says, leaning up against the bars, beer in hand. "I just wanted to ask the big guy if he had any thoughts on what I talked about last night."

Brute steps forward. "Do you mean joining you?"

"Of course," he says, slurring slightly. "What do you think I mean?"

"Never," Brute answers through clenched teeth.

"Hey, it's your funeral, big guy. Enjoy your meal. I'll see you in hell." He stumbles away and falls into the wall before righting himself. He continues to stagger, then slams the back door.

"Do you guys mind if I find him later and rip his head off?" Brute grabs an imaginary head and twists

"No, Brute," Nightstar says. "We can't deviate from the plan. I wanna clobber that guy, too, but we have to escape. Don't forget the memory stick. We need to get it to the lab."

I almost forgot about the lab with everything that's been going on, but Nightstar's right. That has to be our first priority after we escape.

We finish dinner, and the sun starts to set. Music blares from outside. The smell of hard liquor wafts into our cell. The Bandanas are getting rowdy, and their drunken yells fill the yard. That could be a big advantage. I remember Dad being drunk a few times and he could barely function.

Nightstar walks over to me and puts her arm around my shoulder. "Are you ready for this?" She hands me the set of keys.

"I'm more than ready," I say, as I pull my hood over my head and practice turning the key quickly.

The guard's been drinking, and he yawns and begins to nod off. He leans back in his chair and starts to snore. It's time. I hand Nightstar the keys and she sticks her hand through the bars. She carefully inserts the key into the keyhole and turns. I'm amazed at how silent she is. Brute's right behind her, forearms pumping, ready to pounce. The third key works and she swings the door open, and before the guard can react, Brute grabs his neck and lifts him in the air, squeezing until he's lifeless.

Nightstar bolts down the hall to release the other prisoners. I sprint right and find the door where the weapons are stored. I wait for Nightstar to throw me the keys but when I push the door, it creaks open. The room's filled with weapons and ours are on the floor right in front. I lift Brute's axe. "Give it here, kid," Brute says as he holds the handle and kisses the blade. I snatch my sword, bow, and Nightstar's daggers. There's a quiver filled with arrows, and I grab that also, along with a few rifles for the prisoners.

Brute and I run out of the room. The four other prisoners are standing with Nightstar. They're wearing hoods, their faces concealed underneath. Angry screams echo from outside, followed by a few gunshots. They must have gotten Kevin.

One of the prisoners takes off his hood to reveal his face. "We can't wait. We have to go now or we'll never make it." Holy crap! It's Jake.

I can't speak when everyone decides to flee. We dash out of the building, and I strike down a guard with my sword. Nightstar spins and slices the neck of the other. The guard falls dead and we rush down the stairs and sprint towards the woods.

As I run, I can't stop thinking of Jake. How's he still alive? What happened that night? I feel like tackling him and bombarding him with questions.

We hear more gunshots from behind. The roar of an engine is quickly followed by the loud squeal of tires and then an equally loud crash. They're drunker than I thought.

We run into the forest and reach a clearing in the woods and stop to catch our breath. I'm still dumbfounded that Jake's alive and am finding it hard to speak. He steps forward and slaps Brute on the back. "Thanks for saving us. We owe you our lives. I'm Jake." The rest of the prisoners remove their hoods. "This is Todd, Susan, and my girlfriend Summer. As soon as I see her, I feel faint. Her hair's a little shorter but she's still as beautiful as I remem... Hold on. Did Jake say girlfriend?

CHAPTER 28

Girlfriend? What does Jake mean by girlfriend? I want to run over and kiss Summer, but I'm so confused by what he just said. Are they dating now? It doesn't make sense. I take off my hood and step into the moonlight.

"Kyle?" Jake says, stepping back. "How can it be? I thought you were dead."

"Kyle." Summer let's go of Jake's hand and races over to me. She runs her hands through my hair and pulls it out of my face. "I don't understand. You fell. You were killed."

Her touch makes me want to hold her, but I'm still stunned by the whole girlfriend thing. "I thought you were dead. I ran up the hill screaming your name. There were no traces of survivors. How'd you guys escape?"

"After you fell, I climbed back up the tree. The monsters were tearing everyone apart."

Jake steps forward and lifts his shirt, revealing deep scars on his back and chest. "I can attest to that. One of the beasts was about to snatch Summer, but I beheaded him." He holds up his sword. "I saved her life. I don't know where you were, but I saved her life."

"I fell, Jake," I say as I step up to him. I feel like crushing him for even remotely suggesting it. "I would never have left Summer."

He pushes his chest against mine. I can feel the tension between us.

"Calm down, boys." Brute steps in and pushes us away from each other. Jake almost falls from the force. "We just escaped, and this is no time to fight. We have to keep moving."

"Brute's right," Nightstar says. "We have to get to the lab. That has to be our first priority." Jake and I reluctantly agree, and we follow Nightstar into the woods.

Summer's running next to Jake, and every time I peek over at her, she seems really upset. I have to find out what went on with her and Jake. It's eating me up inside. Was she so distraught and Jake took advantage of her? Did they only kiss? Or more? I swear I'm gonna punch Jake right in his pretty boy face when I get the chance.

We finally stop running. Nightstar sits down pulling in deep breaths. "This is far enough. We'll camp here for the night. No fires."

We sit in the dark and most everyone introduces themselves. I'm too upset to speak, and Summer doesn't say a word, either. After the introductions, Nightstar tells the others the information on the memory stick and how we have to deliver it to the lab in Philadelphia. They agree how important the information is and say they'll help us in any way they can. Summer seems to be barely listening, and she gets up and wanders into the woods. I jump up and follow, Jake giving me the evil eye as I do.

"Summer," I call to her, but she keeps walking. "I need to talk to you."

She whips around and immediately jumps into my arms. "Kyle, I thought you were dead. I was so hurt for so long and to see you alive, I'm so happy." She cries into my chest and squeezes me tighter.

"I thought you were dead, too. To see you now, it's a miracle. My prayers have been answered." I take her shoulders and gently push her away. "What about you and Jake?"

Summer lowers her head. "I don't know. He was so nice to me after I thought you had died. He comforted me."

"Do you have feelings for him?"

She pauses for a moment. "I'm sorry. I just need a little time." She starts to walk away.

"Summer, this can't be. We're meant to be together."

She turns with tears in her eyes. "Kyle, I love you so much. I just need to think this through. Everything has happened so quickly. I'm so confused." She grabs my face again and kisses my cheek. "Just give me a little time," she whispers into my ear.

We walk back to the camp, and she sits down by herself. Jake stands, throws me a look, and marches over to her. Summer holds his hand for a moment and I hear her say, "I need some time. Please." Jake stares at me, his face filled with anger, and motions for me to follow him.

As I walk behind him, all I want to do is send an arrow right through his backstabbing heart. As soon as we get out of sight of the camp, he turns and sprints towards me. "What are you doing, Kyle? Summer's mine now. You left her and I saved her."

"Are you nuts or what? I fell down a cliff. I didn't leave her. I know how you felt about her, how you looked at her, even before you thought I was dead!" I step closer and feel his breath against my face.

"Regardless, you were gone." He turns and steps away. He twists back, the veins in his neck bulging. "She's mine now!"

"She was never yours!" I yell, stepping towards him, ready to fight. "You better leave her alone!" Jake steps back and tightens his fist before landing a right hook to my jaw. I reach for my sword, but decide no weapons. I send a jab into his left eye, lower my shoulder, and tackle him to the ground. I get him into a headlock, and he bites my forearm. I figured him to be a biter. He shoves me off and picks up a large stick. He lifts it over his shoulder and swings it at my head.

Brute grabs the stick mid-air. "I don't think that's a good idea." He picks Jake up by the back of his shirt, then lifts me up also, my feet dangling off the ground. We kick at each other while suspended.

"Let me go, Brute. I'm gonna kill him!" I scream.

"That's enough!" Brute hollers so loudly that Jake and I both freeze.

"What's going on?" Nightstar calls from the camp.

"Nothing," Brute yells back. "I got it under control." He turns us so we're staring into his eyes. "Now, both of you listen. This stops now. We need you two strong for the next few days. Instead of fighting each other, be ready to fight the bad guys." I want to say Jake is the bad guy, but don't. Probably not the right moment. "That little lady is back there crying and thinking this over. Whatever her decision, it's what sticks. Got it?" We both nod, and Brute slowly lets us down. As soon as our feet hit the ground, we start swinging at each other and Brute lifts us again.

"Okay," Jake says. "Whatever Summer decides. Just let me down." Brute drops us, and we fall to the ground. I get up and dust off my cloak. I stare at Jake as he does the same, and I know this isn't over. I can't let my guard down. He'll try to fight again.

We walk back to camp where Summer is sitting by the fire with her face in her hands. I feel bad that she's so upset, but I feel even worse that it seems tough for her to choose between me and that jerk. We were so close, and she must know that I didn't leave her. She saw me fall. There's no way I'd choose another girl over her. I hope she feels the same about me.

As I'm contemplating ways to win back Summer, Nightstar walks over to her and sits down. "So you're the famous Summer." Summer smiles and they begin to talk, but not loud enough for me to hear. I inch a little closer, but Nightstar stares at me with a 'don't even think about it' look. I scoot back and try to read their lips. Doesn't work. In the middle of their conversation, Summer breaks down and Nightstar holds her, patting her back. I vaguely hear Nightstar say, "You'll be okay." She then gets up, looks over at me, and shrugs, mouthing, "I tried."

I can't take it anymore. I'm gonna go over there, take her in my arms, and kiss her. I get up and march towards Summer when she stands, walks over to Jake, and takes his hand. Ahh! She chose him. She leads him into the woods. I can't believe this. I have to go in there and stop her. This can't be her decision. Just as I'm about to run in, Jake slinks out, his head lowered. He mumbles under his breath as he passes me, never lifting his head. Summer peeks from behind a tree and motions me to follow.

I push the branches aside, and she's standing among the large oak trees. She sees me and smiles such a beautiful smile. She walks over to me and holds both my hands. Her touch shoots straight from my fingers down to my toes. "I told Jake that I need to be with you, Kyle. I want you to know that nothing happened between the two of us. I never forgot about you. I love you and am so happy you're alive." She reaches up and kisses me. I don't say anything. I just want to feel her against me. She knows how much I love and need her.

The next morning everyone wakes, and Jake has a big puss on his face. I want to march over to him, point my finger in his face, and say, "Ha, I told you so," but I've never been that type of person.

As we walk, I hold Summer's hand and Jake keeps staring at me. He walks by me, brushing against my shoulder. I turn and he has his hand extended. "Truce," he says, his face tensed. "Brute was right. We need to worry about the creatures and Bandanas, not each other." We shake, but I don't trust him one bit.

As we travel Nightstar says that she believes we're about two days from Philadelphia. She thinks the streets will be crawling with the Ragers. We stick to the forest, but we start to see highways and figure it'll be faster to take the roads. We pass by a gas station and go in for food and water. As soon as we enter Nightstar looks for a map. She finds one and unfolds it. "It looks like the lab is on the outskirts of

Philadelphia. It's much closer than I thought and not really in the city. We might get lucky."

We camp another night and head out towards the lab after breakfast. We travel a few more hours when Nightstar holds up her hand. "According to the map, it's five blocks ahead. It looks to me like it's going to be one of these store fronts, not very big." I've seen no creatures so far, and the streets look relatively clear, just a few cars and the usual litter.

Nightstar is up ahead with Brute when she pulls his arm down and Brute drops to his knees. "Kyle, get up here." I crawl to the front, and we hide behind an overturned car. There's a one-story building a block ahead and standing out in front are two heavily armed guards. They have huge machine guns that make my bow look like a slingshot. The guards also seem to be wearing some kind of body armor and uniforms that are definitely military.

"Should we approach?" Brute asks.

"Those guns would tear us apart," Nightstar says.

Before we have a chance to discuss it any further, Summer steps out from behind us.

"Summer, what are you doing? Get down," I whisper, but she continues. One of the guards notices her and raises his gun.

"Freeze right there, young lady," he commands. "Identify yourself."

"We are friendly," Summer says slowly as she motions us to stand. "We are here to help." We all stand up, and the other guard advances with his gun raised. "We have important information for the lab. Please, we just want to help."

"You need to drop your weapons," the guard says. Everyone removes their rifles, and Nightstar places her daggers on the ground with her grappling hook. Brute reluctantly drops his axe. I peek at my hand, not having realized that I pulled out my sword. I slide it into its scabbard and place that and my bow on the ground in front of me. We raise our arms to surrender. "Okay, now put your hands behind your back and lie down on the ground."

My face is pretty much kissing the pavement when a guard marches over and frisks me. "He's clean." He lifts me off the ground and puts me into a line with everyone else. The guards escort us to the front of the store. There's a big sign that says "Specialty Labs" and in the corner of the window is an official government sticker.

The guard pushes a button on one of the side walls, and a screen appears in the middle of the wall. There's the face of a middle-aged man in the center of it. He's wearing a white jacket and glasses.

"Hey, boss, we have some teens here that say they have information from someone in New York. They were heavily armed but seem friendly."

"Okay," he says, fixing his glasses. "Have their leader step forward." Surprising even myself, I step forward and stare into the screen. "Yes, hello… um," I stutter, not a very good start. "We're from New York. We visited a lab there, and a man gave us some important information just before he, um… died." Nightstar tosses me the memory stick and I hold it up. "It's all on this. I couldn't understand most of it, but he believes he isolated a specific chromosome, or something like-"

"Hey, Steve," the man interrupts. One of the guards steps forward and I move aside. "Show them in right away."

The guards usher us inside and lead us down a hallway to an old elevator. He doesn't even press a button, just pushes the door open. Inside is a very different door. It's made of a shiny metal with a digital keypad on the right side. The guard enters some numbers and the door opens. We all walk inside, and it's tremendous. The walls are silver, and as the doors slide close, an even bigger keypad with a screen appears. He takes off his helmet and places his face in front. What looks like a red laser scans his face, and numbers appear on the screen. "Clearance accepted," a robotic voice says, and the elevator starts to descend.

I'm used to getting sick in elevators, but this one moves so smoothly I don't feel a thing. It travels down for about ten seconds before the doors slide open. The nerdy guy from the screen stands in front of us. There's a woman in a white lab coat next to him. "Please come with me," he says, and we follow him down a long hallway. The floors are white, the walls are white, the ceiling's white. It's the cleanest place I've ever seen.

We pass by several rooms and other people in white jackets, I'm guessing scientists, are scurrying around. One room that we pass seems to have cages, and I catch a glimpse of what looks like a creature's claws. I start to question the scientist about it, but he quickly hushes me and ushers us into the last room at the end of the hall. It's a large, white room, of course, with a single desk in the middle.

"Can I get the memory stick?" he asks. I hand it to him, and he inserts it into a computer sitting on top of the desk. The screen pops up and a "please insert password" sign appears. "It's Yankees7," Nightstar says. "Must have been a Mantle fan."

"Yeah, that's good." The man laughs as he enters the password. The same screen I saw on Nightstar's computer loads.

"Scroll down to August twenty-first," I say.

He studies the page. "This can't be accurate," he says as he slides the mouse and scrolls down the page. He lifts his glasses and squints as he reads. Then he clicks to another screen, and all the scientific jargon that we couldn't understand pops up. "Yes, this makes perfect scientific sense." He reads more then covers his mouth before calling over the female scientist and pointing. They smile widely and hug each other.

"What is it?" we all seem to ask at once.

"I think he did it!" he says, his eyes wide.

"Did what?" we say in chorus.

"I think he may have found a cure!"

CHAPTER 29

The scientist takes his glasses off and wipes them clean on the sleeve of his jacket. "I don't know if cure is the correct word," he states. "Maybe antidote or vaccine. Although, a vaccine entails a preparation of a weakened or killed pathogen, such as a bacterium, or a portion of the pathogen's structure, of course, which upon administration stimulates antibodies." I gaze at Brute. A dumbfounded look is plastered on his face. Nightstar raises an eyebrow and stares at him. At this point he might as well be talking to himself. He realizes that this is going way over our heads. "You know what? Let me show you. Come with me."

We follow him as he shuffles down the hallway. "I never formally introduced myself," he says as he shakes my hand. "My moniker's…" He pauses and stares at us again. "I mean to say my name's Henry, and this is my assistant, Jennifer."

"Hello, very nice to meet you," we say.

"We have been trying to isolate the responsible chromosome for some time now, but were never able to. The man in New York that supplied the information to you was a colleague of mine. We lost communication years ago."

"What was his name?" Nightstar asks.

"His name is—I'm sorry was, Richard Starr. He was a student of mine, and he was brilliant, a savant in genetics. Graduated from Harvard at the age of fifteen. He started at the New York lab as soon as he finished school. Then adults began transforming. We were in touch for a while, but the Internet went down. He's been working on a solution since." He holds up the memory stick. "I assume he turned right before he gave you this, which means he was nineteen. That's rather belated for males."

He turns left into a room and makes sure we're all inside before closing the door. The room's huge. There's a tall, white table in the center of it, with computer screens surrounding the base. He approaches the largest screen and types on the keyboard. Each computer screen powers on, with the words "voice activation" flashing across the table.

"Comp1, this is Henry Rice. Confirm." Henry steps towards the screen.

A female, robotic voice emanates from the center of it. "Voice activation complete. How may I assist you, Henry?"

"Display subject 3123 please." A 3D hologram of one of the creatures appears floating above the table. It's so life-like that a few of us take a step back.

"This is one of our subjects. If you noticed the room with the cages on your way in, that's where we hold nineteen of them now. A few of the creatures we captured in the city. Some are scientists that turned while working in the lab. It's inhumane, yes, but I don't believe they're human anymore. We've been experimenting on them for years, and through extensive observations, our hypothesis is that once they've transformed, there's no chance of recovery."

He raises his arms, points his fingers, then spreads them out. It's like he's manipulating a huge floating touch screen. The hologram suddenly zooms to the creature's insides. Its organs are now visible, and when he spins his finger, the image spins with it. He touches the brain of the creature and a part of it glows red.

"Its origin is the pituitary gland. This generates the incredible levels of testosterone. But it doesn't stop there. It quickly suffuses to every organ and every cell." Henry taps the screen, and the red glow spreads out from the pituitary gland to every inch of the creature's body. "You're not you anymore. Isolating the chromosome will stop this process. Richard's work won't cure anyone who has already turned. But it will stop teenagers from mutating in the first place. The young will have a chance, again."

The room is silent after his speech. The fact that we may have a fighting chance is hard to fathom, after all this time of having no hope. I break the silence and ask, "Did you figure out why most adults have turned?"

Henry pauses and then clears his throat. "Um..To be honest, Kyle, not really." He looks over to Brute. "The fact that some are immune is a big part of our study, but it's really a conundrum, a medical or scientific mystery. In the future we may understand, but not now. It's similar though to certain afflictions mankind has had to endure. We don't know what causes autism or why Alzheimer's patients lose their motor functions. There are so many instances in medical science where this occurs. This," he points to the hologram of the creature, "just so happens to have killed most of the human race. That's why this finding is so crucial."

"How long will it take to make the vaccine or antidote?" I ask.

"I don't think either is the most appropriate scientific term. But I'd say my staff can formulate the medicine, for lack of a better word, promptly. We were so close many times. Richard isolating the chromosome is the last piece of the puzzle. You can now understand why we were so elated that you delivered this information."

Henry leads us out of the room and into the hallway. "Let me give you a tour of the rest of the lab. It will be your home for the foreseeable future."

He walks us down the hall and points into the room with the cages. "This is where we hold the creatures. We may never be able to save them, but we continue to try. We've obtained valuable information by studying them."

He continues down the hall and points into the next room where scientists are working with different equipment. "This is where we perform our experiments. The scientists here are older and deemed immune. In the beginning, it was difficult because many of our younger scientists would make headway and then the rage would consume them. We killed them before they fully transformed, but we soon learned to cage them."

"What do you feed them?" I ask, cringing at what the answer might be.

"Whatever we can. Their main source of food is meat. They crave it. Many of the creatures succumb to starvation, but we then use the deceased for sustenance. It's been an arduous task but we've been able to maintain nineteen subjects."

I take a few steps back and stare into the cages. I see the monsters clawing at the bars, trying to escape. They seem as out of control as ever.

"Why don't you sedate them?" Jake asks.

"Because we need to study them in their natural state. Listen." I don't hear anything. "The room is soundproof. They don't bother us at all."

He walks us to the end of the hall and opens the door. Another hallway leads to the left with a door at the end. "This lab is government controlled. We've occupied this space since the early fifties, not me of course, but the lab. Our objective was secretive. We were to find answers to medical mysteries, discover cures for diseases, and prevent chemical warfare." He shrugs his shoulders. "Now we're basically all that's left. There's only one other functional lab on the west coast."

He points to the door at the end of the hall. "That door leads to the barracks. A few of the guards live there, but you'll have your own bed and hot showers." Summer and a few of the girls squeal when he mentions it. A shower. I haven't taken one in years. The mere thought of it gives me goose bumps. "Get some rest," Henry says. "There's so much more information I need to share with you. I'll explain in the morning."

We enter the barracks, and it's very similar to the many army movies I watched with Dad as a kid. Bunk beds are set up along both walls, and there are two doors at the end that I assume are bathrooms. I check out one of the beds and push the mattress down. It seems comfy.

"I got the top bunk," Brute says, winking at me. At his size, the top bunk would quickly become the bottom bunk. We all place our belongings under the beds and sit on the mattresses.

"We're finally going to get a good night's sleep," I say.

Summer pats her cover and lies down. "Yeah, this is great. Henry seems nice. Do you think he's right? Do you think he can cure us? Stop us from turning."

"It seems legit. All that science stuff," Nightstar says. "But no more talking. Let's take showers."

Brute sniffs his armpits and pretends to pass out and we all laugh, but it's true. We stink. I have dirt caked in places where dirt shouldn't be. Next to our bunks are shelves filled with towels. Each of us grabs one and then we run towards the showers. The girls to one side, the boys the other.

I pull my cloak off and try to take off my shirt, but it's stuck. I have to peel it off my skin it's so dirty. In the back of the showers, I notice a laundry sign. "Hey, guys, we can wash our clothes," I yell. Brute's dirty clothes fly through the air and stick to my face.

"Thanks, kid," he says as he steps into the shower.

"You're welcome," I say through his soiled pants. I throw all the clothes in the washer and wrap myself in a towel. I was always shy in gym class and never wanted to take a shower in front of everyone, but not today. I'd run naked through Yankee Stadium if it meant getting clean.

I jump into the shower, and the water runs through my hair and down my back. I get the chills as it hits my skin. The feeling brings me back to the first time I ever took a shower. I'd always take baths as a kid, but on our first vacation driving down to Disney, we stopped at a hotel. There was no tub, just a stand up shower. I refused to take one, but Dad pushed me in. I turned on the shower, and the water was scalding. The hot water hitting my back gave me the same goose bumps, and it felt so good that I could have showered for hours. Dad had to drag me out. The memory seems so real I swear I can hear Dad yelling at me. "Get out of the shower this instance!" How I wish it were really him.

I must use two bottles of shampoo and every inch of me is squeaky clean. I peek at Brute's shower stall, and his head is an inch from the ceiling. His hair and beard are covered in suds, and he looks like a giant Santa Claus. "Hey, Santa, enjoying the shower?"

He looks over. "Ho, ho, ho," he laughs, and I can't help but crack up at the sight of him. I finish and wrap a towel around my waist. There are brand new toothbrushes and combs on a shelf next to the sink. I can't remember the last time I brushed my teeth, and my mouth feels so clean after that I want to run over and kiss Summer.

I throw our clothes in the dryer, and when I take them out, they are so warm that I hug my cloak. I walk back to the bed and snuggle up against it. This place is already beginning to feel like home.

I'm about to fall asleep when the girls come out of the shower. They're all smiles. Their clothes are clean and their hair's shiny. Summer hops across the room and climbs into the bed across from me. "That was so wonderful." She sighs and looks over at me, her face beaming. "I feel so clean, like we have a new start."

"Yeah. A new start on life," I say. "That sounds wonderful." I stare at Summer as she sits on her bed brushing her hair. When she gets to a tangle she sticks out her tongue as she struggles to pull the brush through. She does this every time. It has to be the cutest thing I've ever seen. "Hey, Summer." She looks up with those stunning eyes. I almost fall off the bed but catch myself. "I love you."

"I love you, too, Kyle." She reaches her hand towards me. I grab it, holding it gently. I don't let go until Summer falls asleep. I'm so happy to have her back. I put my head down and stare at her feeling like we have a chance now. So many nights I'd sit up thinking we had no future. Now I feel there is one.

As I sleep, I dream of Summer. We're married and have two little twin boys. It's Christmas morning, and the twins are opening their presents. Brute walks in dressed as Santa, and they attack him, grasping onto his legs, and he pretends to try to shake them off. Nightstar follows, looking beautiful in a flowing red dress, and she and Summer hug. It's the most beautiful dream I've ever had.

The next morning at breakfast, Henry continues to talk about the lab. We were curious as to how everything's powered without electricity pumping through the city. He tells us that power's being generated from a field just outside of Philadelphia. It's covered with solar panels and has fully powered the lab since the early 2000s. Water's being pumped in from the nearby river, and the basement has a large freezer. The food was meant to sustain over a hundred people for years in case of a catastrophe, and he thinks it can feed the small amount of people in the lab for over a decade.

"Let me show you one more thing that I think you'll like," Henry says. He brings us to a room and opens the door, right away you can tell it's the rec center, and it's awesome. There's a pool table and foosball in the center of the room. On the side, there are Arcade-size video games and vending machines, which are turned off, I'm assuming to conserve energy. In another corner is ping pong and a dartboard on the wall. It's a teenager's paradise. Summer and Nightstar decide to play darts, and Summer seems like she's a natural. Brute and Jake's friends play a spirited game of pool.

"Hey, Kyle," Jake says, "I challenge you to foosball?"

"Sure," I say, and we start to play. I'm used to playing with four people and it's weird to have to switch back to defense from offense, but it's still fun.

"Kyle," Jake says as he turns his handle quickly and one of his offensive players scores.

I drop the ball back in play. "What's up?"

"I just want to let you know that you have me all wrong. I know you see me as cocky, but I'm actually a nice guy. I don't want Summer to come between us. I just want to be friends." Jake extends his hand in front of me to shake. I'm not sure I trust him and imagine his fingers crossed behind his back.

"Okay, friends," I say shaking his hand. We keep playing the game, and he seems like he's played before. Probably at the country club. I have to get over this hatred for Jake, but it's hard. Maybe I can trust him.

"How do you like that?" Brute yells as he sinks his eight ball to win. He raises his pool stick, and it sticks into the ceiling. Everyone starts to laugh when an alarm goes off. There's a red light in the corner that spins as it blares.

"What's the alarm for?" Nightstar yells over the sound. We start to inch towards the door when it swings open.

One of the guards peeks in. "We're under attack. Your weapons are in the barracks under your beds. We need reinforcements at the front. Arm yourself. Hurry."

Who could be attacking us? We sprint down the hall and everyone grabs their weapons. I run out of the barracks behind Nightstar, and Henry's in the hall looking nervous and running his hand through his hair. "Did someone follow you here?" he asks, his voice racing.

"Not that we know of," I say, "but we did escape from bandits. I don't know if they tracked us." We follow Henry down the hall, and he runs to the screen next to the elevator.

A guard is on the screen, and I can hear gunfire in the background. "There are too many of them. We can't hold them off. Send reinforcements."

"Can you guys get up there to help?" Henry says as his face is scanned. The elevator door slowly opens, and we run in.

"We'll do what we can," I say, and I push the up button.

As soon as the door closes, I can hear the gunfire and screaming from above. The door slides open, and we can see out onto the street. Two guards are lying in a pool of blood, and one is firing his gun. We step out of the elevator and look up to see a pickup truck plowing into the bodyguard and smashing into the front of the store. The guard gets thrown against the wall and slams into the ground in front of us, covered in glass and blood. Right away gunfire sprays into the hallway, and everyone drops to the floor.

Bullets penetrate the walls around us. The dust from the Spackle starts to fill the room, making it difficult to breathe. "Get back in the elevator," I say between coughs We crawl back in, and Brute pushes the down button. As the door closes I see the Bandanas leap in through the smashed windows.

The elevator descends and its door opens. Henry is in the hallway rubbing his hands. "What happened?"

"They got in," I say. "They overtook the guards. Do you think the elevator door will hold them?"

"I don't know. We've never been under attack by humans before. The creatures never had weapons. Who are they?"

"They're the bandits," Nightstar says. "They must have tracked us here."

There's a loud explosion, and the elevator door shakes. A plume of smoke seeps through the bottom of the door, and the distinct smell of gunpowder fills the room. They must have grenades or some other type of explosives. "That door can withstand most anything," Henry says, his voice cracking from nerves, "but they'll eventually get in."

"Let's fall back," I say. "Prepare for them to come through."

Everyone finds a place where they have a good shot at the door. The huge explosions continue when the lights dim and then flicker.

"They must be cutting the power," Nightstar says.

"Oh no," Henry yells. "Not the power."

"It's okay," Brute says as he raises his axe. "We fight well in the dark."

Henry rubs his hair frantically, knocking his glasses off. "No, you don't understand." He drops to the floor and searches for his glasses on his hands and knees. "The cages are magnetic." He finds the glasses and clumsily puts them on. "If they cut the power," he points to the creatures, "they'll release them!"

CHAPTER 30

I peer into the room with the beasts, and they're still clawing at the bars. "How long does the power have to be out before the cell doors fail?"

Henry cleans his glasses and looks at the cages. "They have a fail-safe switch. It only works if the power is out for a minute or so. Anything over that time, and the cell doors will automatically open."

"So, you never lost power before?" I ask.

"We had generators just in case the power went out, but the fuel went bad. We never had a problem because it's solar energy. You never run out of that."

Yeah, but the sun sets at night. How is the energy stored? Before I can open my mouth to ask, Nightstar says, "Could it be the explosions that are causing the power loss?"

"No," Henry says. "The cables run from the outside. It's not near the elevators. They must be cutting them to blind us. But they don't know what we have down here. They don't know what they're releasing."

The lights turn off again, then quickly power back on. Henry looks up and shakes his head. "They're definitely cutting the lines. Once the creatures get out, they'll easily break through the glass door. There's no place to hide."

Everyone seems deep in thought, but no one suggests anything. We're trapped down here, with no good options. If we open the elevator to escape, the Bandanas will mow us down with their weapons. If we stay, the creatures will tear us apart.

The lights fail, and this time stay out for what seems like forever. The darkness is eerie, but it's the silence that sends a chill down my spine. I can only hear breathing (everyone must be too scared to speak) and the occasional thud of an explosion from above. I reach for Summer, feel her hand, and grasp it. Brute bumps into us and starts backing down the hall. "Nightstar," I say softly.

"I'm right here, Kyle," she says, and we continue to move as a group, desperately searching for a way out of this hallway.

The lights flicker on, and I notice Jake and his friends enter a room. A few scientists scurry around, and Henry's leaning against the window of the cell room, peering inside. He looks towards us his eyes wide. "They're out!" A loud metallic, thump, thump, fills the hallway followed by the sound of pounding against glass. The glass shatters and screams echo past us. "Save yourselves!" Henry yells before the lights go off again.

My hand finally feels a door handle, but it's locked.

"No good, guys," I say as I pull an arrow from my quiver. "Time to fight." The lights flick back on, and Brute and Nightstar have their weapons drawn. The creatures are ripping the scientists to pieces. They have no idea how to defend themselves. Their white jackets turn crimson, and the smell of blood wafts through the hall.

Henry escapes and runs towards us with a beast right behind him, tearing at his jacket. I let my arrow go, but darkness surrounds us again. I grab the handle of my sword and hold it high and to my side. I can't see anything, but the sound of screams and thuds moves quickly towards us.

The light powers on and Brute has a creature over his head, its claws scratching at his forearms. He heaves it down the hall, and it crashes into two other beasts. Nightstar slices one at the throat, and it falls. I push forward and throw my hand at a beast's neck. My sword cleanly slices through, blood spattering my face. Summer's shotgun blasts and it's sound is deafening in the confined hallway. It confuses me for a moment, and my ears ring loudly, but I shake my head clear and turn to face another beast when the lights fail once again.

The creature barrels into me, knocking the wind from my lungs. We crash through the locked door and slide across the floor. I get up, bent over, trying to pull in breaths, and swing my sword wildly. I hit nothing but air.

My leg throbs at the calf, and I feel blood trickling down my ankle. I hobble to the side and lean against a wall. I can hear the beast's hiss but can't see it. I hope it can't see me. I hold my breath. Can't make a sound. Extending my sword to the side, I tap the wall a few feet to the left. The creature smashes into the wall so violently that my whole body vibrates. Natural light suddenly fills the hallway and penetrates the room. The Bandanas must have gotten in. The creature's stunned and as it pushes to get up, I chop down with my sword, cutting its head clean off. Its body jerks wildly, blood shooting like a fire hose from its neck.

"Let's get 'em, boys," someone yells from down the hall. It's immediately followed by, "Holy crap." The door pushes open, and Brute backs into the room, carrying Henry over his shoulder. Nightstar runs in, and Summer soon follows. I hobble to the door, dragging my leg and slam it closed. A beast crashes into it, and the force sends me flying.

Two creatures enter and sniff the air. Brute drops Henry and wields his axe. A beast lunges, and Brute heaves it into the other. Summer fires and wounds the leg of one as it's down, but it leaps and knocks the rifle away. The beast jumps on Summer, and she screams a piercing scream. I charge and tackle the creature. It jams my shoulders into the ground, claws digging into my flesh. Nightstar leaps, her dagger raised, and drives it into the beast's neck. The creature stands, Nightstar clinging to its back. They both slam into the wall and fall in a heap on top of me. Nightstar breathes heavily as she twists the dagger, the creature's blood soaking the floor.

Henry, bloodied and confused, stands and staggers towards us. A beast's jaws pierce his neck. Brute grabs the creature, and Henry collapses to the ground. Brute lifts the beast and drives its head and body down with such force into his knee that the beast's neck breaks. Brute holds up the monster and raises both eyebrows. I think even he's amazed. Blood drips under his feet, and he slips and topples to the ground, unconscious.

I crawl towards Brute, but two more beasts enter, searching for blood. I grab my sword and squeeze with all my might. No one else I love is dying today. I stand and face them, blade in front of my nose. They barrel towards me, and I slice my sword at an angle. The blade enters one at the neck and exits through its opposite rib cage, cutting the beast in half. I sidestep the second one, and it slides on the blood, crashing into the wall and collapsing to the ground. I charge the beast, sword raised, but it slashes its claws at my leg. I jump, my foot hitting the wall, and flip over, throwing the blade at its neck. I land in a perfect pose as its head flops like a fish on the floor. I slide my sword into its scabbard and rush to the others.

"Are you guys okay?" I ask.

"I'm hurt, but fine," Summer says.

Nightstar holds her head. "I'm good, I think. How's the big guy?"

"I don't know," I say as I reach him. His chest's heaving up and down. "He's breathing, but he's out cold."

The shotgun fire from the hallway stops and only a few screams of pain can be heard. "Hey, kid," Brute says as he sits up, holding his head. "You okay?"

"Yeah, big fella. Thank God you're fine. Stay here for a sec. I have to check something."

I crawl towards the door and pass Henry's body. He's covered in blood. One arm has been broken and is bent awkwardly behind his head. His eyes are wide open. I reach to check his pulse when his hand jerks and grasps my wrist. He pulls me in close. His voice is slow and labored. "Kyle, this is all… my… fault. Take this." He slips the memory stick into my hand and closes it. "Bring it to the lab… in Cali—" His voice slips away. I slide my hand over his eyes to close them. I stuff the stick into my pocket. I wonder what he meant by this being his fault. He did all he could to help us.

I crawl to the door, slipping on blood, and push it open. The hallway is a massacre. The perfect white is now perfectly red. Shotgun shells float in puddles of blood on the floor. Body parts are littered everywhere. Not sure which is human and which is creature. "Is anybody alive?" I call out. Nothing.

I turn back and see my friends covered in blood on the floor, amazed we're still alive. "I'll be back in a second. I want to see if anyone survived."

I tiptoe through the hallway, trying my best not to slip on the blood. The smell of guts is excruciating, and I pull my hood over my nose and mouth, breathing through the fabric. It doesn't help.

There's no sign of life in the hallway. All the windows are smashed and shards of glass are mixed with blood on the floor. They crackle under my boots during each step. A few of the Bandanas' faces are visible, and I can't help but think of how ironic it is. They let the creatures escape, but if they didn't come down here, we'd all be dead.

I get to the door that Jake entered and peek in through the window. It looks similar to the hallway, blood and guts strewn everywhere. I poke my head through the broken glass. "Anybody alive?" Nothing. I sigh. It's just more death. And even if I didn't care for Jake, nobody deserves this.

I turn to check the other rooms when I hear a small whimper. I look in but still can't see any signs of life. Must be my mind playing tricks on me. Then I notice a leg sticking out from under one of the desks in the corner of the room. It quickly pulls in when I push the door open.

"Hello," I call. "Are you okay?"

"Don't come near me." It's Jake. I get down on my knees to help him.

"Jake, it's Kyle."

He pulls his legs in tighter. "I know who it is. Don't touch me."

"But, Jake, I'm here to help."

"I don't need your help." He crawls out from under the desk and stares at the mess on the floor. He fixes his hair and snatches his sword off the ground. He doesn't have a scratch on his body.

Why no injuries? All at once it dawns on me. No scratches, cowering under the desk. He hid as his friends were torn apart by the creatures. I stare at him and shake my head. He can tell I'm disgusted.

Jake steps towards me. "Are you going to tell Summer?" Before I say a word, he lifts his sword. "Well, I'm not going to give you the chance." His blade strikes down, but I block it with mine. Sparks fly as the sound of metal upon metal echoes.

I kick him straight in the chest, and he staggers back, slipping on the blood but staying upright. "This is crazy, Jake."

"What's crazy is that Summer picked you." He starts circling around me, sword raised. "Since I first saw her, I knew she was meant for me."

"I knew you hadn't changed your mind about her." I circle in the opposite direction, ready for his attack. His knees bend slightly and he jumps, driving his sword towards my chest. I turn sideways and slap it away with my blade, kicking him again. This time he falls but quickly recovers.

I'm beaming with confidence, but still don't want to fight. "You can't beat me, Jake, but I don't want any more death."

A sinister smile crosses his face as he reaches behind his back and removes a pistol hidden in his belt. "Summer's mine!" Smoke rises from the weapon as a bullet penetrates my left shoulder. Drops of blood splatter my lips and chin. I feel no pain at first, but then it zings from my shoulder up through my neck. The force whips me around, and I twist back to see Jake advancing with the gun, ready to fire again. My only thought: get that weapon.

I dive to the ground and a bullet ricochets off the floor just missing my head. When I hit the slippery blood, I slide and am stopped by Jake's legs. He falls over me and smashes into the floor, the gun sliding from his reach. I grab his hair and drive his head into the floor. He jerks up, and I get to my knees. I drive his head again, this time with such force that a crack spreads out a few inches from impact. He's motionless. I push him away, too tired to check his pulse.

"Hey, kid," Brute calls from the hallway, "where are you?"

"In here," I answer.

I look over to see Brute at the door but his big head drops quickly. He gets up, face smeared with blood. He shakes his hands and wipes them on his chest. "Oh, come on." He slouches in and sees Jake, face first in blood. "I had a feeling it'd come to this. Is he alive?"

I shrug my shoulders. I really don't care at this point.

Brute shuffles over, trying hard not to slip. He places his big paw around Jake's neck. "There's a pulse, but he's out cold, kid. Probably for a while."

Brute grabs my arm and pulls. The pain screams from my shoulder, and I scrunch my face so forcefully I may have popped a vein. "Whoa, sorry. What happened?"

I point to my shoulder unable to speak.

Brute inspects it, then shakes his head. "The bullet went straight through, but it tore apart your shoulder blade. You'll be hurtin' for a long time, kid."

He lifts me from my waist this time, and I'm able to limp alongside him. We navigate our way through the bodies in the hallway, Brute mumbling and shaking his head. "All this death, for what?" We make it back to the room and Nightstar is holding Henry's wrist checking for a pulse.

Summer runs over and hugs me. I wince from the pain. "Kyle, are you okay?"

"I'll be fine."

Nightstar leaves Henry and inspects my wound. "Not again. How many bullets can a human take?" I start to laugh but the pain stops me.

"How are we gonna get out of here?" I ask.

Brute takes a few steps down the hallway and almost slips. He points to the elevator. "Let's check that. See if there's a way out."

We trudge through the hall, no one saying a word. The amount of death is unimaginable. There are bodies with bandanas around their necks and some with red jackets that have small patches of white at the corners. Most of the creatures are headless, but some are blown to miniscule pieces.

The light shooting down through the elevators reflects off the blood, making the hallway seem to glow a purplish red. It feels so surreal. We reach the elevator shaft and a rope dangles down. With the help of Brute, and painful screams on my part, we climb and make it up to the street.

Outside is just as catastrophic as inside. Creature's footsteps are stamped in smeared blood, some heading into the lab, some towards the forest. The realization that they could be close makes me shudder.

Summer rips a few bandanas off of the surrounding bodies and ties together a makeshift sling. She carefully places my arm, and the weight taken off my shoulder makes me walk taller and lessens the pain. She kisses my cheek and holds my good hand.

I look at her, Brute, and Nightstar. I'm so happy they're alive, but know that we're all hurting. Nightstar must have hurt her arm and she holds it against her side as she limps besides us. Brute's covered in blood and bruises. His beard's so red that he looks like a beat up clown. Summer hasn't complained, but she must have hurt her leg badly. I have to pull her along as we hobble down the road.

I stop and turn towards everyone. "We have to find shelter. We need to recover from these wounds and get food."

"To be honest," Nightstar says, "we could use a hospital."

"Let's not forget our little problem," Brute says. "You guys are getting closer to turning, and the lab was just destroyed."

The realization of our situation suddenly hits me. Yeah, we're alive. But we've only prolonged the inevitable. Nightstar, Summer, and I are destined to turn. The chance of immunity is slim. I'll soon lose everyone I care for, again.

I lower my head and slouch my shoulders. Stuffing my hands in my pocket I squeeze the memory stick. I almost forgot about it. This is our only chance.

"You know, guys. There's a lab in California," I say and point to what I think is west. "I've always loved the beach."

Brute puts his huge arms around us and pulls us into a soft bear hug. You can tell he's being gentle but we all, including Brute, moan slightly. Summer looks up, her hazel eyes wide with excitement. "I've always wanted to travel cross country with my friends."